Chambers
The Spirit Warrior

SARAH GERDES

Copyright © 2018 Sarah Gerdes

All rights reserved.

ISBN:-10: 1-7329503-7-7
ISBN-13: 978-1-7329503-7-5

Printed in the United States of America

First American Print Edition 2018, reprint 2020, 2022, 2023

Cover design by Lyuben Valevski
http://lv-designs.eu

ALL RIGHTS RESERVED. NO PART OF THIS BOOK MAY BE REPRODUCED OR TRANSMITTED IN ANY FORM OR BY ANY MEANS, ELECTRONIC OR MECHANICAL, INCLUDING PHOTOCOPYING, RECORDING, OR BY ANY INFORMATION STORAGE AND RETRIEVAL SYSTEM, WITHOUT WRITTEN PERMISSION FROM THE PUBLISHER. ADDRESS PO BOX 841, Coeur d'Alene 83816

DEDICATION

The Spirit Warrior is dedicated to a reader who has a true warrior soul. Afflicted with multiple physical disabilities since birth, which have compounded over her life, she forges ahead, through stays at the hospital, stretches where she can't rise from bed, and overcomes her demons to tirelessly work on her first book. Rachel Parker, you are a profound and inspiring spirit in this earthly world.

Chambers
The Spirit Warrior

CHAPTER 1

Darkness came suddenly and completely, the pinpoints of light silently absorbed by the lava pebbles collapsing the last remnant of our journey in China. The seconds pulsed in time with my heart, the distance from Bao growing, centuries of time separating our bodies.

I shivered.

Drops of sweat ran down the center of my back then stopped in place, frozen from the cold, like the emotions I knew I had to turn off. Bao had no part in my life now. She could not. Neither did Xing, my enemy turned ally, or Zheng He, the Admiral, who was intended for greatness. We'd worked so hard to protect their lives and limit our impact on their destiny, but I'd never know if we were successful. Not until I returned to the present and read the history books. For now, me and my sister Mia were ghosts, destined to slip in and out of places and times, taking what we needed and leaving before we had the chance to alter history and hurt civilizations.

The orb in my hands began to glow. In moments, it would show us a wall of disintegrating rock, revealing our next destination, leading us to our future. To where, I didn't know.

"What's taking so long?" Mia whispered, the words fading into the chill. She touched my arm lightly, the excitement on her face plain, despite being swollen and discolored from the lashing she'd recently received. I'd not had time to heal her, but I would. No need for her to resemble a bruised pear.

I looked down. *Where you are sending us?* The dirty, gold exterior of the softball sized object changed color as gradually as the warmth emanating within my palms. The golden rays of light from between my fingers, jagged figures hitting the walls around me.

"This is going to be so great," Mia predicted.

Her emotions washed over me as clearly as if she'd said the words: she was leaving nothing behind that wasn't going to be bettered. Her confidence had grown with her beauty, expanding with the knowledge and exposure she'd gained from serving the Empress. In the two month's we'd been in fifteenth century China, my eighteen year-old twin had blossomed from a stick figured athlete to a woman with curves, her aversion to makeup replaced with an enjoyment of red lips and tight fitting silk outfits. She'd also reveled in her ability to captivate the new Ming Emperor and harness his emotions with her intellect and attitude.

As she oozed enthusiasm, my father held his rigid stance. I felt his glare on my back. He'd asked for the return of his backpack and I'd ignored him. It was me who had figured out how to use the orb, saved his life and removd us from the enemy. It was I who found the rocks that gave the orb the powers to heal and hurt others as I saw fit. I'd even altered his body to the point of being unrecognizable, transforming his jelly-roll stomach to washboard abs that looked tight enough to crack a walnut, atop his tree trunk size legs. Just because Dad had a new physique and earned back a measure of my respect by not giving in to the torture that nearly killed him didn't mean he was leading this journey.

As we waited, I wiped my right palm on my pants, catching a glimpse of my skin. The top layer of flesh seemed to stretch and tighten, like a plane moving through high altitudes. It was morbidly fascinating.

"Did you see...?" I asked Mia, then stopped. It had to be a trick of the light. "Never mind."

We faced a wall with the chord-like strips hanging from top to bottom, identical to the last portal. Seconds ticked by, more than I'd remembered for the first journey, but then, I had no expectations. Now that I wanted the uncertainty of our destination resolved, time lagged.

A reddish hue came from above, along the ridges of immobile, black rock. I was mesmerized as the stone ceiling seemed to liquefy into pulsing red, the surges of molten lava flowing in a stop and start jerking motion, threading its way down the surface like blood in an artery. It reached the corner and floor, going below my feet, surrounding us like captives inside a virtual intestinal wall around the air pockets.

Then it was gone.

I swallowed and wiped my hands again, this time on the front of my shirt, ridding them of sweat but not the anxiety.

"Cage, what's the problem?" Mia shook my arm.

"No problem," I answered casually, my lips creating a dry, sucking sound. The moisture of the snow melt had been replaced with the dryness we all now felt. "It's hot."

"It's always the weather." Dad muttered behind me, his voice deeper than it had been before our journey began.

"Look at that," exclaimed Mia, not hearing Dad's comment. She pointed at the needle which shone like a star on top of the orb, glinting as it turned. Following its lead, I rotated, Mia and Dad doing the same.

The room was full-bright now, the underground cavern like an indoor soccer stadium. Though I shared my twin sister's curiosity, my mind craved peace and quiet. I was so tired. I closed my eyes for a second, a brief respite from the non-stop action.

In the cool, seductive moment of peace, I felt a distinct presence slip between the layers of my skin, pushing under my shoulder blades. The cold traveled down my legs and out my arms, spreading in all directions, like an injection refusing to stay in its required course.

I jerked, gripping the ball in one hand, shaking my shoulders back and forth.

"Cage, stop moving," Mia griped. "The wall is starting to open." Sure enough, the very center of the rock was disintegrating outward, opening up the portal to the other side of time, and whatever it was intended to stay inside before I passed through.

"Move!" I cried, ripping at my shirt with one hand, as though the presence within could be torn off. Mia had a look of confusion on her face as she watched me fight against myself. "Dad, take her!"

"Cage, no! Dad, let me go. We have to help him," she yelled, struggling against dad as he yanked her towards the widening hole. I felt a vibration within, as though the presence had heard her comment and made known its thoughts.

It meant to go to the other side, using my body as the host.

As Dad pulled her towards the opening, the entity pushed through my blood stream, burning my organs, spreading to every extremity, filling me up. I jerked side to side, hoping to jostle it from within me to the hardened rock where its life would wither and die, stuck in the eternal rock stasis.

"No," I groaned, a guttural sound. The invader had moved over the back of my throat, consuming the air. My fingers uselessly clawed against a being protected by my own skin.

Mia pushed free of Dad who missed catching her arm. I kicked my leg out, connecting with her stomach, pushing her back into Dad, both careening in to the far wall. She had a look of pain on her face, wanting to help me even if it hurt her.

Her love moved through me, driving me to fight harder.

The darkness passed over my chin, moving up my jaw. It had one goal: to take over my consciousness, control my mind, dominate my body.

A pressure, like a head vise threatened to black out my eyes, my view forever corrupted by the shadowed veil. I mentally resisted, but like the weight of an elevator coming up; my efforts were useless. By myself, I was failing. It would own me, and I would lead the way to our deaths.

Think of me. The whisper was pure and firm. *Now.*

It couldn't be…but the words repeated. It was true. *She* had returned.

No! I yelled back. I didn't want to think of her. It was too painful.

The pressure started over my eyes.

Remember me, came the voice again. It was said with the same, calm inflection of the person who had repeatedly told me to treat girls with respect, to push harder at the end of the race when my lungs were exploding, to never give up. A small part of my rational mind told me not to let my ego and fragile heart be the death of me.

Long submerged images of Mom flooded my mind, shattering my well preserved emotional barrier to the past. She was there, picking the large blooms off the magnolia trees, the palm-size pedals of pink with white tips, large enough for her to gather water from the pond.

As my heart jolted from pain, the pressure on my cheekbone stopped, hovering on the edge of skin separating what allowed me to see and control my mouth. The presence didn't like the thought of my mother. It stalled on the edge of darkness, fighting against what she represented.

I searched for more memories of my mom, ones I'd kept locked away, hidden in my personal drawer of hurt since her death, meant to remain unopened forever. This time, it was during one of the many afternoons when Mia and I were home after school.

Mom, as usual, sat by me, across from Mia as she teased me about my long hair and sideburns, kicking Mia under the table when she joined in the teasing. The three of us, laughing, eating homemade bread with butter and chokecherry jelly. I made a grab for the opened jar, wanting more but Mia beat me to it, taunting me in a way that dared me to hit her, knowing I wouldn't and it set us both laughing.

The thing inside me hated laughter. It fled, dropping from my jaw and down my throat, the withdrawal leaving an acid, charcoal aftertaste. I coughed, gagging out the ashes of hate. As I heard Mia ask if I was okay, I blocked out her voice, focusing on the image of Mom's hand touching my shoulder, ruffling my hair in a way she knew was guaranteed to annoy me. I meant to pursue it from my body.

I let more memories flow, those of experiences I had hated in the moment and cherished since her death. The ones that made me cry in anger at night, eliminated only by pressing my eyes tight, hitting the bed, forcing my tears on the soft confines of the pillow. The memories that had made me despise Dad over and over for his unintentional but very real role in her fate.

The entity that remained in my body somehow screamed, the hollow, vaporous sound filling my mind.

Heat rushed down towards my knees and I knew it was about to burst from my body. What felt like minutes had been seconds, time enough for the hole in the rock to open man-height, revealing a bright, desolate new location. A different sensation sucked the air out of my chest, drying my skin, crackling with an arid-dry heat. I felt the energy inside me prepare to make its escape. I had to prevent that, no matter what.

"Get out!" I croaked, my voice harsh and dry, shoving Mia with the force that catapulted her out of the entrance. Off balance, I stumbled from the dark into the stream of sunlight heating my back like a flame. Before my hands hit the ground, I rolled on my shoulder, buckling my chest to protect the orb, wincing at the sharp rocks underneath. My body felt ripped apart inside, as though an inner layer had been taken.

The charcoal taste lingered. I coughed and spat on the ground, doing all I could to get it out of my mouth. In that moment, the sound of metal ricocheting off the rock jolted me. The presence was looking for a new home; a new source of energy for possession. The pinging from rock to rock sounded like a pinball machine.

"Mia, dive to your left!" I ordered, hoping she was quicker than *It* was. She rolled across the hard earth, stopping only when forced by the immobile rock barrier on the other side.

She stopped, but the sound didn't.

I felt anger surging from within the invisible entity, craving a physical body with the fever of a shark caught up in a blood-inspired attack. At that moment, a black shadow flew overhead and I ducked, commanding Mia to stay down. Grabbing a handful of rocks, I threw it at the bird, hoping it would veer away. Instead, it came toward us with the focus of a remote-controlled aircraft. My hand flew up, ready to fend off an attack, the tips of its feathers brushing my shoulder before flying high in to the sky, emitting a shriek of victory.

A sick feeling of regret moved through me. I should have been fast enough to grab the tail and throw it to the ground, bashing its head on the rock until the brains spilt out, killing the spirit inside. A dead animal was a small price to pay for others to live.

Mia was beside me, her hands on my shoulders. It was hard to focus, but she made me look in her eyes. A smudge of brown dirt was on her face where she'd wiped herself.

"What happened? What was *up* with that bird?" It was impossible to lie to her and I didn't try.

"Look," I pointed upward. We remained crouched, watching in silence as the bird dipped erratically, then regained its balance and flew down in the brush of trees below. Too late for a gun even if I'd had one. *He* was gone, having taken possession of the bird, leaving me and my family alone.

I coughed out more of the charcoal lodged in the back of my throat. "What was in me is now in that bird. And before that, Mia," I paused, "I think it was in Dad."

"That was *in* you?" she whispered, her eyes wide with understanding, "and it came through using Dad."

I curtly nodded. "I think that's why Dad was walking zombie like, just out of it, remember?" She nodded. Now, it was temporarily out of sight, like a murderer who had gone inside a store for a candy bar.

"Could have been worse," Mia said, a bit of levity returning to her voice, her feeling of relief greater than my own. "Could have gone back inside Dad." We looked at each other, startled.

Dad!

I spun around and saw Dad still inside the cave entrance, standing in a shocked stupor, a vacant gaze on his face.

"What are you doing?" I yelled, my fear coming out as anger. The rock was closing in on his shoulders. He would soon be entombed in stone. Suicide wasn't an honorable form of death when you hadn't atoned for your sins.

"Dive!" I ordered harshly, breaking his paralysis. Dad snapped awake, awkwardly lurching out. The tip of his left foot caught on the bottom rim of the opening and he fell, crushing his knee on the hard rock surface, his body buckling. He seemed confused and I had seconds.

I spiraled, mimicking a rotating freehanded cartwheel, dropping the orb on the ground as I spun both legs over my shoulders. I passed parallel to the rock face, centimeters from the wall, gripping my father's foot and yanking it from within the eternal confines of the catacombs and out, my nose brushing the rock face as it closed up.

We had made it. We were here. Alive. Where ever *here* was.

CHAPTER 2

A gust of hot wind covered the back of my head, moving around me, causing the first beads of moisture between my shoulder blades.

"Where do you think it came from, originally?" Mia whispered breathlessly. Adrenaline was coursing through her nearly as fast as my own, though hers felt different. She was invigorated. I was sickened.

"Maybe the rock itself activated it during our traveling." I picked up the orb cautiously, as though it might reveal more than I knew. It was covered in a matt of white powder that was now under our feet.

I returned it to the backpack, tightening the straps on my shoulders, wincing against the blinding sun above us.

It travels from within. An inscribed line on an ancient sword I'd read during my time in China. It was a clue, like the others on the sword that Wi Cheng, the Master of Weapons, had requested I commit to memory.

"Other than the great tan you are going to get, what are you thinking?" Mia asked, interrupting my thoughts. My dry lips cracked as I smiled with a little relief. It hadn't taken long for her sassiness to return.

"It was real, Mia. *He* was here, inside me. And if I hadn't been able to get it out…"

"Would it have killed you?"

"No idea. But I'm sure it would have taken over my mind."

Mia stared at me in silence and I knew exactly what she was thinking. I could have been possessed and she never would have realized it.

"You deserve to know," I began. "You have to be prepared just in case it happens to you." Mia listened intently to my words as I described the sensation of the chill, and how the positive thoughts and emotions had forced the evil out. "It, He—and I'm sure it was a he—went into the bird."

"Got it," she said, resolutely looking back towards the bush where we'd last seen the bird. "Happy. Love. Positive." My admiration for my sister surged. During the last journey and now here, she'd meet the challenge with the same guts and determination she had with everything else in her life.

I turned, seeing Dad, his motionless figure in a ball against the rock.

"Dad," I said, bending over. "We have to go." I couldn't risk having the bird return and being caught unaware. I turned him over, taken aback by his face. It was pale, but it was also…older. "Mia," I whispered, the tone of my voice causing her to come closer.

We gazed at his figure. The large body he'd been gifted when I'd healed him now had shrunk. No longer was he encased in thick muscles with a flat stomach. Moving my fingers on his biceps, I pressed, feeling bones, barely concealed under a thin layer of flesh. His face had aged a decade. Deep creases made half-circles under his eyes, the tight, sallow skin replacing the plump, fleshy bags of an overworked scientist. The off-center wrinkle between his eyebrows, as familiar to me as his forgetfulness, had deepened. A new age line ran from the center of his forehead down to his nose, forging a jagged path. Even his hairline had changed, receding from his forehead like the edge of the ocean retreating from the shoreline.

"Did going through time do this?" Mia wondered softly. Her eyes moved again to the orb and back to Dad, searching my own face for more information. I couldn't tell her what I didn't know. "Cage…." She was staring at me, her mouth as wide as her eyes. It was as though she were seeing me for the first time.

"What?" My vanity kicked in. If that thing had destroyed my looks I was….

She fumbled for my backpack, finding what she needed before I asked again. Had I lost my hair or wizened up like a wrinkled, moldy prune? That was seriously going to suck. Mia thrust the mirror into my hands.

"Look," she ordered, her face doing a poor job of disguising her glee.

I reluctantly lifted her hand higher to meet my gaze. In the mirror was someone who resembled me, carrying commons traits of dark hair and green eyes, but the youthful appearance of a teen was gone, replaced with a mature gaze, focused and sure. My brows had thinned slightly, arching back and over the corner to the edge of my forehead. My face appeared to have widened slightly. I had more muscles in my jaw, and the darkness of whiskers, a one day growth. It was like looking at the older brother I never had; the one who was wiser, but whose wisdom had come with the loss of innocence. Then I remembered the image of my hand within the catacombs and looked down, gazing at the tone and color. It was tanned, sun-induced and taut; the skin of someone in his prime.

"What about me?" Mia asked excitedly, the giddiness in her voice matching her actual age, but not her appearance. She reached for the mirror, nearly grabbing it out of my hands. I smiled as her facial expression reflected the transformation that had occurred. Her hair, always blond and thick, was so rich and full it jutted out from her ponytail in all directions. A slight squeal escaped her lips as she ripped out the rubber band. The mass of curls dropped in waves across her shoulders and chest, the sun catching streams of golden, reds and yellows with fractions of white. She patted her jaw. Her cheekbones, refined and arched, aged her several years. Seventeen inside, twenty-one as far as anyone else was concerned. The only grimace occurred when she saw the bruising that hadn't entirely gone away.

She touched it. "Can you heal me?"

I smiled. "Sure, if you can wait until we are out of here."

Dad raised his head, and Mia quickly put way her mirror. He propped his arm on his elbow, awkwardly got to his knees and lurched a few steps before stopping, his breath jagged. Mia and I were quiet as he staggered towards the large boulders behind us. Dad held one hand on the rock and gazed down to the valley. He muttered incoherently before he found a crevice between two rocks and puked, the sound so violent it was as if years of agony were coming out.

Time travel had impacted us after all.

We waited in the hot sun as Dad retched. Mia removed her hoodie, revealing the short-sleeved t-shirt she'd had on when we left Washington State and commenced our unintended adventure to the past. She stripped that off as well, now wearing only a brown undershirt with thin shoulder straps.

"Don't do it," I warned, knowing she'd burn before her skin turned to a golden tan. Mia gave me an impish smile. The warm weather was a nice change from the chill of winter in China, and I guessed she was as glad to be done with at least one part of the uniform.

"Have your feet recovered from the binding?" She shrugged, as though her feet hadn't undergone the torturous exercise.

"Not really," she said, closing her eyes, raising her face towards the sun, the unsightly dark bruises spotting her skin. "But it wasn't for more than a couple weeks. Could have been worse." Without a word, I moved closer and leaned my foot against hers. Slowly, I turned the spindle so it was over the rock of life, no longer needing to open the top half of the orb. Recognizing the inscriptions was enough. *At some point it would be nice to know what the strange lettering meant.*

I watched in satisfaction as the dark blue of her skin turned purple, then pink and finally ivory. Only the freckles remained, and they were present before the lashing. I suggested she take out the mirror and look at herself one more time.

"Why?" She asked, her eyes still closed. The girl was going to take a catnap despite the stench now wafting up from the crevice.

"You might like the view." She cracked one eye open in time enough to see me replacing the orb. With the alacrity of a viper snatching a mouse, she whipped open the mirror and looked at her new self. Her smile of joy was gratifying. "You're welcome."

She gave me a bear hug, releasing me only when I complained about the heat she was giving off.

"I am hot!" she retorted playfully, clipping my ear. "Why don't you get out of your sweatshirt?" I was about to follow her suggestion when the pounding of hoofs coasted up the valley. Soon yells, high pitched and piercing, were intermixed with gunshots and hooting, all three noises bouncing against the rocks until the entire valley seemed filled with the pinball-like sounds.

The commotion affected Dad. He coughed, lifted his head and strained to see over the rock. His jaw clenched and I could see the intake of air moving down his throat. Suddenly, a burst of emotion took the form of food and out it came in a spit of finality.

Mia raised her eyebrow at me and I turned away, unwilling to tell her of my gift to sense the feelings of others. Now wasn't the time.

"See if you can figure out when and where we are," I asked, jerking my head towards the valley. We perched on opposite sides of a barren, rock covered basin, she on the west side, me on the east. It was black obsidian, the same shiny, angular composite as one that was in the orb; the rock that gave life. The familiarity was comforting.

I cautiously peered over the expanse of the glossy-black formations. We were further away from the sound of men and horses than I thought. Where the dark rock stopped, a blue lake began, the water spreading across the valley to another set of mountains in the distance. Dotting the rim were pine trees, indigenous to high, dry plains.

A flash of the tapestry appeared, the visual drawn by Bao on paper that now resided in my pocket. On it had been five locations; each one a visual of a land we'd visit—if we were alive. One was marked by black rocks, a river separating the land and brown plains. That image now lay before me.

My chest burned. The orb had sent us to gather a rock, artifact or both. The next instant I felt a stab of fear and hesitation. Great things required great sacrifices, sometimes of good people. I thought of Boa's father and mother, who made decisions knowing the result would be their death—substituting their lives for their children.

A lone duck flew overhead, dropping excrement on a boulder nearby, the splat a juicy thud. The noisy bird continued its course, lifting with the warm updrafts, diving in and out of the long reeds growing along the lake's edge. Cranes lounged by the shoreline, dipping their wings in the water, plunging in and out, eating what lie beneath the marsh. The spicy, arid aroma of the brush failed to cover the stink of a swamp as it wafted on the air and towards us.

A whoosh and a click caused me to instinctively duck. Two arrows landed in succession, both stopping with muted thumps to the ground. One landed nearby Dad. He reached out and flipped it over. His face was still a greenish color, now it turned white and his mouth pressed thin, stretching wide in anxiety. He threw it away as though it were poisonous.

"You recognize it?" I grumbled, already knowing he did. He squinted his eyes shut as though the sun prevented his answer.

Yells brought me back to observe the area below in search of the source. Guttural sounds mixed with gunshots, the popping like a bottle rocket instead of the pump of a modern 9 mm. An occasional cry of agony heralded the outcome of the gun or arrow hitting its mark.

"Mia, what's on your side?"

"It's fascinating." I suppressed an impatient retort. Torture was fascinating if it were being endured by the right person. She heard my exhale of frustration and spoke. "America obviously, late-eighteen hundreds. War."

I joined her, absorbing the scene. Two groups of native American Indians were on either side of a long, wide knoll, separated by the trail of black magma and a forest of pine trees and rocks. One group had shaved heads, the other with faces painted red with white stripes. Joining the group with the shaved heads were white men in faded blue uniforms.

"Look there," Mia pointed. "You can tell the time period by the jackets, and since I know you're going to ask anyway, I'll propose between sometime in the eighteen seventies," she estimated, her voice indicating complete authority.

I strained to make out the uniforms, but history wasn't my forte. The jackets were brown or dark blue, it was hard to tell. A covering of dust could have made black jackets white around here. I glanced at her side profile.

"You're good, Mia, but to get it down to a window of a decade? How can you be so sure?"

"The hats give it away," she said without missing a beat.

Rock crunching indicated Dad was coming up from behind. I held my breath. "Short hats?" he asked.

"Yes, and if you don't believe me on the time period," she continued, her voice oozing superiority, "the US Army pants predating this time period were darker and the hats a little fuzzy and roundish. I know it's after eighteen sixty, because jackets no longer had the x's across the front, and are longer, looking more like tuxedo jackets. See there?"

I raised my hand. "Believe you. What about the location? Anything that's going to help us figure out if we'll be shot or captured?"

"Along the border of Northern California and Southern Oregon," Dad offered, his voice flat and resigned, as though the truth could no longer be contained. I turned to him. His eyes were fixed on the scene below, darting between the movements in the valley. I felt fear, anxiety, reproach and…regret. He knew exactly where we were and what was going on. "1876 or 77, approximately."

"Don't tell me anymore," Mia requested, her eyes narrowing. "The Modoc Indian wars." Mia's momentary satisfaction of historical recall dissipated like the sun behind an on-coming cloud as she whipped around. "Dad, how do you know that?"

"I, well…" he hedged.

A yell and several shots were fired as she stared at him, the dawn of betrayal rising up from within her.

"You've been here before?" she whispered. "You've been…." She couldn't get the words out. A rising flush of guilt moved up Dad's neck and colored the greyish hue of his face. It might as well have been a visual of what Mia was starting to feel, the heat of her anger as real as any molten lava from within an underground volcano.

Her emotions felt familiar. All the resentment, bitterness and hate I'd felt about the missed matches and track meets, the unexplained tardiness to dinner, were now seeping into Mia's consciousness. The only difference between me and my twin was that I'd long ago decided he was a complete, self-absorbed jerk, harboring my disgust for three years. Mia had maintained her undiluted, staunch trust and love for him throughout.

"Dad, do you have ties to this place?" I asked. "Something we need to know about?"

Dad shoved himself off his knees, pressing his back against the rock. The color of his face made my lips pucker. It had turned again, the hue of the under belly of a slug in the Washington winter. He wavered, bending over, his hands on his knees. I felt the quickening of an unbalanced system. The lack of food, spiking and dipping of his blood sugar changing his emotional state from one moment to the next. He was lightheaded, and I inhaled a breath of patience.

"Breathe in," I counseled, feeling more parent than child.

Dad steadied himself before speaking. "Wait a few minutes," he told us. "These are short, spit fights. It'll die down." He drew long, inhales through his mouth that I hoped he wouldn't exhale my direction. "They always do."

The afternoon sun had crested above us and before long would be descending in the west, beyond the mountain range. It would give us a reprieve from the heat, but then we'd have only an hour of light until it got cold, and fast.

"This is not going to *die down*," Mia retorted, her voice bitterly sarcastic. "The wars end up with an entire tribe obliterated and the white settlers taking everything." Her anger had gone deep, like an enormous fish pushing itself into the darkness, the inside becoming as black as its surroundings. Successive waves of hurt and betrayal moved through her, displaying themselves on her face.

I gripped Dad's arm, staying to his side to avoid his breath.

"Answer me. What's making you sick?" Two months ago, I would have been caught up in an angry vortex, just like my sister. Not after China. Not after being a witness to death, torture, dismemberment and zombies. Anger served no purpose now. I had demonic possessions to worry about.

Dad rubbed his fingertips against his forehead. I sensed him pushing out feelings of guilt, and….pain. A lot of it. Images of women crying came to the forefront.

"Scar-faced Charley. Captain Jack, Curly Joe," he muttered. Mia's eyebrows creased, then widened. He wasn't having a moment of delirium. He was repeating names Mia recognized. She opened her mouth to talk but was interrupted by a harsh scream from a male voice. She gasped and I joined her in looking down to the valley. In the time we'd looked away, the battle had been decided.

A bald Indian stood over a kneeling captive. In one hand he held the shoulder, the other a blade. The veins on his neck and temple protruded, the blood pumping with the thrill of victory. The captive had shoulders broader than me, the lean, taught muscles rippling under a leather top. His dark hair hung past his shoulder, a part woven in a long braid to one side. Early twenties I guessed. Behind him, U.S. Army soldiers stood warily and at attention, watching the natives.

"The guy holding the knife looks....*vicious*," Mia whispered.

A soldier with a jacket cleaner than the others strode up to the captive. His manner was officious; a commander used to giving orders. He was asking questions of the captive that weren't being answered. The Indian moved his knife to the warrior's forehead.

"They're going to scalp him," Mia predicted.

"Looks that way." The macabre scene should have had me on the edge, my body filled with the possibility and anxiety of inevitable death. Now...

"I can do without seeing it." I turned away. It was the perfect time to get down the mountain.

"He's just sitting there," Mia said, more to herself than us, her voice a mixture of awe and surprise. "No fear at all." Whether it was a fascination with his physical stature, or his calm demeanor, I couldn't tell. An odd stab of jealousy coursed through me.

"Your admiration will end when he dies," I said coldly.

Dad pulled it together enough to wedge his head between me and Mia. He moaned. "I can't watch," he mumbled, turning back around, sliding down the face of the rock. I glanced at Mia, making eye contact. The benefit of being a twin was an innate understanding of the others' thoughts, at least some of the time.

"You *know* him?" Mia hissed. After a moment, she glanced down to the scene below, then back to Dad. "Where is the dad I had when you were hanging on the torture wall in China?" She caught my eye and I nodded. Dad had recently risen to the occasion when the lives of me and Mia were in jeopardy, his selfless, brave act saving the two of us from death of the hands of a fanatic. Now he'd reverted from his temporary manliness back to the tepid academic he was.

"This isn't then," he murmured.

"Cage…" Mia pleaded, touching my arm.

"Are you kidding me?" I asked, incredulous. "Beyond the fact that he means nothing to me and I have no way to help the guy, it's interfering. Changing history, remember? The primary thing we *can't* do?" She had a lock on my arm like a vice grip, pressing harder.

"He's a single Indian," she argued. "How important could he be in the grand scheme of things?" I glanced at Dad, the only person who'd know the answer to this question and he had clamped his mouth shut. "What is *with* you?" Mia demanded of me. "You saved the Emperor within minutes of us getting to China and he was a complete stranger, and now when you can save someone I *want* you to save, you hesitate?"

"*Want* to save? Why? A sudden, spontaneous infatuation?"

An emotional bomb went off within Mia. Perhaps this is what happens with aging up.

"Look, I'm not against fighting," I added, wanting to mollify her. She cocked her head, hearing the lie in my voice but not knowing the truth. My stomach was crying in desperation for food and I'd not slept in twenty-four hours. "But it doesn't matter if this guy lives or dies and we aren't supposed to interfere."

Dad jerked with alarm, his head automatically shaking no. "Cage, he has to live. I—we--" He shut his mouth. A wash of regret rolled up and through Dads face that was so large, it might as well have been a tsunami.

The dull edge of the blade ran along the captive's forehead. The corners of his mouth raised in a smile as the blade went from one ear, back to the top of scalp. Then another thought hit me. A crazy thought. One I had to pursue.

"Dad, look at me," I demanded. "Were you close to him?" Dad's eyes grazed the ground, searching in vain for solace in the grey dust. Mia groaned with impatience, each second one tick away to the warrior losing his scalp. "I'm doing nothing until you answer."

"Yes," he finally acknowledged. "And his family." His voice cracked on the last word.

Mia pushed me then, tapping my fingers. Her eyes rested on the large, ruby ring on my finger. She cocked her right eyebrow.

No, I mouthed. I wasn't going to use the ring and stun people one by one. Besides, the power of the ring required me to be much closer to the target to have an effect. Then she looked at my backpack. I scowled, subtly shaking my head no. I wasn't going to annihilate an entire valley of warring people without knowing who was good and bad.

"*Do* something or I will," Mia hissed, her eyes intense. Of course, she would say that. Do first, think later. Just like she did in China and it almost got us killed.

The sweat on Dad's face became pronounced and he slid down the wall, hitting the ground. He was running from something of his own doing. I made a conscious decision to search his emotions. Was the man with a knife to his head Dad's son, fathered before us, or with another woman? No. Dad wasn't a player. He loved Mom, her world had been his world. Another rise of emotion came up and out of Dad towards me. It was worry and….regret. Someone had depended on him and he failed.

I stopped, not wanting to know more. Dad seemed to have a pattern of flakiness that caused others to suffer early mortality.

"Dad?" I asked.

When he spoke, his voice was clogged with emotion. His agonized look was one of a person who faced drinking acid, preparing to do it, all the while knowing it was going to kill him. "Cage, you need to help him."

"Why? What's he to you?"

Dad convulsed once, his face blanching grey to white. The words came out in a thin, breathy tone, sounding as though he had an enormous pressure on his chest. "My scalp should be coming off. Not his."

Free will and choice had just been eliminated. Whatever Dad had done, some guy was going to pay for his mistakes.

"Mia, your pack." Without a word, she nimbly unhooked the fanny pack from her small waist, dumping the contents on the ground. I needed to see everything, hoping she had an item I could use. From her pouch tumbled two rolls of gauze, a tube of antibacterial cream to prevent infection, a strip of moleskin used to patch up blisters, a small pair of scissors, a whistle, a tube of lip gloss and a starter gun used for track meets. All necessary items for an elite soccer player.

"The whistle," I requested, reaching for the gun. The small, palm-size black weapon looked like a miniature pistol from the 1940s without the bullets. It was a super-charged cap gun, blowing a foul-smelling plume of smoke with each shot, but it was seriously loud. "Does this work?" she nodded. Reaching deep into my own bag, I removed the cracked mirror, holding the plastic casing gently.

The Indian had lifted his knife into the air and was slowly lowering it, the sharp point glinting toward the warrior squatting on the ground. My movement was momentarily slowed, caught off guard by the captive's manner. Mia was right. He was calm, even…accepting. He didn't flinch from the point of the blade. Instead, he sat motionless, watching it lower to his face. His manner told me he knew pain and death were inevitable.

I held the starter gun, the whistle, and the pocket mirror, wedging myself tightly between the black, jagged rocks, feeling the sting of the obsidian as it cut into my arms and legs. Warm liquid ran down my arms as I pointed the gun directly at the birds in the water. The entire lake looked like one big mass of feathers.

"Both of you, get back under the overhang. Ready?"

The gun emitted a pop loud enough to start the Olympics. Lifting off the water like the rise of a tidal wave, thousands upon thousands of wings darkened the sky. As the great form soared and scattered in all directions, screeching cries overwhelmed the valley. The Indians and soldiers reacted in panic, scattering to the protection of the trees, all but the man holding the knife. He watched, the tip of the blade paused on the warrior's hairline and remained there, pressing into the flesh.

I flashed the mirror in the sunlight, directly to the kneeling captive's face. I didn't want him to know we were here, but if he was going to get away, I had no other choice. The flash caught his attention. He looked up, searching for the source. For a split-second, we made eye contact. It was an intense glare of knowledge and understanding. It reminded me of the look I received from Wi Cheng, an old soul, communicating with one, older still.

As a group of gray pelicans passed over the knife-wielding Indian, I blew the whistle and fired again. The birds erupted in their own distress, raining down gobs of white and yellow dung, which landed on the bald head of the knife-wielding captor who raised both hands to protect his face and eyes.

It was enough.

The warrior jumped up, knocking his captor backward with a pummel to the chest. The crap covered man fell back over the edge and rolled down a steep incline. By the time he stopped, our guy would be long gone.

"Cage, look!" commanded Mia, breathless. The escaping Indian was running back to his tribe who flanked him on either side. "You did it," she squealed, alternately hugging me and jumping up and down, watching the backside of the man run in to the trees.

Hope he was the good guy, I thought, handing Mia her items.

"We need to get out of here," I ordered. It wouldn't take a brilliant mind to guess the prisoner had help. If the escaping Indian saw us, maybe someone else had as well.

The sound of air being sliced was the only warning I had before a dark arrow hit my chest, going right through my shirt. Mia's stifled words were cut off as the end of the arrow waivered and dropped on the ground.

"It---" started Mia.

"--broke off at impact," I interrupted, overriding her words. She pressed her lips, keeping the secret of why no blood was drawn. Dad's eyes were wide and I had no intention of explaining. Picking up the wooden part of the crude missile, I thrust it against the rock as I would a defective tool.

"Dad, which direction?"

"This way." We slipped down the soft dirt trail, passing a wild burrow that roamed in the canyon, who looked up long enough to determine we were no threat. By the time we reached the bottom, we were dirty and out of breath. Mia's shoulders were pink from exposure to the sun.

As we ran through the rocks, Mia spoke. "You said it was you that should be scalped, not him." Her voice was quiet, but had lost none of the rebelliousness. "What could you have done to deserve that?"

"I killed someone."

Mia stumbled at his words. I caught her from the back, steadying her as Dad turned us to the East. I urged them both to keep going. Faint noises behind us were getting louder, increasing in pace and intensity.

"Just past the hill," Dad said, his breathing strained.

We ran through a stream, scrambled up the bank, diving straight into a thicket that cut down visibility by half. Our clothes snagged on branches from the pine trees and Mia exclaimed as a branch snapped her in the face.

I heard cracking behind us and a muffled command. "Hurry!" I pressed. Mia picked up the pace and in the process ran right into Dad. He tumbled off balance and Mia and I both heard a crack followed by a low howl of pain.

"My foot, my ankle!" Dad groaned, doubling over on the ground. He attempted to get up and failed.

I sprung to him, thrusting my shoulder under his armpit, asking Mia to get the other side.

"Do we have enough time to get there?" I asked.

He clenched his jaw. "Yes, another minute."

"Mia-lift." Dad pushed off as well as he could. Up the hill we alternately pulled and lifted, ignoring the branches that now lacerated our faces and arms.

"Hear that?" Mia whispered. The noise behind us was a dull padding. Our pursuers were close. She surged ahead with the will of an ox wanting to get the harness off from around its neck.

"Over there—the dark brush," Dad directed, jerking his head up and to the right. It was a wall of trees, the green exterior blending into a black, the sunlight blocked by the interlocking branches that formed an impenetrable barrier.

"No opening," I grunted.

"Under the trees. Drop me. I can do it." We reached the edge, setting him down. Dad was immediately on all fours, lifting his bad foot up, awkwardly but rapidly moving forward. First, his head disappeared, then his shoulders. "This way." His words came muffled under the layers of growth.

I glanced behind me, expecting to see a line of white-striped faces against the twilight.

"Mia, go!" I said, giving her a push. She went down and I followed, entering the dark underworld.

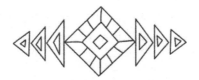

CHAPTER 3

The low branches served as a roofline above my head, the sensation reassuring. The floor beneath me was springy, nature's Astro turf, but the pine needles that falling on the back of my neck pricked, the sharp, spikey ends like ants crawling on my skin. I heard Mia's muffled breathing and imagined the sharp needle tips brushing her pink shoulders.

"Go lower," I suggested, unsure if she heard me.

Dust particles wafted up from the ground, tickling my nose. I inhaled through my mouth, the moisture filling my lungs, the warm, wet sensation at odds with the dry land. It felt good, and I did it again, fast and deep, capturing as much of the vapor as possible.

"Gah!" I exclaimed. My hand had landed on a large, prickly item and I retracted it as fast as possible, scuttling to the side. Mia asked what had happened and I told her.

"A porcupine?"

"Can't be," I grunted. I'd have been threaded with long, poisoned darts. We started forward and then it was Mia's turn to cry out. "Dad, wait."

At first, the near darkness made it difficult to see the outline of the object. It was burnt brown in color, the size and shape of a football, the outside comprised of wooden scales instead quills. It was an oversized pine cone, droppings from the giant, old growth forest, untouched by deforestation or pollution.

"Brush the ground with your palm," I encouraged them both, the sweeping movement clearing the way as we continued crawling.

It wasn't long until Dad announced we'd arrived.

Mia and I emerged from the confining undergrowth to stand in a small clearing. The perimeter of trees sprang from the Earth like pillars at a coliseum, shooting straight up to the sky, now black, dotted with ornamental lights. The half-moon shone bright, illuminating the dark, green grass underneath my hands.

Mia brushed off her arms and shoulders, muttering about the sticky sap. She looked like a wild animal, her hair spreading in all directions, frizzed out from the moisture in sections. Dad was the antithesis, sitting calmly as he removed his shoes and socks.

"The bone's cracked," he diagnosed, staring at his skin. The ankle was swelling, the blood rushing to the injured area like food coloring through water. It was Mia who had caused him to fall, but she was not about to apologize. She squatted in front of him, her fingers interlaced.

"Did you think we were too young to understand what you were doing?" she asked him, picking up exactly where she'd left off before we made our escape. She didn't sound hurt over his dishonesty. She sounded *offended*. I felt her animosity continuing its growth inside her, an emotional cancer accelerating as it spread throughout her system.

"They won't come here?" I interrupted, hoping to distract her from the no-win conversation.

Dad shook his head, pointing to the ground beyond me. "No. Look at the water."

I twisted around. At first glance, the bubbling spring appeared to be ordinary. A faint breeze on my back felt like a gentle nudge forward, and I leaned closer. The liquid was ivory, the milky substance bouncing off thousands of white crystal rocks, causing it to reflect like a light. Trinkets with tiny beads, a fraction of the size of my fingernail were visible, as were the remnants of feathers and emulsified leather. I went to touch one.

"Don't," said Dad in a rare moment of authority. They had to be Indian artifacts, placed here for a reason.

"This is a sacred area?"

He nodded. "And the reason they won't come here. This place is for the spirits of the dead."

Mia came to my side, peering at the water. "Let's hope it's not the cursed ones," I muttered. Mia grunted. "What's the story behind the heat?"

"The tribe showed me a series of underground tunnels. The water below is from hot springs. The boiling water stretches for miles in every direction, warming the top of the caves that are under our feet. The white rocks in the spring were created from shoots of steam, though the tribe believes it's the spirits that make the rocks glisten, not the rocks themselves."

"Does the spring have another outlet?" I asked, turning away. "One where we can drink without soaking up a soul or two?" Our destiny didn't matter that much if we perished from lack of food, water or sleep deprivation.

Mia put her hands on her hips, leaning on one leg. "Great, Dad," she griped, forestalling his answer. "No water. No food. A broken ankle and you killed someone. What else are you going to tell us? You have another kid here too?"

He raised a hand, looking stricken. "No! Of course not! I would never—"

"Don't," she interrupted, raising her palm to his face, the most insulting act of defiance I'd ever seen from her. Mom would be appalled, but then, it was she who taught us about the tie between action and consequence. Dad was getting the consequences of putting me and Mia through three years of lies. I'd like to tell Mia what I'd learned, that his intentions weren't purposefully bad. They were just…misdirected.

"We do have *some* water," Dad stammered softly. "It's over there." He pointed to a smaller, almost invisible outcropping of liquid near the rim of the trees. The watering hole was the size of my palm, but clear and shimmering. "The purest water is volcanic. It's more like hot tea, but it will do the job."

"Mia, you go first," I suggested. As she walked away, I bent down near Dad, gently lifting his ankle. "Where does it hurt?" I asked, buying time. The wound wasn't nearly as horrific as his previous injuries, where bones jutted through tone muscle and tissue, skin hanging from his body like clothes on a hanger. Dad pointed. *Not that it matters. The orb will heal it all.*

Without a word, I slipped off the backpack, removed the orb and adjusted the spindle over the rock of life.

"Mia won't be happy," Dad said in an undertone only I could hear. "She's right in wanting me to suffer."

"Don't worry, you will," I replied, the comment causing Dad to smile a little. "But not at the expense of keeping us alive." I slowly turned the top half to the right. The ebony rays of the moonlight shone down on Dad's purpling skin. In seconds, blood flow underneath the skin accelerated. The grotesque shaping of the skin receded as the fractured bones reconnected. Soon, the veins rose to the surface, the color a healthy blue contrasting against the light pink of his skin. I expected the veins to recede, resembling a youthful hand, but they remained in place. It was the skin texture of an older person, the top layer thin, the blue vein lines resembling rivers snaking through an arid land.

Dad flexed it back and forth. "Incredible," he whispered.

"We'll have to get out of here in the morning," I told him, receiving only a quiet acknowledgement in return. "There's a reason we were sent here and it probably has little to do with you redeeming whatever it is you did." Why his skin and body hadn't reverted to his pre-travel was still a mystery.

One of many I have yet to solve.

Mia came back to the wellspring, ignoring Dad as she inspected the artifacts in the water.

"Mia, let me heal your back." Her shoulders were red, even in the moonlight, the nicks and scratches covered in dried blood. She shrugged, giving me a 'don't-bother-me-with-the-little-things," look. Obstinate girl. Then I realized she was using her wounds as an object lesson for Dad. They were symbolic of his failure, each point of blood a tool in making him feel worse.

I sighed. This was going to be a long trip. I returned the orb to its protective location on my back and went to satisfy my thirst.

"If this place is sacred," I heard Mia say accusingly, "when do the Indians actually come here? Only when someone dies?"

"The burial ceremony for the spirit takes place within twenty-four hours of death," Dad answered, his voice subdued. "So yes, only when death occurs."

"Good thing Cage saved that guy since you weren't going to." Her voice was laced with a challenge, belligerent and harsh.

Dad cleared his throat again. "Legend has it the spirits guard this area against the enemies, consuming the bodies of those who enter without permission."

I looked around, imagining invisible beings, spying upon us, waiting for more time to determine if we were friend or foe. The thought was strangely comforting.

After drinking as much as I dared, conscious not to make myself sick, I cupped my hands full of water, bringing it over my face. The warm liquid was soothing, a temporary relief from the situation. I was physically exhausted, emotionally drained and mentally worn down.

"Not smart to have us invade their sacred burial ground when their ancestors hate you already." I laughed involuntarily, glancing at Dad to see if he was going to keep taking her criticisms.

"Okay Mia. I'll make you a deal. If you can stay awake for a little while longer, I'll tell you the entire story."

"Everything?" Mia asked skeptically, raising her eyebrow.

"And before I pass out from exhaustion?" I added, reminding both of them I'd not slept in a day.

"Everything."

CHAPTER 4

Dad insisted on starting at the beginning and I was too tired to argue. I removed the nunchucks from my back pocket, and threaded my hand through the strap of the backpack, wrapping it once around my wrist. I stretched out on the Earthen mattress composed of dried needles scattered on top of the warm moss, my head on top of my free wrist. Mia was content to listen lying down, using my stomach as a pillow. Dad sat adjacent to us, his legs crossed, his hands folded on his lap like he was starting a lecture.

"Before your mother died, she sent off a package to herself. It was a wooden box, filled with straw, the kind that's flat and white, that we only saw in China, you know?" I didn't, but I got the idea. The stars above us were bright against the black sky and I felt myself fighting to keep my eyelids open. With the threat of our pursuers gone, my body started to relax inch by inch. "She sent it the same day she died. I didn't even know about it for weeks." Dad pushed up the corner of his mouth at the memory. "When it did come, I put it in the basement and forgot about it for six months."

"What had mom written on the outside?" asked Mia.

He shook his head. "Simple shipping paperwork. Nothing to give away how important the objects inside were to anyone."

"I'd have opened it the first moment I had a chance," proclaimed Mia, jutting her chin out. We both would have.

Dad sighed. "I'm not like you Mia. To me, it was another painful reminder she was gone."

I raised my free hand above my head, stretching. I tried to put myself in his shoes and visualize what he went through. Stricken with grief and guilt, he'd been a broken man, intent on avoiding the last object Mom had touched. Heck, I'd been doing that since she died. I avoided looking at flowers. I'd put away her pictures, anything and everything that reminded me of her.

Dad picked up a handful of pine needles with one hand, dropping them in the palm of his other.

"As I said, the box sat in the dark in the basement for six months. I actually assumed it was full of photographs which were the last thing I wanted to see. But then I had to get a research paper for a project Draben wanted. It was dark and I ran smack in to the box. For whatever reason, I felt it was time." He pressed his lips together at the memory, chagrined. "The thing took a crowbar to pry open."

"We don't own a crowbar," Mia pointed out.

"Exactly. When I got one, I found a metal box in the center, pine shavings all around. It was orange with rust, dirty with grime and no lock. Inside was the orb, the plates, the compass and the broken mirror. I spent most of the night trying to figure out the significance of each."

"No note?" I asked, dubious. It was unlike Mom to leave out instructions. Ever since first grade, she'd put notes in our lunch pails, or reminder sticky notes on the fridge. Order was her thing. Forgetfulness and mediocrity were not.

Dad shook his head, the outline of his hair making strange waves against the blanket of darkness behind him.

"Nothing. I eventually went to bed but found myself returning to the box time and again. I wondered if the orb had money in it, or jewels. I thought about taking it to the school of antiquities for verification, but it never felt right.

"Each night, after you two had gone to bed I'd go back and take it all out," he admitted, dipping his head sheepishly, like he was staying out late at night, past his curfew. "I became obsessed with it really. The nights seemed to be getting shorter, like there wasn't enough time to learn about this thing that your mother had never mentioned to me. Never even *shown* me."

I moved my shoulders back and forth, scratching an itch. To have your wife send you something strange without a note, after her death had to have been weird.

"So, at first you were in grief," Mia interjected, "too self-absorbed to care about us. Then you finally opened this box up and began traveling around and we didn't even notice the difference, did we?" Mia was now angry at herself for not catching him.

Dad coughed, the dry, catching sound echoing in the small grove. "Mia, I focused on the only thing I knew how to do. Work."

"Yeah, but—" she interrupted.

"But I had to work to keep the bills paid, Mia," he responded right back, forestalling any objection. "I couldn't be home with you after school and even though you were old enough to avoid day care, what would you have done had I suggested a house sitter to watch over you? You would have rejected that option, right?" Mia and I were silent. Of course we would have. We'd been fourteen at the time of Mom's death. "So," he continued, satisfied that he had at least one point in his favor, "I did what any single parent does. I worked."

"Either way you missed all our events. The important things in our life for three years."

"Yes, and for that I'm sorry. But Mia, what if you were in my shoes and lost your partner? Would you have done anything within your power to try and figure it out?" Again, Mia was without a quick comeback.

"I wonder what else she was hiding," I said. Mia bashed her head on my chest.

"That's something that kept me going Cage. What was she involved in? I mean, I don't deal with antiquities or artifacts, only volcanos. These things looked like they were worth a lot of money, but I couldn't just call up the local museum and start checking it out. So, I did the next best thing. I went online."

As Dad described the Internet sites he visited and that none of the items appeared on the stolen antiquities lists, my mind wandered. Where had Mom kept a box that large for the length of their marriage? In my visions with her, she spoke as though she'd known of our mission during this time for years, so why had she not told Dad? What was the point of keeping it from the family?

It was hard to think and listen to Dad's explanation so I concentrated on him.

"Once I was confident the items weren't on the stolen antiquities list, I continued to conduct research on the potential origin of the items. The less I found, the more obsessed I became. Soon the evenings weren't enough. I began carrying the things in my backpack, spending every free moment I had alone with the orb in particular, much of that in the catacombs while I was doing research.

"Then about a year ago, I was in the middle of a cave, taking a break and I pulled it out. I started fiddling around with the thing when it turned to one side. I'd done it before at the house a thousand times and nothing had happened. This time, it started to glow, the cave grew bright and the sound of dropping rocks echoed. I could hardly believe it, *didn't* believe it. The world I knew, the one that was barely livable save for you two, was now changing in front of me. When the hole in the rock appeared, I walked through."

"You just went?" I asked. He nodded. Dad had given no thought to leaving us behind, just did it. Just like Mia. Do first and think later. I wanted to hate him for it and couldn't. If Bao were on the other side, and I had the chance to see her again, I'd have done the same.

"Once I made it through, I had no idea where I was or what I was going to do. Almost immediately I regretted my decision to enter into the darkness but when I turned around the opening was closed. I was stuck here, alone. Or rather—in the valley. That's where he found me."

"Who?" Mia asked expectantly. "The warrior Cage saved?" There it was again. The not so thinly veiled interest in the guy.

Dad's eyes wavered as he met hers. "His name is Kintpuash. He and a group of warriors were out hunting and brought me before the council of elders. As you can imagine, it was impossible to communicate something as incredible as I'd been through, but I tried with images and drawings. Kinptuash took my backpack, dumped it on the ground and the elders started sorting through the items. Curly John—"

"The medicine man, right? I remember that from U.S. History."

"Yes, Muleo is his native name," replied Dad, evidently impressed Mia recalled the information so easily. "Think of it Mia, you will meet him in real life. A person you've read about." Her blue eyes seemed to go as grey and lifeless as the crushed ash beneath our feet.

"Ridiculous the settlers had to give them such stupid, degrading names."

"That's what happened back then," Dad replied, somewhat impatiently. "You do recall Captain Jack don't you?"

Mia rolled her eyes. "I got an A in American History."

"Great. Now you'll get your bachelor's degree in real life. Where was I?"

"The book," I said wearily.

"Curly John—rather, Muleo, picked up the plates very carefully. He opened the book, gazed at it, then fiddled with another medal holder. Out dropped a pen-like device. I tried to stop him, worried he'd ruin a priceless artifact but he ignored me, and actually seemed to know what he was doing. He started writing on the metal and when he finished, he passed the plates around. Each time they got in the hands of an elder, the man exclaimed out loud or crushed his eyebrows deep in thought. Finally, it got to me and I will say, I was shocked. On one side were the medicine man's drawing and on the other side, the English translation."

"What did it say?" I asked.

"*Are you peaceful or are you an enemy?*' I wrote underneath on the left side that I was peaceful, but the words didn't appear."

"It didn't work for you," Mia surmised.

"No, and I thought it was all over for me, but one of the elders spoke and shortly after, a very regal-looking Indian woman came in to the room. Her name is Winema, but the name she's known by outside the tribe is Toby."

"I know," Mia interjected. "She married a white settler. Fluent in English and was a translator between the tribes, Army and settler." She looked at me, pausing. "What in the world were you doing during U.S. History?"

"Not listening?"

Dad chuckled, then continued. "That was it. That was the start of my relationship with the Modoc tribe. The first time I stayed with them for a few hours only, worried that you two were going to wake up and find me gone. When I returned and saw time stood still, I—I—"

"Started lying," finished Mia, her voice acid.

Dad cleared his throat. "It was clear my trips had no impact on time. They liked me coming, and I was hopeful that they would help me learn more about the orb."

"Obviously *that* didn't happen," Mia pointed out, her voice rich with contempt. "Cage figured it out in days, not months."

"You're right. I had no idea that rocks were supposed to be inside. Worse, I was wrong to have kept going back so many times, but after a while, it became comforting."

Mia let out a snort. "I can't believe you were spending time here, with them, instead of us!"

Dad focused his gaze on the water. "After a while, I became familiar with their symbols and they began picking up some words that I could communicate with them directly," Dad explained as though he were pulling in a lifeboat from the ocean. "Kinptuash understands English much better than he speaks, at least he did when I was last here. Two warriors were almost always with him, Kaga and Boncho, who has a scar on his neck, here," he said, drawing a line along his neck. "They understand English pretty well, but defer to his leadership. After a while, the whole group got used to me coming and going and I ceased to be so much of an oddity."

"I don't recall either of those names," Mia said, her tone doubting Dad, who shrugged.

"They are warriors, not the leaders of the tribe, maybe that's why. Anyone else in that time period stand out?" As much as Mia didn't want to converse with Dad, her ego couldn't help shining through.

"Sconchin is the leader. Two others, Scarface Charlie is the war chief and Hooker Jim led the raids but I don't recall their tribal names. That's odd, isn't it?"

"Not really. They are easy to remember and most history books have chosen to use the names used by the Army and settlers."

Of all the places and times, we were sent here, where Dad knew everyone. Perhaps that meant he'd gotten close—or we were close—to whatever we were to find, and he'd missed it.

You have exactly twelve months from the time the door of evil opens. Words from the ancient archivist, told to me in a dungeon in China. Words that meant nothing then. I adjusted my shoulders again, causing Mia to grumble with irritation. When did the door to time first open? Certainly not when Dad first used it, because the window would have already shut. Did it start when I received the orb, the transfer of stewardship an invisible key?

My body involuntarily tensed. We spent approximately two months in China. Ten months left. But there was one big difference: in China, I'd seen no evidence of the Serpent King.

It had to be him. He'd come through with us and I had to collect three more rocks to fill the orbs. Four more artifacts, according to the tapestry, but then what? I had only the words inscribed on a sword to give me hints of the final outcome, an inevitable confrontation with the source of evil.

Assuming I made it that far, alive.

Thinking of the time…. "Hey Mia. Do you know what we missed?" She rolled her head back and forth on my belly. "Our birthday. We can now legally vote."

"Hurray," she grumbled. "That's going to do us a lot of good. And you didn't even notice Dad, did you?"

He coughed. "Well, we were in China…"

"Fighting bad guys," I interjected. "Saving rulers. Little things."

She bonked my chest hard and sat up, wrapping her arms around her legs she had drawn against her chest. "How many times have you been *here*?" she asked Dad, her intensely, quiet voice breaking my line of thought. Her eyes were the equivalent of fiery darts covered with an ice-like precision, a prelude to something more ominous.

"Dozens," he answered, rubbing his temple with his fingers. "I got lazy, greedy with the thought of understanding what your Mom meant for me to do with the orb. I was so convinced that the Modoc's had the power or wisdom to bring her back to us."

Mia could barely contain her fury. "They didn't, or Mom would be here."

"You are right, again," he answered, the finality in his voice an echo in the clearing. "Whatever the orb requires of the holder, age or wisdom, I don't know. It didn't show me where to travel. I had no idea it had powers that Cage unlocked. When Draben took you through the wall, I thought it would be easy. I knew the Indians would have saved me from Draben. When I learned what he wanted, I figured this place would…"

"What?" I asked, when he faltered. "See how he fared getting scalped?" Dad was harsher than I thought. Good for him.

Dad smirked. "Yes, essentially."

"At least you don't have to worry about Draben telling anyone of the orb," I said, pulling my right knee into my chest, stretching my lower back. I repeated the motion with the other leg, then let my feet drop open. The visual of Draben's limp body, transformed into a zombie by me before being torn apart, was now hundreds of years decomposed. It wasn't going anywhere, our family secret immortally preserved in another time.

I rolled up and into a sitting position, my legs crossed. "What I really want to know is who told you about the Serpent King? You had me ask Draben, so you couldn't have learned it from him."

Dad's face paled in the moonlight. "No," he whispered, then cleared his throat again and spoke up, as though he'd caught himself exposing emotions he'd rather not show. "That was Kinptuash.

"The day before I last left this time, he showed me an area outside the valley. It's barren; black with obsidian and still smelling of burnt trees, remnants of a forest fire that burns annually. The rocks on the ground are placed in a particular arrangement." He shrugged his shoulders, squinting his eyes as he visualized the scene. "Oh, I suppose you can see it from above in a helicopter, like the artifacts placed by the Hopi's in Arizona of our day. From five hundred feet up, the images are unmistakable."

"The last day you were here…" I reminded Dad, getting him back on track.

"He took me to a high plain overlooking the blackened valley, showing me the pictorial on the ground. The rocks were of white, like those," gesturing to the fountain. "He told me a legend existed. That a darkness would come, one that would cover the land like the black obsidian we saw everywhere. The darkness would bring death. At the time, I thought he was referring to the US Army, and the death of plague and bullets brought by the white man. He told me no, that it wasn't a man, it was Serpents."

"You mean like, *actual* serpents?" Mia asked, raising her eyebrow.

"Why not?" I asked before Dad responded. "Moses used his staff to destroy thousands of poisonous serpents in the dessert. Why not a legend that predicted the coming of a form of death—poisonous serpents in the form of a white man? Either form—beast or man—can be deadly?"

"Cage," scowled Mia, "you missed the part where, according to the Bible, Moses' serpent first ate the staff-turned-serpents of the evil priest first. That's what allowed him to eat all the serpents."

"Details," he said, laughing at his omission.

He waved his hand over the Earth, as if replicating what he saw from above. "I asked Muleo. He drew a picture in the sand of a man on a horse. In one hand, he had a staff. Around him were many figures. Muleo told me he was Ubel, known in this world as the Serpent King. The figures around him were his priests." Dad paused then, looking from me to Mia. "Hanging on that rack, with snow falling and my body freezing bit by bit, I was in so much pain I could barely think. I was sure my words weren't going to make any sense. But when you brought Draben back to life and he answered all your questions, I realized he might know much more about the legend than me."

In a flash, Mia raised her arm and smacked her forehead. "Forget the stupid snake and King for a second. Aren't you more worried that we are going to wake up tomorrow and be chased around the valley?"

"Of course. That's the last part of what I need to tell you both. When Lapuan's woman became ill, she was lethargic and tired. I figured mono, pretty common with teenagers. The chief was worried enough to ask me if I had some medicine to help Nolina, so I started looking for solutions on my trips to and from."

"Why not let nature take its course?" I asked.

Dad turned to me. "Nature had taken its course with your mom. If you knew my death or Mia's death was possible, what would you do?"

Mia and I looked at one another. The question needed no answer.

"The Modocs had become an extension of my own family. I wanted to save her. Save her like I couldn't save your mother."

His noble intention didn't pacify Mia. "Forget the fact that you didn't know how to use the orb," she pointed out. "Besides, if you really felt guilty, you'd have been the first one to jump up and help save that warrior when he was about to be killed."

Dad's face looked pained and conflicted. I briefly wondered if it were because Mia was calling him a coward, but then felt another emotion. A wall—a barrier. Information he wasn't sharing.

"Could Nolina still be alive?" I asked.

Dad shook his head. "I very much doubt it. She was on her deathbed. They were waiting for me to help save her. I never came. She most surely died." I felt his doubt, knowing he believed his words. He'd traveled through time, witnessed a man raised as a zombie and conversed with men and women long since dead. I wanted to tell him to have a little faith.

"I'm just going as far as the woods," he said, standing and walking away.

"Call of nature," I said to Mia, watching Dad's retreating shadow.

"Let it be a long one," she muttered. Not even in her worst times had I seen a look of such extreme bitterness on her pretty face. She hugged her legs even tighter, resting her chin on her knees. "I was such an idiot, Cage. I can't believe I trusted him the entire time. Believed in him. Stood up for him!" She shook her head, grinding her teeth. "All the while you were right. Another fact that gets me."

I laid back down. "Don't let it. I was angry for years. At least you had the benefit of being happy in your ignorance when it was completely pointless for me."

Mia jerked her head roughly, as though slapping the thought away. "He had no right to try and do this alone, you know. We could have helped him. I mean, Mom probably gave that box to all of us. Not just Dad. Furthermore, *you* now have the orb. *You* are the only one operating it. Dad could do the time travel part easy enough. Maybe I could too."

It was my turn to look up at the skies. This was *not* what I needed right now. I sat up and retrieved the orb from my backpack.

"Here."

Mia hesitated only a moment, her belligerent, disbelieving stare turning to unforced enthusiasm. She eagerly took the object in her hands, rolling it over several times. She didn't bother ask me what to do. Mia immediately began turning the top, almost roughly.

"Be careful," I cautioned. "The pointer might break."

She didn't respond, but was more cautious when she unscrewed the lid, having seem me operate it when going through the tunnels. She reverently lifted the top, inspecting the rocks within.

"What are they for?"

This was the moment I'd been dreading. To tell her or keep it to myself? Dad would eventually ask the same questions. Then what?

"You can't possibly be afraid I'm going to take your *power*?" Her slurring of the last word pricked my ego and I suppressed an exhale of irritation.

"The black obsidian can heal or hurt," I said, my voice as even as if I were explaining a math problem.

Her eyes lit up, excited with the prospect. "It was how you brought Draben back to life?"

"Yes, but he was a zombie. No soul. The grey rock, the pumice, controlled the water on the sea. I don't know what else it can do."

"I want to try it." She looked up at me, expecting me to challenge her. A surge of protectionism came over me, making me want to hover around the ball myself, shielding it with my back. I rationalized she was my sister, not some thief who was going to turn around and hurt me. Besides, what right did I have to determine who held the orb within my family? The orb had a will of its own.

"You only have one problem," I told her, sitting back down on the ground, as nonchalantly as I could. "Something to use for your experiment."

She shook her head, squinting her eyes in concentration. She glanced around the clearing, for what, I had no idea. She set the orb on the grass, moved to the far edge, by the other spring. She rolled up her sleeve as she sat down.

"Mia, don't—"

Before I could stop her, she slipped the edge of the rock from one side of her wrist to the other. Grabbing her hand, I held it up. The blood came to the surface slowly, in pin-point size clots. Had the edge been sharper, her vein would have been sliced, the opening gushing blood.

"Let go of me Cage," she demanded, giving no hint of pain. "I don't want your help."

Unreal. She turned the top of the orb clockwise, watching her left wrist as it lay flat on her leg. I held my breath, wondering what was going to happen.

Nothing.

Mia kept turning the top half until it had moved a full circle around.

The moonlight caught the crease between her eyebrows. She then turned the top half counterclockwise. This time, my heart raced faster. It might cause her pain or paralyze her, just as I had done with the Prince of Yan and his guards. As she rotated the metal, the blood on her wrist remained the same. At least no more damage was being inflicted.

"Are you not telling me something that's important?" she demanded. Gone was the sarcastic, teasing-I-love-you manner. She was in her win-at-all-costs mode.

"Mia, settle down." She was about to launch off on a tirade about my use of the phrase settle down when I cut her off. "You didn't want my help and now you do. Which is it?"

Her chest was heaving from her failure.

I motioned for her to hold the object firmly. "Take it, just like you did. Open it up, locate the black obsidian rock, replace the top and turn the spindle over the rock. Clear your mind then wait and see what happens."

She raised her left eyebrow, lowering her chin enough to cast a shadow on her eyes. "That's it?"

I rolled my own eyes to the glowing lights from above. Determination and pride had momentarily taken over reason if she really believed I was on some power trip. "What do I have to gain from not telling you the truth?" Mia's eyebrow lowered and her lips slid to one corner as she considered my statement. "You want to do this? Then listen." I waited for her to acknowledge me before I repeated the step-by-step instructions.

Inch by inch, the top of the orb turned the full circumference. We gazed at her wrist. Nothing changed.

Strange. Healing the protruding bones from Dad's leg had taken only a quarter turn when I did it, the skin sealing itself and reviving his flesh in another quarter turn. I'd stopped then, unwilling to see if any further rotation of the orb would cause him to grow wings and take flight.

"It looks like the orb doesn't like you either," said Dad. He'd come from behind Mia. Pretending not to hear him,

Mia turned it once again. The top of her hand was white from pressure, as though it would make a difference. Dad sat down on the other side of the sacred fountain. "Now I'm not going to feel so inadequate for failing with that thing." Mia's face clearly communicated her dislike at being placed in the same category with Dad.

"When you tried, on the training grounds, it had the rocks in it?" Mia asked Dad, who nodded.

"And that proved the orb wasn't going to respond to me." Dad seemed unconcerned with his lack of talent, as though it were a weight lifted from his shoulders. "What really bothers me is why I could travel through time but do nothing else. I can't read the inscriptions either nor make the tablet work."

They both directed questioning eyes on me.

"Spill it," said Mia, recognizing the signs of hesitancy. "After the crap I went through, I deserve to know what happened and why it works for you."

Confronting the inevitable, I spoke. "I don't know why it works for me. I can only relate what happened," which I did. I told them the easy part; finding the stones on my journey with Zheng He. Recognizing the patterns of the rocks and the indentations within the orb itself. They'd heard from Qi Tai that I'd raised a six-armed thousand-year-old beast to life, but not how it was raised from its stone form. Mia's eyes widened with amazement and more than a bit of envy as I retold how I'd sat on the stone base of the statue, holding the orb in my hand.

"The next thing I knew, the legs had turned to hair colored flesh, the snort was hoofing and the beast was making a decision to chop me up or take down others in the hallway."

"What would you have done if it had tried to hurt you?" Mia asked, her eyes wide. "Turn the orb the other direction to kill it?"

Dad grinned from ear to ear, familial pride plain on his face. "The man-bull never tried attacking you did it?"

"No," I answered, remembering how it has paused just long enough to stop my heart.

Dad seemed pleased with the answer. "It had an unspoken allegiance to you." I told them how I'd found the beast after the battle and healed it from the life-threatening wounds. I also related how the severed hand reconnected, the tissue as strong and healthier-looking that it was before.

"What did Zheng He mean about controlling the storms?" Mia asked, her voice carrying an element of skepticism. "Withholding things from us?" I glanced at Dad, mentally cursing him. This was the collateral damage of him lying. Now she was paranoid I was doing it too.

"The night the bull was transformed from a creature of stone to a living animal, Zeng He got the letter explaining your disappearance and the order we return. He had me imprisoned in the ship, handcuffed inside the main cabin. When the storm came, the ship was getting slammed by the waves. He was sure the ship was going to sink without my help. Zheng He ordered me to calm the storm and I just figured it out. I used the other stone, the pumice. When I turned it one direction, the storm got immediately worse. The other direction lessened it. Equal and opposites, just like the other rock."

"Opposition in all things," Dad murmured, more to himself. Perking up, he interlaced his fingers. "You know what's interesting about this Cage, is that it's not just dead creatures once living that come to life," Dad said thoughtfully. "The stone bull and the dragon, both inanimate creatures."

"It doesn't explain why one obeyed me and the other tried to kill me along with everyone else."

"Ahh," said Dad, his eye's brightening as they did when he gave a lecture at the university. "On the contrary, that might be the very reason. What if the difference in attitude had nothing to do with the creature, but had more to do with the way the creature was formed—or more importantly, the *person*—who formed the creature. You said Zheng He told you monks created the stone temples, the thousands of Buddha statues. Who created those statues? And what types of statues were they? I'd bet that the monks had something to do with the carvings themselves," he went on, gathering speed as he spoke. "And they might have chanted in prayers while they did it. Most certainly the monks said prayers morning and night and throughout the day, is as the custom. Beyond that, the Buddha's are nearly always about good things—love, hope, fertility, strength."

Dad was right on that count. I'd never seen a Buddha of hate or killing.

"On the other hand, the dragon in the square was created for one reason only. To protect the Emperor and his royal family. The dragon was likely carved by a master artisan whose sole intent was to produce a finished sculpture fierce enough to destroy any living or non-living being that posed a threat to the ruler. Don't you see? When it awoke, it went after every threat, you included, with no thought as to who raised it or why. In the end, it was true to its mission, dying in the process of fighting for the life of the Emperor."

"What you're saying is that neither one had a soul, so they were products of their creator, or the intent for which they were created."

"Exactly!" Dad enthusiastically agreed, his voice pleased with his theory.

"It doesn't totally explain Draben though," I countered, seeing a flaw in the logic.

"Of course it does," Dad countered. "He said he didn't have a soul, and the orb was the only way to get the soul back. Once you have the body and the soul, the person is whole." Dad was positively triumphant at his conclusion, but the knowledge didn't give me comfort. I now knew where he was going with this and what he thought the powers of the orb could deliver.

"Dad—what you're thinking…" I trailed. "It's not possible. Not with the current rocks." I didn't want to crush his dream of reuniting with Mom, and certainly I'd like to be with Bao, but only if she was alive, healthy, and in the same condition I left her. Not some monster with eye balls dripping out their sockets and gore oozing from her stomach. Mom was now three years in the grave, the flesh gone.

Dad looked like I had struck him with a hand, the reality of my image hitting him as though he'd never considered Mom rising up as a zombie like Draben.

"You—we don't know, Son," he said, hope still clear in his voice. "So much is still to be learned about the orb." His look wasn't one of jealousy. He exuded a pride that it was me, his son, who had cracked the code, or at least part of it. "You are just figuring it out. Think of what is in front of you. What filling the other holes will bring and what they can do. No telling how much power can be gained."

"Cage found the powers of both rocks on accident," Mia interjected. "Not because he was trying to do anything with it. Here," she said, thrusting the orb back at me. She was taking it as a personal insult the orb hadn't responded to her.

"Do you want me to heal your wounds now?"

"Why bother?" Mia untied her shirt from her belt loop and put it on. "I just hope I do more than end up as a servant or someone's intended concubine this time." She balled up her hoodie for a pillow and laid down, her back to me and Dad.

Her anger wasn't completely fair. If it hadn't been for me knowing how to operate the thing, Dad would be dead, along with lots of other people, herself included.

Dad raised his eyebrow at me, a single, man-to-man glance that said it all. He knew better than to chuckle or try and reason with her. For the first time in years, we felt the same way.

CHAPTER 5

When my eyes closed, it was with the heaviness of a warm blanket draping me from shoulders to feet. The fuzzy texture seemed to creep up and around my frame, molding itself against me like warm clay, the breeze lulling me to sleep. The last visual I had was of the underground tunnels, full of warm water, the steam pushing up and through the surface to our protected environment.

"Cage, wake up. We have to talk." My eyes refused to open. Dad's voice was right in my ear, his breath tickling it in a way so irritating I flipped up a hand. It connected with bones, followed by an exclamation of pain. "That was unnecessary," Dad scolded. "I think you split my lip."

I cracked an eye, humor stirring my body from its hibernation-like dormancy.

"What's going on?" I grumbled, not bothering to whisper. The only things that woke Mia were her stomach or soccer matches.

"It will be light in a couple of hours. You understand what they will do if they find us, don't you?"

The visual of the warrior with the knife came to mind. "Yeah. I got that part," I responded gravely. "But the one on the ground, the one I saved, is he after you too?"

"I don't know. Maybe. But you shouldn't have to suffer along with me." Dad paused and I cracked an eye. "Well, why did you bring us here?"

Sighing, I sat upright, crossing my legs, meditation style. The cold air immediately cloaked my back, causing me to shiver. I wanted the warmth of the moss but knew I'd fall asleep again if I laid back down. Dad was across from me, his eyes staring at the backpack. He made no motion to get it, his look one of acknowledgment it was now mine to protect, not his.

"Are you kidding me?" I yawned. It never dawned on me he thought I'd brought us here on purpose. "The orb picked the location and the time, just as it did for you. Maybe we are here so you could set things right about the girl."

Dad fiddled with his fingers, locking then interlocking them. "Could be. Do you mind if I look inside the orb?" I searched for his intentions and felt nothing. Dad smiled at me as though he knew exactly what I was thinking. "It doesn't work for me, remember?"

I unscrewed the lid, holding the top in my hand as I gave him the bottom portion. He lifted it to his eyes, turning it at an angle in the moonlight. He placed the tip of his forefinger on the inside, just as I had, feeling the texture of the dents.

"Pumice isn't unique on its own. My question is why pumice from China and specifically, the Datong volcanoes? Did you really have to journey there to get these exact specimens?"

I shrugged. "I only operate the thing."

"When did Mia develop the ability to see hidden objects?"

"You referring to the time at the courtyard?" Dad nodded. "She saved the Empress's cousin. A holy man blessed her for placing her life in jeopardy. She can 'see what men want' was her words. To date, her new gift has displayed itself in what you saw—she can see through clothes, and who knows what else for anything valuable."

"That's what men want," agreed Dad. "Whatever is valuable." I only nodded, hoping he'd let me get back to sleep. He handed me the object and I put the lid back on, replacing it in the backpack. "She's pretty mad at me, justifiably so. I was on your crap list for three years. You think hers will be shorter?" I'd never heard Dad like that. Now that he did it so naturally, it made me laugh.

"She'll come around. Eventually." I laid down on my side, head on my bicep.

Dad glanced at Mia, the jowls on his cheeks tightened as he drew back his lips. "Look. If anything happens like it did in China and we get separated…"

"Don't do it," I said bluntly. He was as transparent as a kid waiting until his parents went to sleep before he snuck out of the house.

"Do you blame me? I'm a dead man anyway."

"So, you're going to help them along? Look, Dad," I began, propping myself on my elbow. "It appears that we have a choice, to align ourselves with one group for our time here, and that's the Modocs. Our other option is to go it alone, and I don't give us high odds for survival."

Dad ran his hands through his hair in frustration. "I just don't know. What I saw earlier today doesn't make sense. It's as though the balance within the valley has somehow shifted."

"Explain."

He gestured with his hands, the moonlight aiding his explanation. "The tribes each have certain parts of the river they fish, what areas each hunt the animals and generally co-exist. Sometimes tribes raid one another's campsites but it's stealing horses, the equivalent of toilet-papering the house next door. Something must have happened. Pulamon used to be a friend of Kinptuash, and I have no idea what made him so angry he'd try to kill him."

I thought of Xing and his one-time desire to kill me. Hate is generated for a lot of reasons. Not all of them as obvious as a person dying. "What about the settlers, as Mia said. Could that have changed things?"

"Sure, and I saw some of that. When the tribes left for seasonal hunting, the settlers moved in, built structures and refused to leave. The Klamaths fought back, the settlers brought in the Army and the tribe ceded land only after lot of tribe members died. Sconchin, the leader of the Modocs, learned from this and voluntarily gave up almost half of the most prime areas for fishing and hunting to the settlers, thinking they made the best choice for their people. They retreated into the rockier formations."

"How do they survive then?"

"When I was here, they were going out by night to raid the other lands, but they were smart," he said admiringly. "The warrior in charge of raiding is Hooker Jim, as Mia noted. He'd take a few animals here and there, under the cover of night, never too much to cause a stir. And those horses," he said, shaking his head. "A female Indian trains the horses, or really, it's like she speaks to them silently, keeping the manes as silky as any of the Emperor of China's finest robes."

"Happy horses are important," I answered without any real feeling.

"Horses, Cage, are everything. But it's more than that. The female Indian, Kahinsula, she's got a gift, like you. It's special. No one gave it to her, it just is. She can ride better than anyone, including Kintpuash and come to think of it, she's about your age, maybe slightly older, but given how you look…" he chuckled again. "No one's going to mistake you for a teenager anymore."

Probably not. "Raiding isn't a long-term strategy."

Dad's eyes grew darker as he lowered his lids. "No, and it's only a matter of time before they run out of food or get pushed to the point of utter destruction or submission. I hope we aren't too late."

"Is that the end?" I asked wearily.

"Yes, get some sleep."

I did, and it was deep. My dreams took me to Bao, who was sitting on a marble bench, under a cherry tree within the Emperor's sacred zoo. Bright pink blossoms cascaded gently down either side, tossing this way and that of her narrow shoulders like fairies dancing on Christmas Eve. She was smiling, her left palm outstretched, beckoning me to her. The smell of lilies passed through the air, riding on her request until it reached me and I followed the scent back to where she sat.

A part of my consciousness wondered if this was a gift from the orb, giving me back stolen time for a memory that now lived in only in my dreams. That same part of me didn't care if it was a physical truth. The smell, the touch, our emotions, felt as tangible as if it were real.

I walked steadily towards her, my pace hiding a nearly overwhelming desire to run. *Soon now.* My arms would wrap around her, the soft, dark hair would touch me as she nuzzled her cheek to the crook of my neck and we would hold each other. The rising temperature within me was tempered by a deep adoration balancing my physical desire.

Anticipating our reunion, I smiled and her ruby lips parted, the dark liner at the corner of her eyes tilted up as her cheeks lifted with joy. Then she froze, her eyes distracted by a dark cloud in the sky above. Her face changed from welcoming joy to fear as we both watched the falling leaves turn to ash. The warm breeze turned thin, leaving a chill without moisture. I tried to run towards her but my legs felt heavy, like I was running as hard as I could without the movement underneath. The more I tried, the slower I became until my legs were motionless. Alarmed, Bao looked at me, her eyes expressing a terror that echoed in my mind. The whipping wind was gathering forms that had shape and direction, coming around her, towards me then back, accompanied by an eerie whistle of pain.

They were souls. I felt emotions within the air. Loss. Grief. Anger. Why? My mind cried out. Why disturb us, the living? Swishes of air traveled beside me in all directions, assaulting me with feelings of bitterness. Their bodies had been separated from their soul, damning them to an eternity alone, without the possibility of reuniting with their families.

It was not our fault, my mind shouted. *We had nothing to do with it! We are still young! In love!*

My words were ignored. The speed of the souls moving under the tree increased to hurricane level, the ash hitting Boa so quickly she was blanketed in grey. Soon she would be covered, her body indiscernible.

Fight, I yelled to Bao, but her ears were already covered, so too were her eyes, the beautiful long lashes hidden far underneath the suffocating objects. Her body gone, no longer relevant, her soul would be….

Nooo! I shouted.

I jolted awake, panting. A dream. It was just a *dream*. My chest pounded from the exertion of my heart, the back of my throat constricted and hoarse. Had I yelled out loud, as I did in my dream or was it because my throat was dry? Lying motionless, I looked up, unwilling to do more. Was the legend of the sacred grove real after all? Had my mind been invaded by the spirits of those long dead, entities who entered the mind and body of the living? Only one person might know.

"Dad?" I asked, still looking up at the sky. "Dad, wake up," I repeated, raising my voice above a whisper. I turned to where I'd last seen him. The ground was empty. I craned over, peering in the darkness though it was unnecessary. The light of the moon was still bright, illuminating the entire area. He wasn't on the other side either. Probably another call of nature. He'd promised he wouldn't leave, that we would go in to the Modocs together.

Unable to sleep, I stood and began a series of Gi Gong breathing exercises, counting to twenty as I stretched out my arms as though they were rolling a large ball in front of my chest and waist. Whatever poison was in my lungs—real or imagined—I wanted it out. I took as long to expel the air as I did to take it in, visualizing every particle gone from my body. The entire effort took several minutes. After ten repetitions, I stopped. The charcoal taste and feeling inside me might have left, but it was being replaced with tension in my middle back from the obvious. Dad had left us.

"Mia, wake up," I said to my sister, nudging her still body with my hand. She groaned irritably. "Mia, we've got to go."

Mia turned over, her voice groggy. "I love this heating pad," she said, nestling her shoulders in the warmth of the moss.

"Get up and drink as much water as you can. It's going to get hot and I have no idea how far we have to go." She made no motion and I shook her.

"Go where?" Mia grumbled, but eventually rose, rubbing her shoulders to combat the morning cold before remembering her pillow. She slipped on the coarse, brown top and looked around. "He's gone?" Mia's countenance changed abruptly, snapping her awake. "He didn't take the backpack did he?"

"No. I had the strap looped between my hands." I went to drink from the spring, splashing my face. A nice, long hot bath would be welcome at this point. It was an experience I wondered if I'd ever have again.

"Maybe in a roman hot tub," I muttered.

"Roman what?" Mia asked.

"Nothing." The sun was rising and the items inside the water sparkled. "Oh, man." I called Mia over and she followed my gaze down to the water. She let out a breath of anger and shock, moving her fingers under the trickling water, plucking a small, gold object from a shelf on the rock.

"How *could* he?" Mia asked, holding up mom's wedding ring. I knew the answer, but it took me a moment before I said it out loud.

I looked her straight in the eye. "He's trying to save us. He thinks the Modocs will kill him and us too, just for being with him." Mia held the ring in the center of her palm, staring at it. "Put it on," I suggested, picking up the nunchucks from the ground and putting them in the backpack. We were done here. I put my hands on her shoulders. "We get what we need. We find Dad, we leave. Agreed?"

Mia nodded. "What? You're not going to add the part about not falling in love, no killing and no changing the future?" In my moment of silence, she smirked. "Gotcha."

We dropped, noiselessly shuffling along the ground, the silence broken by the calling of birds.

"How do you know this was the way down?" she hissed softly.

"The ground is indented." The moss had kept the depressions of dad's footsteps long enough for me to trace it to the edge of the clearing. "He can't be that far ahead."

My instinct told me Dad was playing this out like a game of chess. He was making his move, hoping to negate the issues with the Modocs before they came in search of us.

We neared the edge of the underbrush and a high shrieking from the sky startled me. It was an animal going for a kill. I put my hand out behind me, stopping her. "Be still." We remained low, watching the hawk swoop down and then soar high into the hot, morning air. A branch nearby barely moved when the bird gave a shrill cry and dove straight down. Its wing span was as long as my arms outstretched, its red tail as distinctive as its cry. If Ubel, as my dad called him, could inhabit animals and use their characteristics to do his bidding, the eyes of a hawk, eight times as powerful as a humans, would easily spot us. Until I knew the secret to keeping our physical bodies from being re-possessed, we were vulnerable.

The bird's talons stretched out as it neared the ground, clasping an object within its claws and flew back in to the air in a graceful arch.

Mia moved to my side as the bird went the other direction. "Is that what you were getting at last night? The being—whatever his name was—the entity, was inside you, and now the bird?"

"I do. Look there," I pointed. A long object hung from the claws of the hawk. The bird of prey deftly navigated the winds in the warm air and found a resting place on a lonely tree jutting from a rock formation. It pricked out the snake's eyes. The silence was complete again as we waited. The bird stopped its killing, darted its head around and I could swear...looked at me, watching for moment. The bird screamed once, then ferociously attacked the dead animal in its talons.

"*Weird*," Mia said under her breath. Nothing seemed weird anymore to me. Experiences seemed…connected.

"Why didn't you tell Dad about it? He never asked what happened in the tunnel, which I thought was odd. And you stopped me from mentioning the shirt." Her tone wasn't accusatory, it was interested. "Don't you trust him?"

"It's only partly about trust," I answered. The truth was I didn't want Mia getting sick with the knowledge of what we were up against.

We reached the edge, stood and stretched. I dug within my pants. "Hold on a minute. It's light enough now and I want to check one thing."

The paper was unharmed from the last pursuit in China, the thin, archival material crisp, the edges sharp. A familiar scent wafted up as I unfolded the document, bringing back the flood of memories, the stroke of my lips on Bao's cheek and neckline, my hands on her lower back. Her eyes, sparkling with her affection for me, her lashes moist from the tears of separation felt as fresh as…yesterday.

It *was* only yesterday that I'd left her. My longing for her hadn't diminished in the twenty-four hours since I'd said goodbye. If anything, it had increased. I wondered how long it had taken her to relinquish her feelings for me. A week to forget the sound my voice, a year before the image of my face became blurry. Had she lived out her life in happiness? Marrying, having children, or serving her Empress until the day she died.

"You miss her that much?" I hadn't noticed Mia watching me as I absently gazed at the paper. Mia's soft voice was gentler than it had been in weeks.

I gave her a crooked smile. "We had a choice to do the right thing and we did. Just like now." Mia grabbed a handful of hair, removed the rubber band from her wrist and pulled the mass back from her face in a ponytail.

She sighed with resignation. "Nope. You'd never let us do the wrong thing. Staying with Bao or bringing her along would have been wrong. Leaving Dad would be wrong." She stopped talking and stared. "Well? Are we going or not?"

"Give me a minute. I'm looking at this diagram Bao made of the tapestry. It gives us clues." Mia bent over my shoulder, tracing the edge of the paper with her fingertip. On the right and slightly lower were two black lines dividing the imagery.

"That looks familiar."

"It was in the valley we saw," I finished for her. "Last night Dad felt inside the orb and he thinks the texture matches what this rock might be."

Mia peered closer, the morning light illuminating the dark underbrush. She pointed to a figure. "That guy is very detailed, so is the clock-thing. What does it mean?"

My stomach constricted slightly, and the reaction bothered me. She was my sister. My twin. Why was I compelled to hide parts of the story from her when she had a right to know the entire saga?

Safety. Her innate curiosity and enthusiasm for anything adventurous was present at all times. Unfortunately, that was also part of the problem. If she knew what lay before us, I'd be hard pressed to stop her from going straight to each Indian tribe, searching for an artifact, all the while running from one rock formation to another to get what we needed.

I glanced at the rising sun, my pulse quickening with the reality we were going to face the opposition shortly. "Promise me you aren't going to do anything rash without talking to me first?" Mia scolded me by rolling her eyes. "I'm not saying you're stupid Mia. I'm asking you to be responsible. Can you do it?" She vigorously nodded her head. It would have to do. I pointed to the clock.

"This represents fifty-two years. Fifty-two years is the gap between the window of evil to this world. It's when Ubel, who I actually think is the spirit of the Serpent King, can enter this world, its spirit possessing any living being. The tapestry in China depicted him as very handsome, powerful, compelling, a leader anyone would be proud to follow, which would make sense. The spirit could enter any physical body, and we all know the more handsome you are, and dynamic, helps out."

"The Prince of Yan," Mia added.

I nodded. "Exactly. The existing Emperor had been fair and just, but he didn't have the age or commanding presence of the Prince. We saw how the people wanted to follow the invader. He made them feel safe. Mia," I went on, "I read the inscriptions on sword that was thousands of years old detailing his conquests of entire civilizations and Mia, it matches history. *Real history* that we both know about."

Mia's full lips parted and I felt her pulse quicken, its steady beat strong not palpitating. She was in control of her emotions, absorbing the information while remaining logical. The possibility this was a far bigger piece of the puzzle than simply gaining a rock or artifact now was dawning on her.

"Dad doesn't know does he?"

"No." The sun made a flat line across the plains below us, beginning to bake the Earth. She had minutes to take on faith what I had weeks to absorb. "I don't know why he couldn't read the inscriptions, but in China, I learned so much. We are a part of a lineage—a family—that has fought this evil man for a thousand years. Other families were a part of our force, but they were killed, one by one. We are the only family left. Mom kept the orb and the notepad for us, in that box. I believe that somehow, when I got the orb, it coincided with the beginning of the cycle- or maybe even activated it. It didn't happen when Dad had it or the cycle would have already ended."

Mia's breath was heavier now, the blood flowing thick and fast, her thoughts captivated by my words. "You—we—are going to be fighting this—thing—that can move in and out of bodies? For how long, the next fifty-two years?"

"No, we have about ten months." At this, Mia's shoulders straightened, her eyes darting above my head. She was now my ally in this, not just my twin who was going to blindly follow my lead.

"By coming here, we aged up, and it has to be for a reason. I wonder…" she said, looking around.

"If our skills have changed?" I asked.

"Or improved. Do you think this mean we will be old by the time this is over?" I had no answers. "Okay," she said, regrouping. "We go through time and find what you need for the orb and then this source of evil, this Ubel, is eliminated, right?"

"That's the concept. If we get what we need then yes, he'll go back to the other side for another fifty-two years—

unless…" A flash of words on the sword came to me. It could end, but I wasn't ready to believe the requirements inscribed on the sword. Not yet. I pointed down to the illustration.

"His destruction has been limited to the windows of time where he's been on the earth. But in those time periods, massive outbreaks of disease have taken place, wars have been started, civilizations destroyed. The Chinese archives listed mass devastations and they were linked with the opening of the window. In each one, a supposed bad ruler was in place, but what if….just what if that ruler was good and was inhabited by Ubel? All the destruction occurred and then after that time period was up, bam, it went back to normal? If the person on that horse is as good looking and powerful and persuasive as I think he was, people will blindly follow him. You know that once a person is overcome with the thirst for power it is an unquenchable desire."

Mia pulled her eyes away from mine and looked down at the paper. "Those people look like the living dead," she said, her words barely a whisper.

"You saw what Qi Tai was intending to do with an army of zombies. Imagine what a person with ten times his power and influence?"

"All this going on while Dad is worried about penance for some girl he didn't save." She shook her head in anger and worry.

"Now you understand why I keep emphasizing time. We don't have much."

"Four more places, including this one?" I nodded. She glanced once more at the tapestry then looked around on the ground. "If Dad was trying to hide his tracks, he did a bad job of it."

"He wasn't," I told her. "I think he wants us to follow him, but arrive after he's had the hard conversation. Be careful with your footing," I cautioned. Animal prints were all along the path, donkey and deer I guessed, mixed with Dad's.

"Stop," whispered Mia, touching the back of my shirt. When I turned, she was already bent over, using a rock to dig below the hard surface.

"Not now Mia."

She hushed my comment, focused on her objective. Impatient, I watched as she dug her nails into the ground and soon pulled up a rock.

"Look," Mia said, showing her find. The light glimmered off the chunk of dirt. It was gold, the size of a quarter. "We might use it for a negotiation." For a split second, I thought she got the better part of the deal in China. Sure, my shirt saved me from death, but she had the ability to see valuable objects.

"Or, we save it for our return." If we lived through this, I'd like to benefit in some way other than wisdom.

"Can you imagine?" Mia conjectured, as we resumed walking. "Who knows where we will go? I could get us silver talons from Rome, diamonds from India, gold from this time. Any one of them would guarantee a life far from what we had back at home with a rented house and an old Toyota."

I thought of the fifteenth century jade in the Emperor's Palace. It would have brought me millions, but how would I justify it in my possession? Stealing wasn't my thing, so it would have to be given to me, like Mia's gift.

"Wait a sec. I see another one ..." she paused and dug, grunting with effort. Eventually she lifted up an object. "What do you think of that?" It was a piece of gold the size of her fist.

"Will it fit in your pack?" The sides of her carrier bulged in agony, the zipper protesting as she struggled to close it without breaking the seam. She snapped the clasp together and neatly tied her shirt around the back, leaving it dangling like a tail over her butt.

"How far do you we have to go?"

"From this map, I guess an hour, but I'm heading in a general direction." I was about to warn her of her pink shoulders, but the color had already turned to a nice, even tan. She looked like a California surfer, albeit one with a few scratches from the sand.

She laughed at my glance. "Why don't you take off your own shirt Cage? You could get a vicious bronze if you let yourself."

I wasn't opposed to having a tan, I just didn't see the point. No girls. No bathing suits. Who was I going to impress?

"Let me go first," was all I got out before a warm hand cupped my forehead, a foot was placed over my right ankle and the edge of a blade angled at my throat. I stopped, my body motionless. Though my arms were free and I could have dropped, spun and maneuvered against one attacker, I had no idea how many others were around.

Unaware of what was happening behind her, Mia kept walking. An Indian appeared like a ghost on the wind, covering her mouth with a palm, looping her arms behind her back in an effortless, gliding motion that would have made my martial arts master proud. When he turned, I felt relief and worry. He was a member of the tribe my father liked and feared. He was with the Modocs.

CHAPTER 6

Mia tried to move her body, obstinately resisting against the arms that gripped her from behind. In one fluid motion, the man spun her around. He had a scar on his neck and a part of his jaw line. His wide hand was over her mouth, from nose to chin, the pressure depressing her flesh.

"Boncho?" I guessed. His already dark eyes blackened. In my peripheral vision, I noticed his fingers twitching, and I imagined him moving his digits in some way to protect himself from evil spirits.

The other warrior beside him remained motionless.

"Kaga?" He only stared.

Mia struggled within Boncho's grasp. Before I could warn her, she clenched her teeth, crunching on the flesh that pressed against her skin. Boncho's eyes flitted, the muscles underneath his skin rippling as his eyes held mine. Instead of releasing her, his fingers pressed harder. Blood ran down his wrist, a drop, then another, hitting the ground silently.

Impressive.

Mia's eyes followed a movement behind me, but I didn't need to see the person. Watching my sister was enough. First, her eyelashes fluttered, then a slight blush appeared at the base of her neck, working its way up her throat, then under and around Boncho's hand. By the time it reached her eyes, the man was at my shoulder. Mia's shoulders rose slightly.

Kinptuash moved between me and my sister. Today, his face was natural, free of the white paint. His shoulders were level with my own, though broader. He wore a half-sleeve leather shirt, sewn at the sides, the straps hanging below his relaxed arms.

"We have no weapons," I offered, hoping to avoid a search of my backpack. The light of the torch shadowed his face as Kinptuash studied me.

"Mmm-mm." Mia squirmed against Boncho's grasp. When Kintpuash glanced at my sister, I followed his gaze. The dark blood had oozed between his fingers like paint seeping through wooden slats.

Kinptuash spoke in low tones, the vowels and consonants fused together like words in a song. Boncho removed his hand, turned his palm over and kept his eyes flat as the blood dripped from the ripped flesh. His skin had small indents where Mia's teeth had been.

Mia drew a breath to talk, but Kinptuash silenced her with a glance. She cocked her head up and to the right, the confidence she'd gained in China on full display with another man, in another time.

Kintpuash stared at her quizzically, but instead of softening, he pointed to Mia's left hand. A pink flush colored her cheeks and she pursed her lips. She raised her hand and turned it over, palm up.

Kinptuash took her hand in his and lifted it to his mouth. His eyes never left hers as he bit in to her flesh. Mia's eyes remained steady, as though a strip of glue held them to her upper lid. She'd prove herself a stronger warrior than his own man, even if it meant the bite went clean through to her bones.

After Kinptuash removed his blood-stained lips from her hand, he stretched the torn flesh, continuing until she involuntarily jerked. It was enough. He stopped, rotating her hand, the blood hitting the dirt directly on top of Boncho's blood. She nodded at Kintpuash in understanding.

When he released her hand, Mia did the unexpected. She extended her injured hand, palm up, in front of Boncho. The warrior took a moment to consider her offer, then he covered it with his own. They had a truce. We could move on.

"Kinptuash," I said, dipping my head slightly. "We—me and my sister—desire to go to your camp. I believe my father, George Fleener, might already be there."

The warrior looked to the east. His jaw muscles remained smooth, whatever emotion he had deep he kept deep within, like a giant animal of the sea, well underneath the waves.

"Traitor," Kinptuash responded, his voice flat.

He turned and led us back in to the valley of the lava bed forest, the way from which we came.

We silently jogged in single file down the steep trail when we reached a narrow valley of grey smokestacks. The chest high pillars had wide bases, resembling the ant hills that I'd seen in pictures of South America, but these mud-like cones were narrow and uneven, the rim haphazardly placed mud. Faint plumes drafted up one of the grey stacks and by the time we ran by, the stench of sulfur was strong.

As we covered the terrain, Kintpuash's words kept repeating in my mind. *Yes, Dad would be considered a traitor until the truth was known.*

Kinptuash didn't slow his pace as we continued through the ever-changing terrain. At the end of the narrow valley we came to a wash, the dry, soft sand flushed out by massive downpours of rain in the spring. Kinptuash held up his right palm and I stopped. Mia nudged her way to my left side, peering over my shoulder, Boncho to my right.

We waited as Kinptuash walked cautiously forward through the area. Seconds later, a rattlesnake sprung from its hiding place, flying through the air, sinking its teeth into the Kinptuash' leather covered ankle. The snake writhed in fury at the obstacle placed between his fangs and the skin he desired. Kinptuash removed a large blade from the leather strap at his waist, but before he could use it, a rock hit the head of the snake, causing it to release its fangs and drop to the ground. Kinptuash was caught off guard, spinning to find the source that had thrown the stone as the snake slithered away. Mia was smug, the rock had come from a kick of her shoe, its mark precise. Kinptuash regarded her intently. Not what he expected, I was sure.

Kintpuash's inattention was a mistake. Another snake coiled to strike behind him. Without hesitation, I slipped the knife from Boncho's belt, held it by the blade and sent it whirling to the reptile. Kinptuash' eyes followed the blade as it went by him, the tip penetrating the snakes head as it reared back to strike. The force of the knife lifted the rattlesnake up from its position, slamming it against a boulder. The clang and thud of the knife was followed by silence as Kinptuash stared at me.

"Nice one," muttered Mia.

Kinptuash retrieved the knife from the snake's head. Giving the weapon back to Boncho, he dropped to my feet, raising the hem of my pants. He touched the thick material of my shoes, releasing the pant leg. Mia didn't wait for him to touch her feet. She lifted her pant leg, extending her foot, moving it in a circle for a good view. His fingers traced the leather, stopping on the canvas, grunting. The thick soled slippers with thin sides weren't going to withstand fangs of a rattlesnake.

Kintpuash spoke and in a single movement, Boncho lofted Mia on his shoulders as easily as if she were a pillow. We sprinted down the center of the wash without another word until we reached the other side where Boncho placed Mia on her feet, moving again the minute he did so.

Once on the rock terrain, the trees thinned. Soon we'd be in the full sunlight with little covering other than the boulders.

We ran over two more rises when Mia started coughing, a dry, hacking sound. Kinptuash stopped, quickly removing the leather sack around his pouch. He unplugged the top, placing the bottom of the sack and gave it directly to my sister, who took a long, healthy drink. She handed me the sack and I lifted. Nothing came out. I tried again, then upended it. Out came two drops. Kinptuash looked at the ground where they fell and Boncho grunted.

"Oh sorry, Cage," her apologetic look echoing her words. As much as I was a parched desert rat, it *was* funny. "I didn't do that on purpose."

Kinptuash took back the empty leather water bag as Boncho loosened his own pouch. I took less than I wanted. When it was his turn, Boncho lifted it up and down to assess the amount remaining, giving me a glance of appreciation.

Seconds later we were on the move again, the black rocks changing to soft grey dust. It reminded me of the ash from Mt. Saint Helens in Washington. Small puffs of white dispersing in the air, the fine, white particles sure to get in our lungs if our pace was any slower.

Gradually, the ash ground turned into enormous black obsidian rocks. We were somewhere within the onyx colored expanse depicted in the tapestry, a place of significance known only to me and few men, long dead. Had Dad been here, I'd have asked him about the importance of the formations.

All the while, I was considering how and when I'd be able to stop, gather a few samples and compare the textures to the inside of the orb.

"Kinptuash," I half whispered. "My father was with us this morning but is now gone. Do you know where he is?"

Kinptuash abruptly halted. I nearly slammed in to him as he turned around. His face had hardened, the plains on his high cheekbones tightening and his eyes drew back.

"I think that's a yes," Mia said pointedly. "He might already be dead, if that's what he was trying to accomplish. But then, Kinptuash did say traitor."

"Mia..." I said, stunned by the callousness at her words. She put up her wounded hand in the same fashion she'd done to stop dad from speaking the night before.

She started to talk but closed her mouth with another look from Kintpuash. I got it. If I'd been a woman, with a guy looking like he should be on some billboard wearing underwear, sporting his bronze tan and ripped abs, I'd lose my voice too.

"No more words," Kinptuash commanded us in perfectly good, although accented, English. "We go to your father."

With a glance from his leader, Boncho darted off through the trees, quiet as a deer. Kaga, the lean warrior behind me held his position. We stood still for some time until I heard a bird calling.

Kinptuash gestured and we followed, sprinting across the dark land, down a steep incline and alongside a marshland. By the water's edge, aside towering pine trees, we carefully avoided the ravine to our right, a hundred foot drop that ended at another stream. As we neared the top, I heard the sounds of shooting guns and the pop of metal. It was loud enough to cover any noise of our advancement through the woods.

Another bird call and Kinptuash put out his hand, stopping our progress. He dropped to the ground, and we did the same, creeping up the last ten yards. Kinptuash quietly lifted needles and leaves off the ground, placing his handfuls noiselessly on Mia's head as though he were dropping ornamental feathers. She started to complain until he pointed to the sky. That blond hair would stand out against the dark underbrush. Mia nodded, gathering a scoopful between her cupped hands and covered herself. Boncho took position to my left and Kaga to Mia's right, with Kinptuash in the center.

We peered over the ridge. Our father was down below, flanked by men in navy blue uniforms on one side and the Klamath warriors who fought against Kinptuash on the other. Standing in front of my father was the Indian who had pressed his knife against Kinptuash' scalp, Pulamon. That same knife was now at my father's throat.

Mia's breathing became erratic and fast, like a racer who has just crossed the finish line in first place. Angry at him though she was, he was still Dad, his life was in jeopardy and she was watching in full color. Kinptuash put his large, brown hand on her shoulder, pushing her back down.

My father was talking with an army officer, a tall, elegant looking man with dark hair, slicked back. He stood eye-level with Dad, the medals on his dark jacket placed in perfect order. He struck me as a man who was calm and in control, somewhat above the scene before him. The man crossed his arms, widening his stance. Dad's expression appeared to be at ease; his jowls loose. The man's face was going flush as the conversation continued.

Just like Dad. Making friends wherever he went.

Throughout, the warrior maintained the knife against Dad's neck, his look one of unrestrained hatred.

"Who is he?" Mia asked in a hushed voice.

"Pulamon," I answered her. "Dad told me last night while you were sleeping." I felt Kintpuash's gaze on me and knew he was trying to determine if the situation were expected. In other words, were we in league with the warrior who had tried to kill him?

The warrior Pulamon stood taller than my father, his body sinewy, bulging muscles fighting for space against one another under the woven shirt. His dark skin practically glistened against the sun, made more intense by heat-induced sweat. Though he held the blade against my father's neck, it was done so lightly and with skill, the edge tipped at an angle with one finger, the thumb creating the pressure. He was as adept at using a weapon as any warrior in ancient China. Though the methods and techniques differed dramatically, the results were the same. Fighting in this time was going to test my skills; nunchucks were useless, unless the user had super-human capabilities to swing the weapon in milliseconds.

Pulamon jerked his head to the side of the campsite where a female Indian walked beside a tall white man with grey hair. The officer yelled over my father's shoulder and the woman walked to Dad, standing to his right.

"Winema," Kinptuash whispered. She was translating Pulamon's words for the officer. "General Canby," he said, pointing to the tall man.

We watched the interaction; the officer speaking and Winema's translation. It produced a howl-like yell. The officer placed his hand on the small revolver positioned on his hip.

Pulamon unwillingly withdrew the knife from Dad's forehead, relinquishing his grip on his shoulder. Dad stood, brushed off invisible dust from his shirt and puffed out his concave chest, pushing his shoulders back. His look was confident, even arrogant.

"I thought you said he was going to the Modocs," Mia whispered.

"That's what he told me."

"Liar," Mia hissed.

Kinptuash gave a staccato-like sound and we went quiet. Dad gestured to the lands behind him and in front of him, then to the ground. Whatever Dad was saying seemed to have an effect on the officer. When he finished, it was as though he successfully made his case. The officer called out and soon enough, a woman came up to Dad, offering him a drink. Another man gestured for him to sit at the table.

Kinptuash emitted a low growl, the sort of sound that went along with a big cat before hunting its prey.

My feelings echoed his.

I inhaled an uncomfortable reality. Dad was trading his death warrant with the Modocs by creating a position of power within the enemy camp. There was only one problem. Knowledge was the only value he had to give.

A female offered Dad a wet towel, waiting as he washed his face. He tossed it at her, waving another woman off after she'd placed food in front of him.

Mia snapped her tongue. No situation, no matter how grave, had ever induced Dad to be condescending to another human being, even Draben, who had tried to kill him.

As Dad ate, General Canby joined him. He appeared to be deferring to Dad's comments, leaning in to hear his words and nodding his head at appropriate intervals. When Dad finished, he leaned back, patting his stomach and had the audacity to place his feet on the bench of the table.

If he was playing a role for the benefit of his captors, he was doing it well.

"Come," Kinptuash ordered. We moved away from the ledge, retracing our path through the meadow and valley.

Although I believed myself to have as much stealth as anyone, I felt awkward, large and out of place as I followed behind Kinptuash, his smooth rhythm never swaying as it melded with the land.

His skill reminded me of a phrase my master often repeated. *The goal of a martial artist is to become one with nature.* To feel life in everything around us. In the rocks. The trees. The water. Those that felt the spirit of nature were one with it, ebbing and flowing, able to connect each thread of life. Kinptuash had that grace as he ran along with amazing speed.

He wasn't one *with* nature. He *was* nature.

Abruptly, all three warriors stopped.

First, the silent whir of an arrow grazed my neck, followed by the sound of a thick thud. I was already crouching when a metal object came towards me, the whir-whir sound of a spiral motion. I instinctively knew if I leaned, it might hit the person behind me, so I sliced up my hand in a vertical motion, the flat side of the blade glancing off the back of my palm. I heard it bounce off a rock, and by that time, I was rolling to my right.

Attackers were coming in from all directions, two already fighting with Kinptuash. I glimpsed his short blade, held backwards, slicing up and into the chest of one man as his long blade spun above him, the end connecting with the forehead of another. I felt a presence and warmth above me, spun and raised up my forearm to shield a blow. It connected with an ax-like pole, the tip of the blade crushing down into my left shoulder.

Warmth gushed from my wound as I kicked my foot an inch above the ground, knocking the man off-balance. Using my gut muscles, I pushed up through my chest, then into my arm, raising the metal edge out of my skin, pushing the man off me. He howled in rage, his voice cut off when I turned the edge of my foot and crushed his throat.

"Cage!" Mia cried. "There are too many!" Where the man before me lay, two took his place, and in my peripheral vision, Mia was held on either side by warriors, one taking a small blade from within a leather sheath. I didn't want to kill them or change the face of destiny, but if it meant saving Mia...

Without thought I directed my ring at two men, watching their movements freeze, arms in position, but the man with the blade was on the other side of her, blocking my line of site. He removed the tomahawk, gripping her hair with the other. The downside of my action was I'd frozen the two men as they held her, and as long as they were paralyzed, she would be within their grasp, unable to escape.

I threw a hatchet and it sunk into the man's shoulder. Mia instantly swiped her left foot back, knocking the Indian forward. She struggled with the immobile hands that held her. Her attacker was wounded, but wasn't giving up. From the ground, he gripped her ankle, pulling her down and the other opponent held both her legs.

We were losing the fight. Boncho was on his knees, a pool of blood at his feet. His heartbeat was fading, and his opponent fiercely gripped his neck pushing out his lifeforce. Kaga and Kinptuash were still fighting and those I'd stunned on the perimeter were now being joined by others.

"Ka-yaaa!" came a voice bursting from the trees. A warrior with his face painted half white and red in the same pattern as the Modocs rode straight towards us, flanked by two other riders.

I yelled, pointing to Boncho. The rider tracked my finger and rode to the wounded man. I ran to Boncho, pushing my good shoulder under his arm, giving him a lift as the rider leaned over, his arm in a U-shape. The rider hooked Boncho's arm and lifted, launching him to the horse.

The animal had barely slowed during the rescue, and now raced towards the edge, past the frozen warriors that lined the perimeter. I turned to see another rider slow beside Kinptuash, whose opponent now lay motionless. Kinptuash took the rider's hand and easily hoisted himself up and then they too were gone. I spun, seeing Kaga with his arm up in a defensive posture, weaponless. As his attacker drew down his knife, a whirling sound came from behind me and I instinctively ducked. The javelin went straight through the man's midsection. He lurched forward as Kaga turned, seeing his rescuer on a horse draw near. He was soon horseback and rode out of the clearing. In seconds, the only sound were the groans of dying men around me.

"Hurry, before it wears off," Mia said, tugging me up. I located my nunchucks which had fallen out of my back pocket, replacing them. A low moan caused me to turn and my focus went straight to the man who had been pierced by the javelin. His eyes were deep chestnut, reminding me of a large maple tree, his body as solid and strong as the base that kept it immobile during violent storms.

I hesitated.

"It's not our fight," Mia said, yanking me away.

"No, it's not. That's why I'm doing this." I'd saved one of the Modocs and I was making it even with the Klamaths.

"This will hurt," I said to him, staring into his pain-filled eyes. "But it will be quick. Mia, help me." She saw what I was doing and got on the other side, lifting his shoulder. "Hold him there." In a single snap, I broke off the arrow point on the other side. "Lower him now." As she did so, I pulled again, ripping the javelin out of his stomach. He groaned in pain, his chest arching up.

"This is the fun part," I said more to myself. Slipping my pack and the orb out, I knelt, resting my left knee against the man's leg. I checked the placement of the spindle on top then started to turn. The power of the ancient device was immediate; the muscles began to reconnect on the inside, weaving tightly, drawing them up and in as the healing made its way to the surface. I didn't need to turn the man over to know the skin on his back would be closing. A murmur came from the edge of the trees.

"Cage, hurry, they are regaining their energy."

"Another second." I gave the top half one more turn, saw the closure and was about to put the orb away when a hand shot up and gripped my throat. I rolled to my right, away from him, the orb clenched within my hands. The man came with me, unwilling to let go, and together, we came upright.

Lifting up my right elbow and twisting my torso, I dropped my full weight on his arms, collapsing his grip. Hate, fear and wonder were in his eyes when he met my glance.

"Mia," I groaned. She gouged her knee in the soft indent between his shoulder and chest. His hand involuntarily released just enough for me to jerk back. Without hesitating I turned the ring on him. He stopped mid struggle and Mia bounded up.

In minutes he'd be fine, along with the others that I'd stunned.

"There are more in the woods that I can see," Mia gasped. We were surrounded.

I told Mia to get beside me. In one counterclockwise turn, the wave of pain flooded the glade. The next, it was silent. Even the birds seemed to have gone still.

"Run," I said firmly. "Where the horses went." I was sure the Indians would find us. The only question was if we could reach the safety of the Modoc tribe first.

CHAPTER 7

We'd been running as hard and fast as our athletic bodies had allowed. The effects of the ring would wear off in minutes, each thirty second spread time for us to increase the distance. Periodically, I'd direct us on a new course where I could clearly see the indents of the horse hooves, getting lucky when we crossed through streams then through valleys.

"I can't see the indents any longer," I admitted.

"I figured," Mia said, her voice ragged with effort.

I encouraged her to keep going. We had no other choice.

We ran through the jutting peaks of oddly shaped lava, a life-sized maze. I zig-zagged randomly, avoiding the soft ground. No footprints, no ability for the Klamaths to track us.

The image of the tapestry came to me, one resembling the landscape.

"Why are you slowing?"

"We're here," I realized. Feeling her eyes on me, I turned. "This image. It's on the map."

"What type of rocks do you need?"

I shook my head. I wasn't sure of anything. "I don't know, but this is on the map. Now is not the time, but look for anything interesting and watch where you step." The liquid lava that once covered this area had air bubbles that popped and hardened, and not all were obvious. One errant step and a twenty foot fall would be deadly.

"You came."

Mia's intake of breath matched my reaction. It was the Indian who had lifted Boncho. He was alone and seemed neither surprised or unhappy at our presence. His eyes moved between me and Mia, scanning us. We both lifted out hands, palms up. He nodded, curtly.

"Follow me." His voice was melodic, and different than Kintpuash.

"Will we be safe?" I asked, touching his arm. In a split second, the point of a knife was indenting my midsection, and the man was eye level.

"Boncho is dying. If you can save him like you saved the enemy, you may live."

I down swiped my hand, knocking the blade away, kicking my right ankle around the back of his left, dropping him. My elbow across his chest, holding his still, his legs in a locked position. His chest heaved. The man wasn't a man at all.

Still, I kept my forearm flat against her chest. "Can you guarantee our safety?"

Her mouth flatlined and her eyes held mine. "No." Strength. Fearlessness and truth.

I released her. "Show me."

Hidden with a mass of boulders was the entrance invisible to the uninitiated. It opened into a large cave resembling a bullhorn laid on its side. Stories high, the walls of the stone were rippled, up and over the arch above us, similar to the inside of a gourd.

A grim-faced warrior came into the light, his tight skin accentuated with a single strip of white on each side of his face.

"Kahinsula." His deep voice matched his looks; two black braids bound with leather draped past his shoulder, stopping mid-chest, the pistol slung at a diagonal glistened and I saw the rifle across his back.

He looked like my vision of a war chief. I searched for a scar on his face but his skin was smooth. He shone a torch close to my face. His interrogating gaze turned from me to Mia. He absorbed her blond hair the way oxygen burned a flame brighter.

Without a second's hesitation, he had a knife and lunged for her. I grabbed his wrist, arching it over and to the right. He recoiled like a snake, dropping to gather the momentum to push up and into me. Before he could, I had already moved left, sliding my leg under his calves, lifting him up, then dropping him. But just as I'd anticipated him, he'd landed on his hands, the position a military push up, then he rolled forward, somersaulting his way into a crouch, leaping with a long dagger towards Mia. I jumped in the path of the blade, swiping my hand down in a rotary curve. The force knocked the knife to the wall, clanging somewhere in the darkness but a smile was on his face and I felt a tug in my midsection. When I rose to my feet, Kintpuash held the man in a hammerlock, his grin still wide until his eyes left mine and he looked down. His smile left, replaced by a scowl then a scream. I had a knife as long as my forearm sticking out of my stomach, and I was unharmed.

He struggled within Kintpuash's grasp.

"Lapuan," Kintpuash growled, squeezing so tight the vein in Lapuan's neck bulged. A nod from Lapuan, the sign of defeat, and Kintpuash released him.

There was nothing else to be done. As the entire group of onlookers watched, I removed the blade. It was as dry as a comb. I was tempted to run my finger along the edge of the thin, obsidian to show the men I was mortal, I could bleed and die, but that would only assure Lapuan he could kill me or my sister. No need to give him a tip on how to do it.

I extended the blade to Lapuan, handle first. If he wanted to fight me, again, I'd do it. A daytime battle was better than having my sister's throat slit in the middle of the night.

No one moved to take the blade.

Hate oozed from Lapuan's skin, an aura of crimson red pushing out from his chest. An image of a young woman started to come into focus but then phased out, turning grainy. It was like the radio was playing but the sound had changed from clear to fuzzy.

Kaga came forth, palm extended. I forfeited the weapon and he replaced the blade in his belt, stepping back.

"Come," Kintpuash said, releasing Lapuan roughly. The warrior strode ahead of us, into the darkness. Kahinsula followed her leader, and we made a single file. We moved up and down, through dips and valleys, like ants in a life-size maze. Several times, I nearly got my face sliced in two when

Kahinsula moved to avoid a cream-colored icicle-shaped lava drop reaching to my waist. Above me were sky bridges, where the liquid had separated into upper and lower tunnels, like a modern highway overpass. In another sections, windows within the lava seemed to appear out of nowhere as if a bubble had popped sideways instead of above.

The thin, cold air crackled with voices.

One cavern opened up into many small pockets within the rock like giant scoops had been taken from the walls. In each crevasse, members of the tribe were busy at work, the areas lit by hand-made candles resting on stones hanging from leather straps. A group of young girls wove baskets, handing the finished product to older women who took them and filled them with what looked like dried fish. Large animal skins stretched on the floor, hides of different colors and weights, some were pelts that seemed thick and bushy, while others were small and wiry.

Into one corner we went. Kahinsula spoke and room was made. She lowered the torch, close enough for me to see that Boncho's warm, chestnut skin had turned grey. His expression conveyed the worry of a man fighting to keeps his eyes wide, because if he let them close, they may not reopen.

I knelt, removing my pack. Kintpuash went for his weapon, but Kahinsula spoke, and his hand remained in place. Mia touched his arm.

"He will heal your man."

An elderly woman gently wiped away the blood on Boncho's face, but that did nothing to stop the gushing of liquid that stained the rush-filled mat underneath my legs.

The orb was in my hands, the spindle still in its necessary place.

"Breathe," I suggested to him, watching his eyes. My knee slipped on the blood, and the top of the orb turned. The older woman inhaled, then let out a sigh of relief. The red liquid stopped flowing.

That was interesting.

"What is it?" Mia asked me. I glanced at her, speaking in Mandarin.

"I wasn't touching him." Prior to this, in China and here, I had to be in physical contact with the person I healed, or so I thought.

All motion in the room ceased as the tribal members saw the gift of healing. The hole in Boncho's chest closed in on itself, the jagged, torn skin pulled tight and firm. The discoloration went from purple-ish red to a dark brown.

Boncho's eyes flickered and he squinted. His left hand went to his chest, searching for a hole no longer there. He turned to see his shoulder, as if to verify the wound on his back was also healed.

"It's fine," I told him. Without asking, Mia lifted his hand, turning the palm over.

"Look," Mia suggested, opening her palm as encouragement. He lifted it closer as though he weren't seeing it correctly. He then faced it palm forward to Kintpuash as evidence. Mia's bite marks, once fresh and open, were closed.

Kintpuash crouched down to me, examining the orb. Confident it wouldn't work for anyone else, I gave it to him.

"Kintpuash," I began. "I saved you and healed one of your warriors. I need certain things your tribe might have. Can you help us?"

"The elders," he said in a muted voice. "She stays," he commanded, glancing up at Mia.

"No. She can't defend herself if Lapuan returns."

"No one can defend her," said a new female voice. A woman of cream-colored skin entered the room. She wore a blue denim-like skirt, and top a stark contrast to the leather of the others. She had green eyes and her brown hair had tints of blond and red.

"Winema?"

She gave me a slight nod and smile. "My tribe uses my native name. The white men call me Toby. You may call me either."

Mia put a finger on her arm. "Why can no one defend me?" Winema's lips grew thin, as though she wanted to say more but she only nodded her head. Mia looked back at me, shock and anger combined. "You. Are. Kidding. Me."

I nodded.

"The council will know what to do." Winema said, with a bit of compassion.

Mia closed her eyes for several seconds, taking in a long breath as she did so. I didn't have to hear the words she was thinking. She was going to pay for Dad's mistakes, perhaps with her life, and without the orb to heal her, she'd be dead.

"No matter what happens, don't bring me back if I die. Returning as a zombie isn't on my bucket list."

It wasn't on mine either.

"She comes," I said, touching the orb. The threat was understood. Kintpuash nodded to Winema.

"Follow me," Winema requested. We walked in single file within the rock corridor. The coloring changed, the floor turning grey to black.

"Cage, it looks like an underground river of ice."

"Or a lake," I murmured, not seeing the edge of the slick surface.

"There are hundreds of gold rocks below the surface," she whispered. "I think the clear objects are diamonds."

The rock around us narrowed, and I realized we were walking on a narrow bridge, a narrow path above the ice. Once we stepped off, I came face to face with hanging icicles.

"Watch your head," I said, ducking. Mia barked a split second after. "Told you."

"I heard that," she retorted.

The glass surface was replaced by a rock wall to my left, the red stone unlike the other lava walls I'd seen. Curious, I reached out, gliding my fingertips along the surface. Odd patterns and etching caused me to look closer, the light from the torch on the cavern wall aiding me.

I squinted. The images were pictographs, carved delicately but deeply.

"Check out the wall Mia."

My sister turned her head. "The pictographs? Do they mean something to you?"

"Not yet."

As I watched, I did a double take. The flat images became two, then three dimensional. A cougar hunted alongside a warrior as a partner, not an adversary. One paw extended, as if pointing the way, a feline version of a hunting dog. In another, a man writhed in pain, the end of a spear sticking out of his chest, the white and black feather of an Eagle attached to the handle carelessly waving in the wind.

Kaga placed a hand at the base of my back, pushing me along. I picked up the pace, but didn't stop absorbing the living mural on my left. The next image that came to life was a woman, being swept down a river, her head above then slipping below, her hand raised in the air to be saved. In the last, the last, an eagle soared down from above, its talons extending at a ninety-degree angle for a cougar below. The cougar swiped, slashing the bird before it was able to flap back.

Kaga drew the torch up to my face. With a grunt, he placed his hand flat to the wall, slicing it up and down one time. No more looking, he was telling me.

The images didn't care what he directed. I had the very real impression the images *wanted* to be seen, as though my observance was releasing their secrets after thousands of years as static, one dimensional carvings.

I kept my head straight forward but my eyes went to rock. They moved again as soon as we did.

"Why'd he have a problem with you looking at the wall?" Mia asked me in English. "They're just pictographs."

"The images moved as I watched," I responded in Mandarin.

"Lucky you," she sarcastically responded. The girl was keeping score of gifts and I was ahead.

The arm of the drowning person woman raised from beneath the surface of a river.

Save me, she cried, the hand lifting from beneath the water in a final attempt to live.

Unconsciously, I stretched out my hands and was a finger length away from helping the person when I ran full in to Winema.

The hand slipped below the surface and was gone. The water no longer moved, the curves of waves frozen in cresting arches. I ran my finger across the top of the rock, wondering if the person were alive, had he—or she—been someone in the past or in the future. When the image had come to life, the hand was above, and now it was gone. Had I caused the character to die by my inattention?

Winema gestured for Mia, and gave me a glance. I felt reasonably sure she'd be safe after what had just occurred. At the very least, they'd want to keep me alive and healthy to heal their wounded, and killing my sister wasn't going to be a good motivator.

"Come," said Kaga, I followed him through more tunnels where the old and young eyes alike warily peering at me. We reached a dead end, where a grey haired man sat on a dark, woven rug. He was scraping wood against metal, a tray of food to his left. He didn't glance up as we approached.

"Eat and rest,'" Kaga told me. He spoke his language to the old man who continued his task. When I sat, the warmth of the floor penetrated my clothing. A tray of food was set beside me without a word. It was full of smoked fish and berries and a flat bread.

I devoured it. Since the man continued his focused task, I laid down, savoring the salmon, which was better than anything restaurant dish I'd had in Seattle. The warmth enveloped me like it had in the glade, although this heat was dry and complete, the underground equivalent of a sauna with Earth's rock as the housing.

The visual comforted me and I closed my eyes.

CHAPTER 8

A hand moved my shoulder and I awoke. It wasn't the old man who had kept me company the night before, but a fully-healed Boncho. I glanced around his frame. He bore no signs of a struggle or near loss of life, and I was glad of it. In some small way, I felt like every act of healing I could do was somehow making up for my father's perceived inaction.

I was ready to go wherever Boncho led, but he paused. He put a hand on my shoulder, and squeezed. Words of thanks didn't follow, because I already knew how he felt.

With a tip of my head I acknowledged his sentiment.

"Follow-me," Boncho requested in perfectly good English.

Mia and Kahinsula were already standing beside a thick, intricately woven rug hanging from points on the rock ceiling. Boncho slipped off his shoes and I did the same.

Within the cavity of the rock, a semicircle of very old men sat on the ground. A blazing fire burned in the center of the room, its smoke drifting upward, disappearing into a hole in the middle of the rock ceiling.

Kinptuash gestured for Mia to take her place within the ring of old men. Lapuan eyed her with the wary emotion a hen has when a fox is let in the coop.

I went where directed, settling myself into the open space, appreciating the thick rug underneath me. Scents, natural and thick, swirled up when I moved. I breathed in through my nose. Barley, usually placed in meditation bags, and used for accelerating strength, as the joints grew more limber, was mixed with sage and pine. All three were used to detoxify the body as the dust particles were absorbed.

I pushed my feet into the wool, releasing more of the material inside. I inhaled from my belly to chest, expanding my chest. If this was some type of ritual for our last rights, I was going to make the most of it.

My movements created a microscopic dust cloud, giving me a surge of clarity as my body rid itself of toxins. I visualized myself helping it along, expelling the negativity out of my lungs.

Stretching my feet further, I gasped. Uncovered lava rock penetrated the shell of my sock. The submerged rivers of heat must be connected to the hot springs in the glade of spirits, keeping the area warm year-round.

My outburst was ignored. The dark-eyed natives were staring in to the fire. Deep lines crossed the foreheads of each man, telling of a life spent foraging the dry land for food and fighting for their lives. Long jowls sagged from high cheekbones, once tight and proud.

Sitting directly across from me was an elder with wide-set eyes, so dark brown they were nearly black. His face was framed by a mass of hair like ribbon unwinding after being around a cardboard spool. Curly John, I guessed. I made a mental note to not call him by his white man name. He would be Muleo to me, regal and knowing, how a medicine man and spiritual leader should be. Next to the chief, he was the most important and powerful person in the cave.

A fuzzy halo of light seemed to surround and lift from Muleo's body. I leaned forward, expecting the aura to dissipate, but it stayed, like a frame to his picture. He watched my inspection of him, our eyes locked until a strand of thick gray hair dropped onto his aged face, catching on an eyelash. The man huffed it out of his face, but it dropped again. A muffled laugh escaped Mia's lips, no louder than a soft cough. The man lowered his eyelids a shade, just enough to silence her.

Next to him, an elder smoked a long pipe, drawing in the air, closing his eyes. The device was no longer than a flute, carved of wood. Two leather sashes, about a hand width apart, were tied around it, and a red feather hanging off a red bead. At the opposite end, a patch of white fur resembling rabbit fluffed out, and from this, a short leather band with two black and white glass beads held a long, white feather. The end of the pipe was carved in the shape of an eagle's claw, painted a realistic yellow. It had three talons that extended up and around the red ball. The craftsman had intricately etched the wood to resemble the texture of the majestic animal, the lifelike nails appearing to razor-sharp.

The embers grew bright as the man inhaled one last time before he passed it along. As he took his turn, and then passed it to the elder beside him, the room grew thick with smoke. When the pipe reached Mia, she extended both her hands, palm up, accepting the item, then turning to the man on her other side in a gesture of offering. A few grumbles were heard, and Mia looked at me.

I glared back. To reject the symbol of harmony was to put our lives in danger.

Mia gave me a shrug, and a 'I'm going to die anyway so what's the harm?' look. Taking the pipe, she pulled down her sleeve, wiping the end clear of leftover spit. She wrinkled her nose, put her lips to the end and inhaled. It was short and weak, not even strong enough to make the embers flare. She exhaled as fast as she could and stretched out her hands to the man beside her. He was about to take it when a gruff voice penetrated the silence.

All eyes in the room went to Muleo. He shook his head no.

"Looks like you need a do-over," I mumbled. "Don't worry Mia. If what I know is correct, you'll feel more like a kite than a piece of hammered rock." I heard a rumble, positive Boncho was the source.

Kinptuash extended his hand to her. Taking the apparatus, he exhaled, his chest dropping inward, then placed the pipe to his lips and breathed in very slowly. I counted ten seconds until he pulled the pipe from his mouth, then he held the smoke in his expanded lungs for another few seconds. He then parted his lips, pushing the air through the narrow opening towards the center of the room. When it hit the fire, the glow of the flames turned from red to green.

Mia frowned in concentration. He'd just schooled her in the art of smoking a peace pipe and she didn't like it one bit. She thrust out her hand, her lips thin. I knew the determined look in her eyes all too well. She exhaled loudly, paused, then began sucking. The girls' soccer-developed lungs were going to help her beat them at their own game.

The embers in the little vat of the pipe started to blaze at her exertion, her cheeks going sallow. A snap was followed by a spark that shot out of the bowl, causing one of the elders to pull back. It was longer than ten seconds and Mia wasn't done yet.

I inwardly cringed, hoping she'd still be able to function when this was over.

"Mia..." I warned. She shot me a look that required no interpretation, waited another second, then removed the pipe from her lips and locked eyes with Kinptuash. The counting began. Kinptuash opened his lips and exhaled, giving her the hint. Slowly, she turned her head left then right. She was going to do this on her terms or not at all. Crap. In ten minutes, she was going to be catatonic. Finally, she spread her lips in a smile, the air flowing out like the breeze on the wind.

The pipe resumed its rotation around the room, where it was used by Boncho and Kaga. By the time it reached me, I'd considered every alternative to actually inhaling. I wanted to remain in control, aware of my surroundings and able to defend myself and Mia. Instinct told me that taking so much as a whiff of that stuff was going to fry my brain, at least temporarily. Still, in my decade of martial arts training, I'd learned to retrain different parts of the stomach, guts and lungs in order to extract as much power and energy as possible. I could easily fake the part about breathing and holding the smoke, except for those darn embers.

Politely accepting the pipe, I inhaled slowly, replicating the actions of Kinptuash. As the air came in my mouth, I arched the back of my tongue, pressing tightly against my throat. The action deliberately narrowed the hole leading down to my lungs, lessening the amount of toxins to enter my blood stream. The rest of the smoke collected in my mouth, burning my tongue as I held it for a fair approximation of Kinptuash' actions. The build-up caused my eyes to water and my nose threatened to spew out fire like a dragon, but I pulled in air through my nostrils, sucking a little clean air each time. This prevented the smoke from escaping, straining my lungs, stomach and throat to the point of pain until I felt an exhale was believable. It took every bit of discipline I possessed to curl my lips around the smoke and expend the toxins in an even, unrushed way. Without the years of practicing Gi Gong breathing, the feat wouldn't have been possible.

The men said nothing, their silence an approval for my poise in participating of their tribal gesture.

The pipe was laid on the ground in front of the oldest looking of the men. His hair was mostly grey, the portion above his ears knotted on the back of his head. The rest hung down past his shoulders, its coarseness reminding me of a horse's mane that had been neglected and allowed to go wild. When he lifted the pipe to his withered lips, his inhale made Mia's look like a simple intake. The embers burned red and never changed, and it had to have lasted over a minute, reminding me of an Olympic swimmer. He held the smoke nearly as long, all the while keeping his eyes closed and his lips sealed tight. There was no doubt in my mind. This man was the leader of the Modoc tribe. He was Sconchin.

When his brown eyes flashed open, he blew the smoke directly in to the fire. It whispered and swirled as it intertwined with the natural heat from the flames in the pit. As the air hung above the flames, the chief spoke. His words sounded musical, with lilts and dips starting with quick jumps and ending with sudden stops.

I followed a waft as it moved up in a circular motion until it found its way out the hole in the roof. We must be very far away from other tribes or civilizations for the smoke to go unnoticed, especially during the day. Above us, it was lunchtime, hot and dry. The smoke could be seen for miles as it contrasted against the glistening obsidian.

When the man stopped speaking, Kinptuash rose, stepping in front of the group.

Mia and I watched in fascination as he bent over, emulating his position as a captive. He jumped up and made a pop, identical to the sound of the starter gun. Then his arms flew out and around him, dangling above his head, representing the thousands of birds flying in panic. The men laughed as Kinptuash spit and spat droplets which rained from his fingers, the bird dung drizzling over the faces of their enemies and down to earth. Pointing to me, Kinptuash let out a *cling!* He jabbed his fingers directly to his eye, and I understood he was telling the group about how my mirror trick had caught his attention. With a pounce, push, and shove, Kinptuash continued the story of the ordeal, how he pushed his captor over the ledge and escaped.

When he finished, it was Kahinsula's turn. She didn't stand, but used her hands to accentuate her story, including my healing of the Klamath. She pointed to the backpack now sitting in front of Kintpuash. Then it was Lapuan's turn. He rose, jabbing at myself then Mia, his teeth clenched and eyes dark.

Eyes squinted, mouths pressed or drooped in angry, determined lines. Foreheads collapse in waves of concern.

As the tension grew, I felt no fear. My hands were on my knees, palms up, the fingertips touching, my natural condition for meditation and peace.

Sconchin gestured for the pack, removed the contents and selected the pen. He flipped it upside down and the pen slid out. Opening the plates, he proceeded to draw. In a few seconds, golden, reddish letters appeared on opposite page. The words were still appearing when Sconchin turned it around and faced it towards me.

The translation was as clear and bright as neon, the color of liquid lava.

Kaga wants to know how you possess the ring that is etched in our stone walls. It was worn by a woman, not a man. Many years ago.

My fingers were interlaced and I felt for the ring, tracing the ruby with my thumb, an outlet for my curiosity. He'd just given me the secret to operating the plates, and clearly expected me to give him a response. Still, I wondered if they would work for me, just as the orb had done. But what if it failed…I'd be just like my dad.

Then it dawned on me they had probably already tried this with Dad, or maybe hadn't, because the ring wasn't in his possession.

Mia sighed loudly, breaking my thought process. Without asking permission, she walked on the outside of the men directly to Sconchin. She bent down to pick up the plates when he seized her arm, the skin indenting with his grip.

"Look. Let's start talllking." Uh-oh. The inhalation from the peace pipe had already dampened her linguistics but was unable to subdue her mind. When Sconchin kept his hold, she stepped in a narrow space between he and Lapuan and sat. The angry man clenched his fist as though he were preparing to backhand her when Sconchin shook his head, waving down Lapuan's temper. The man subsided, doing so under silent protest.

"You had all the fun before," she said to me, blinking hard. "My turn." She deftly opened the plates, retrieved the pen and started writing.

"Wait, Mia," I requested.

"What?" She asked, the irritation in her voice as clear as a bell in a cathedral. She'd taken my question as an insult to her abilities, not the fact that she had no way to answer the question Sconchin had asked.

As she depressed the tip of the pen on the metal, she spoke out loud for my benefit.

"We are here with our dad, George Fleener," she said as she wrote. "He meant to come back to you but was prevented from doing so. We are both very sorry for what happened to Nolina."

Her facial expressions were overstated, as though she were on a stage, wanting to convey her every emotion to those in the back of the theatre. Sconchin peered over, watching the text fade. "We are here to find more rocks and certain objects before Ubel inhabits Cage again and becomes possessed."

Was she crazy? "No more Mia," I commanded. I dreaded the images that were sure to come, quickly wondering through scenarios on how to explain the rocks within the orb.

Sconchin digested my outburst and looked inquisitively at the plates. Mia eyes dropped as well, staring in disbelief. The plates had absorbed the words without offering a translation.

Relief coursed through me from head to chest, while Mia's confusion and humiliation moved up her neck and face in the color of pink.

I was still fiddling with my ring, waiting. The stillness of the room was marred only by the smoke that shot up through the center of the fire pit.

"He's wondering what to do." The muttering was to my right, and sounded once again like Boncho. I cracked open my eye, peering at him.

"Yes, that's correct," I replied to him. Boncho's eyes widened, his lower mouth dropped. It could have been my own.

"Wait, Cage, you just spoke in their language. That's impossible."

Trust it. The voice of my guide, my female protector, spoke to my heart and my mind. I looked down at the plates, leaving them untouched. Then I saw...a glow. The ring. It had an ember fire within, the light dancing. I'd touched it...what had I done?

"We are waiting."

I glanced across the fire. The chief was talking to me. I'd think about the ring later.

"My name is Cage Fleener," I began, slowly and with purpose. After a moment of eye contact with Sconchin, I moved to the others around the circle, Lapuan included. "I am the son of George Fleener, who came to you through the power of the orb. We are here to find objects necessary to keep people of all lands alive, not just of the Modoc lands." I paused, watching the reactions. They were rapt with attention, eyes narrow in concentration, or closed, listening.

"How are you doing that?" asked Mia, shocked with wonder. "I'm...I'm hearing you speak in the Indian language, but it's coming through my head as English." I continued without answering.

"I do not know of a woman who came before, wearing the ring on my finger, but I can guess." I raised my hand for all to see, turning the wrist back and forth. "I believe she was my mother, in a different form. We come here now to find precious rocks and other items you may have to help us in our journey."

Sconchin's eyes nearly closed as he absorbed my words, popping open again when Lapuan spoke.

"If you come peacefully, why is your father with the enemy tribe, and those that have taken our lands from us?" His voice was deep and powerful, a raspy edge to the consonants. "Are you here to lead them to us for our capture?"

"George does not know where we now live Lapuan," intervened Kinptuash. "If he was looking for us, he went to the wrong location, and found the Army."

"Yes!" Lapuan said, his voice rising. "You told us he is now the leader of their group and Pulamon was stopped from killing him," Lapuan then pointed to my sister, his finger an inch from her face. "*She* is the one who should be killed."

Mia stared at his finger for a moment. I wondered if she were going to bite it, as she had with Boncho's hand.

Sconchin called for attention. His brown skin was wrinkled, but tight, in a burnt way, reminding me of the skin on a roasted turkey. He could be seventy or one hundred, it was impossible to know. The burden of leading a small group seemed a much larger, emotional task than running a kingdom with millions of people. Here, the deaths and struggles were intimate; here, the contribution of one person meant the difference of eating that night or sleeping in warmth.

"Kaga, you wish to say something."

The silent warrior spoke, his voice rolling like the waves on the sea. "Nolina was called back by the spirits after the white man left. She is where she belongs."

"No!" shouted Lapuan, jumping up. "That is where she belongs," he said, pointing to Mia. "Where she sits, the daughter of our friend turned enemy. Let her spirit take the place of Nolina, and bring my woman back to me!"

The aura surround Lapuan was purple, and I saw it as clear as if I were seeing my own hand. Still, I had no image of her, like I'd had with General Li. Another nuance I'd have to consider if I made it out of here.

I refocused.

Energy has a color. The thought took hold and captivated me. I'd heard of blind pianists hearing colors within a note, and painters talk about the infinite colors in their minds eye, but I'd never really believed it, and certainly never experienced it until now. Lapuan's color was initially purple, the color sorrow and pain. Now it changed to crimson red.

I looked around the room. No one else reacted except Muleo. His green eyes stared at me, straight through the fire. My senses told me he was seeing everything I was.

"What are they saying Cage?" Mia grumped. "Why can I understand you but notttt themmm?" I was about to respond when Sconchin interrupted.

"Why did your father break his promise to us?" he asked.

"My father did not tell us of Nolina until last night. He'd never spoken of his travels here to either me or my sister Mia before then. He said he had tried to help and meant to return."

Lapuan let out another yell, this time his voice contained scorn. "When it is too late! Too late for our tribe. Our lands. Our people. What can he do now but bring more misery and pain?"

"We do not know that," said Kinptuash, his deep voice even. He looked at me. "Explain. Why did he not return?"

I let out a breath, my lips vibrating with tension. "My father was taken against his will by an enemy. That man desired to travel using this," I said, lifting the orb. "To become wealthy and powerful. My father refused, and was taken before he could return to you. My sister, Mia and I, followed him. It took many weeks to return to this time."

Kaga adjusted his position. The glow of the amber light gave his silhouette definition. His face was narrower than the others, and the color of his skin slightly darker, a richer, deeper hue. Whereas Kinptuash was broad in the shoulder and deep through the chest, Kaga was lean, and his torso, though constricted, showed muscles taut beneath his form-fitting shirt. His hair also set him apart. While the others wore braids in front, leaving a portion flowing in a thick mass, falling like rushing waterfalls in the spring rains, Kaga's was fine and straight, not coarse. He had a single braid on his left, tied at the end with the red feather from a falcon.

Fitting.

"What is it?" Lapuan asked Kaga, his voice harsh. "What do you know?"

Kaga pointed to the orb, the ring and the plates. "The son is doing what the father cannot. He can control all. Heal and kill, as Kahinsula witnessed. Boncho lives because of this man. We could die."

As the others began to grasp the significance of his statement, Mia sighed in frustration, demanding I tell her what was going on.

"Kaga told them the orb responds to me and that I have the ring. They never worked for Dad."

Mia rolled her eyes, the whites splinted with jagged red lines. "Tell me something I don't already knowww."

Waiting until Mia finished, Sconchin spoke. "Kaga means Chronicler in our language," he offered. "His gift is to see from the past so that he may keep a history for the future. Sometimes, the past and the future do not meet. They…move over one another and it is dark for us."

"Lapuan," continued Sconchin. "You demand justice for Nolina. What is it you want?"

"For the father to suffer the same consequence as Nolina." Death, rapid or slow, it didn't matter. The bright fire of revenge burned in his eye. "If not him, then her."

"Will this death come from your hand?" I asked him directly. He considered my question, skepticism making his fingers twitch.

"I want to see his spirit fly from his body, capture it, and bury it in the ground so it cannot live again."

"What are they sayyying?" Mia demanded, her body swaying.

Sconchin looked at me. "She need not know." His eyes lowered, as though he felt bad sitting beside her and being purposefully deceitful.

"Is that the decision of the counsel?" I asked, waiting until Sconchin nodded his head before proceeding. "Mia, the decision has been made to take Dad back from the Klamaths, and…. trade his value for horses, or…whatever the tribe needs to survive." Sconchin was pleased with my comment, his eyes flat and unmoving. Kinptuash grunted and scowled. He was unhappy with the lie.

"Why is that man so angry?" she asked, pointing to Lapuan. Mia was unfazed by the menacing stare of disapproval he gave her.

"That's Lapuan. The girl dad was supposed to help was Nolina." As I spoke, I realized I'd continued talking in the Modoc language, even though Mia had asked her question in English. Of course, they were listening to my words, thereby had a good idea of what Mia was saying to me.

"He has a right to be mad. I'd want to kill dad if I were him," she said, nodding her head approvingly at Lapuan. The action made him frown, and I could see he believed she were making fun of him. "Lying to them. Lying to us, breaking one heart wasn't enough. He had to break two." She was slurring badly, but I understood her.

"He never meant to break your heart Mia," I told her softly. "He tried to do what was right. He failed, but he *had* tried."

"Sure," she said, her bitter edge unmasked. "You only forgave him because you are now the great commander, controlling our destinies."

"No," I responded, feeling a swell of empathy for her statement instead of anger at the insult. "I forgave him because I finally realized he hadn't abandoned us because he lacked love. He did so because he was trying to bring back mom. He was doing it to reunite the family, to make us whole."

Mia's face raged with anger though her eyes swelled with tears. Her carefully crafted, well-guarded shell around her tender heart was so thick and high, she'd never acknowledge it existed, let alone crack. All that pain she had closed off, channeling her love and devotion towards me and Dad was now exposing itself. She'd felt the loss of mom as a fourteen year-old girl, at a time when she was becoming a young woman, when she probably needed Mom a lot more than I did.

I felt the depth of Dad's betrayal on her psyche, first emotionally, then how he had abandoned us physically. She was alone. Terrifically and emotionally alone.

Out of the corner of my eye, I noticed Lapuan's face taking on a mixture of feelings: anger, compassion and sympathy, before smoothing back in to a flat, plain of fury.

Kinptuash gazed at my sister intensely, no doubt catching the tones of her voice and her heartache that was so clear.

"I'll be with you Mia. We've got to *try* to keep the family together."

Mia shook her head. "Why? What has dad to do with anything that we need? Nothing. Not anymore. We proved that. And Mom? You can't bring her back without a soul, a walking piece of rotting flesh? No, Cageeee," she slurred, trying to refocus and talk intelligently. "You can't make Nolina and Lapuan come together. Not now." The hopelessness in her voice, the emptiness in her face echoed about the room, a white ghost of torn emotions bouncing off the black walls.

"What is she saying?" asked Lapuan, his voice less gruff. He'd heard his own name and Nolina's clear enough, and everyone in the room was a witness to Mia's raw emotion.

I cleared my throat. "Lapuan wants to know what you are talking about." Mia raised her eyes to his, the tears still present. She couldn't talk, but she nodded her head. "Mia is upset I can't bring back Nolina for you. Just like it is impossible to bring back our mother for us. They would each have a rotted body and no soul." A flicker of emotion passed across Lapuan's eyes, a momentary softening before once again hardening. He wasn't going to trust Mia, not yet. He'd made that mistake once before with Dad.

"Mia, no matter what happens with Dad, I hope you can forgive him. He has good intentions." At that, Mia's eyes blinked and she snapped her head back, as though the mention of Dad and forgiveness in the same sentence pulled her out of her momentary emotional reflection.

"He sure didn't seem like he had good intentions down with the Army did he? But sure. I'll forgive Dad. When he gets back, *if* he even wants to come back, make sure he gets roped to the back of one of the horses and dragged over dirt with snakes will you? After what we've been through, he deserves it."

The last statement was said with such bitterness that it had a paralyzing effect on Lapuan. Every elder in the room focused their eyes on her.

"Can you translate her words?" asked Sconchin politely, his deep, rolling voice moving through the room like a mist of warm air.

Unwillingly.

"Mia asked that if you do get my father back, that you tie him to the back of a horse and drag him across rocks and rattlesnakes before we trade him."

The room was silent. A daughter was expected to be for her father, not against him.

It was Boncho that broke the silence. "He won't be much good to us," quipped the warrior.

Kinptuash coughed, probably his version of unexpected laughter. Had I been told he was capable of humor before that moment, I'd not have believed it. Lapuan took Mia's comment seriously, evaluating her presence and my own reaction to her words.

"Then, you would see your father die at the hands of the enemy?" Sconchin asked Mia, glancing at me for translation. His voice was tender, like the father asking a sincere question of a petulant, angry teenager.

Mia struggled to make sense of the question, to reconcile it with the hurt and resentment of the last twenty-four hours. Her lips moved to form the words that came more as vocal cracks. "I don't want him dead. I want him to suffer." Sconchin looked to me for assistance.

When I translated, the gravity of her statement wasn't lost on the group of men. She'd convinced them she was as betrayed by Dad as they were.

Suddenly, Mia's face contorted with a thought, and her eyes momentarily brightened from the pipe-induced glaze.

"Cage. Translaaaate as I…talk," she instructed. "He needs to make amends for not keeping his word…to either of us. Give them something they want more, in return." I took a breath and translated as best I could. Kintpuash frowned, but it was Lapuan who spoke to Mia.

"What do you have to offer?" He asked her directly. When I conveyed the question, a half-smile on Mia's face appeared, in spite of her hindered condition. She managed to spin the fanny pack around on her waist to the front, awkwardly unzipping the holder. With a tug and a pull, she retrieved the mammoth piece of gold she'd found during our walk. She held it up for all to see.

"This is what we'll use to get him back." She hurled it at Lapuan, keeping her glazed-over eyes even when he easily made the one-handed catch. "Tomorrow," she slurred. "We get him back. Get what we need and leave him here for you to do whatever you want with him."

Mia didn't leave room for rebuttal. With the last words, she closed her eyes and fell right into Sconchin's lap.

CHAPTER 9

After I translated her words, the room remained as still as a graveyard, save for the crackling sound emitting from the fire. The dense grey smoke wafted through the cavern, turning into a yellow fog that hung in the air. The eerie particles were eye level, somehow stuck in my line of site, disabling me from clearly seeing the faces of the elders, but I felt them watching me.

I looked at the motionless body of my sister. She was a sleeping angel, her long, dark eyelashes resting on her porcelain skin, her full red lips parted ever so slightly. Kinptuash noticed, so did Lapuan.

If revenge was an endearing characteristic, it had served its purpose with him. The large, well-muscled warrior moved his head forward and back, his distaste for us subjugating itself to the possibility of getting his true object of hate within his control. If she were going to be his ally in exacting revenge on my father, he'd side with her.

"She's justified in her anger," I told no one in particular. "My father wasn't honest with us. For years, I blamed him for the death of my mother, but I recently learned he wasn't at fault. Yesterday, Mia learned the truth. Forgiveness won't come soon, or easily. Sconchin, what more do we need to discuss?"

Muleo leaned to Sconchin, whispering. It was the first time I'd seen a side profile of his face. His nose stuck out like the beak of an eagle, the top arching off the center between his eyes before dropping over and down to a sharp point. Three white scar lines, originating at his ear, swooped down his cheek like a Nike swoosh pattern, the bottom one curving along his jawline then up to his chin, the middle scar right above it, ending just below the corner of his lip, and the third to the right of Muleo's nose, at the start of his cheek.

Food. Please let us have one last meal. I'd like to die full.

The herbs in the peace pipe were definitely having an effect on me, because only an altered state of mind would be thinking about food when the sword of death hung nearby.

"Your sister said you need things from us," said Muleo.

The notion of lying occurred to me, just as I had done out of necessity when we first arrived in China. Instinct told me that ploy wasn't going to work here. The Modocs didn't use artifices of silk and diamonds to guard their thoughts and feelings. They were in tune with the mind and body and spirit. My words had to be in harmony with my thought and intent.

"Yes. I'm hoping you have them."

I visualized the images of what Bao had drawn on the paper. A head plate, a shield for the breast, a staff, and a bracelet. Aged from time, shiny or matte, Bao said the pieces had engravings on them, but had not the time to replicate the images in her rush to return to my side. One might be hidden in a dark corner or perhaps worn by one of the elders. A look around confirmed the headbands worn by the aging men were made of leather, not metal. The spear and arrow tips were from the black, obsidian lava. No resemblance.

Lapuan spread his lips wide enough to reveal his large white teeth clamped together. He reminded me of a lion on the prowl who saw another get his quarry. I held up a hand, forestalling a confrontation.

"I do not come to *take* something from you or your tribe, Lapuan. What I need has been preserved for thousands of years, by your people for this exact cause. It will be something you will *want* to give me."

"You saved Boncho, so we will spare your sister. But you desire sacred things. These are not given to others," Muleo responded. "Only when a member of the tribe has made a great sacrifice do we bestow gifts."

If that was the measurement, we were in the hole. A deep, gaping black one.

"We must see your spirit," Muleo continued. "To know if you are worthy of that which you seek." *My spirit?* I was just getting my mind to absorb the reality my soul had inhabited multiple physical bodies through a millennium. If they were going to separate my body and soul, there was only one way to do it. Mia's prediction was right; one of us had been sentenced to death. I'm glad she'd passed out.

"What does a spirit do?" I asked, buying time.

Muleo nodded his head to Kaga. "Our people believe that this life and the next are as one," he began. "When the body dies, the spirit lives on, coming back, living with us here. Some are good, others are evil." I nodded, with him so far. "Spirits are in all things. The trees. The animals. We speak and talk with them, living with them in unison. It is how we are one with this world."

My mind was getting fuzzier, but I tried to summarize. "You want to know if I'll get along with spirits if I'm dead?"

He glared at me, as though I was missing a simple concept. "The unseen spirits co-exist with us in this world. If you come back, you will know this."

So, I'm going to die, and my spirit will hang out with the animals, somewhere, all around us.

I turned to Kahinsula, focusing on my words. "Can you put Mia someplace safe?"

Muleo answered, his eyes now seemed to glow as bright as the embers in front of me. "For what happens next, she must remain." Well, at least she was going to have the luxury of sleeping in blissful ignorance while I got split apart.

I crossed my legs, resting the backs of my hands on my knees. I searched for thoughts and emotions to help my understanding, but it was unclear.

The peace pipe. It was affecting my gifts. I had lost my ability discern emotions.

The evil spirit, Kaga had mentioned. I wondered….

"I believe a great, evil spirit lives, that he came through to this world with me," I began. "My father said your people call him Ubel, the Serpent King."

A gasp in the room was cut short by Muleo's raised hand, requesting silence. "Yes. He is as old as time. He fights the people of the Great Spirit, who resides at the center of the universe, and is in the heart and the mind of all people, and all living things. Ubel wants to take his place."

"Ubel wants to kill me and my family. I need to kill him first."

Muleo bowed his head momentarily, as though reconciling all he knew with my request. When his eyes met mine, he was devoid of emotion. "You must cross-over. To see if you are a spirit warrior."

Cross over to…what, exactly? For the second time I thought it was a good thing Mia was knocked out.

"What must I do?"

Sconchin parted his slips, a low humming emerging through the slit. "Ahhhhoommmm." One by one, the men joined in. It was similar to a vibrating chord in an organ. Even Lapuan participated, his a baritone pitch pushing sound to the walls of the cave.

Sconchin's voice dominated. It reminded me of an ocean, moving in a single direction with powerful, but unseen undercurrents that could be harnessed and used for great destruction. As the intensity in the room increased, Muleo pulled aside his shirt, exposing his skin. Carved into his flesh was the image of a feather, the scar thick, like it was done with a hot poker. As he traced the outline, the image turning from black to neon sign.

"This, I was born with," Muleo began, pride in his voice, power in his eyes, his words clear, reminding me of a violin cutting through a men's chorus. The other elders bowed their heads and even Sconchin seemed to defer to him. "My father had this, as did his father before him."

Acid crept up my throat and threatened to come into my mouth. I'd have to take my shirt off for them to brand my body.

I squinted, peering forward at the glowing image. "You are going to do that to me?"

Muleo's eyes dropped slightly. "No, you will earn it within the fires of affliction."

The scar looked like it *was* the affliction.

"What happens to my body?" I asked.

"If you come back, you will have it again." Right. Not even the rock I had could put my soul back in the body, even if I was around to operate it.

"Cage," said Kaga, his voice soft and firm, "eternal destiny is not the result of chance. It is by choice."

In other words, if I failed, I'd die a physical and spiritual death, but if I lived my question will be answered. Awesome. I looked at Muleo. "Did you offer this to my father?"

"No. He had the orb and we thought he was the one. We were waiting for the sign. It never came."

Of course it didn't. Dad wasn't the man of legends.

"You will not be given what you seek until it is earned by your spirit," said Sconchin, his face as hard as his voice. I nodded my head, acknowledging I understood.

"How are you going to kill me?"

"You are mistaken," said Muleo, his voice chastising my assessment. "We are not the ones who kill you. Watch the fire." Muleo's cheeks hollowed as he drew in a long breath from the peace pipe. Odd. They could have pushed me into the flames or asked me to walk on the coals. That, I was ready for. But hypnosis?

I obeyed his request, watching the flames. When the smoke from his mouth came in to contact with the heat of the blaze. It turned the air blues and greens. Muleo exhaled harder, his green eyes changed to a cat-like yellow.

"It comes soon," whispered Kaga. "Be ready." Muleo gave an enormous huff, and the fire in front of me exploded.

In that moment, my body felt as though it had been caught in the backdraft of the heat. An itching, then burning began in the tips of my fingers, as if the fire were licking each one. Not a moment after, the itching turned to a crinkling that moved to every piece of exposed flesh, save my chest, where the protective shirt rested on my skin. Yet even it was not enough to stop this burning. It crept under my clothing, to my armpits, across my chest and down to my navel. In less than the time it took to blink, my shirt of protection caught fire in a single whoosh and disintegrated. The heat went up my face and across my scalp. I wanted to scream for it to stop, to jump in to the flames and end my life quickly rather than smolder from within.

"You must not look away," counseled Kaga, his voice intense. It conveyed a confidence I didn't feel. My ears barely heard them, as they felt seared into their sockets, and all I saw was the blackness brought on by the obliterating pain. My world was getting smaller. Dimmer. Closer to ending. I fought against it, just as I had the dark evil of the Serpent King's soul as it at tried to overtake me in the catacombs.

Ubel, I told myself. The word had a strange power, even in my thoughts.

This was far worse than drowning under the water after Xing had given me the near fatal blows to my head and stomach.

Pain can be endured, I repeated to myself, holding on to the chords of sanity. They were the words repeated a thousand times by my marital arts instructors. *Push through it.* The fibers that held my tenuous link to reality rebelled, but the words came back.

Push *through* it, not *against* it.

Whether my eyes were open or closed, I could not tell. Mentally, I willed them shut, for the room had gone dark, as the swords of pain continued through my muscles, then bones. When it became unendurable, my extremities reflexed uncontrollably, my fingers drawing in upon themselves like an old man withering. My ears, already feeling collapsed, now pressed sharply inward, causing a sharp popping to occur. My eardrums were gone.

The body must die for the soul to come forth. It was a line inscribed upon the ancient sword I'd read in China.

The moment the words took form in my mind, someone in the room screamed and I felt my body rise up from the ground. In the abstract, I realized the scream had been mine.

Was it an exultant cry of liberation? The burning sensation ceased entirely, as though my outer shell had been discarded and dropped off, releasing what was left. I looked around, seeing the others watching me, or rather, watching my body stay immobile as my spirit detached from its human shell. I felt light and free, faster and more powerful than I'd ever experienced. Only Muleo watched my spirit rise and hover. I wanted to stay and swirl around the men before me but it was not to be. Muleo inhaled from his lower diaphragm, a deep influx of air that stretched out his entire stomach. In a fluid motion that lasted a tenth of a second, the air rose to his chest and he puffed it out, throwing the image of the feather towards the fire. With a whoosh, the plumes from the fire were as wide as I was tall. I gave another scream but no sound came out. My soul was being sucked directly into the flames.

CHAPTER 10

I found myself in the flatlands. A light breeze pushed against the grasses in front of me, the hues of yellow, browns and oranges sparkling against the stems, reaching up and accepting the warmth. The living pieces, each one attached to a living Earth.

It wasn't my imagination, words were being spoken, rising up from the ground, drifting on the air. Millions of sounds were suddenly all around me, soft and quiet, not intrusive or loud.

I fought the sensation of being overwhelmed by the magnitude of life, concentrating on one or two of the blades, wondering if I could discern more in this new state of being.

The breeze is beautiful today, said one soft voice. If I could call it a voice, for it had no harsh beginning or punctuated finality at the end.

It won't be long before the rains come, responded another, not far from my foot. I felt compelled to walk, but immediately worried I would kill an important life with my weight. I tried to move quickly and lightly in order to leave as little impression on the ground as possible.

"I'm sorry," I whispered, looking below and around me, everywhere at once.

We understand, rose up a reply in unison, a chorus of innumerable soft voices speaking at once. *We are strong*. Did I catch a hint of laughter from the blades that found humor in my ignorance?

The trickling sound of water moving over rocks hit my ears, which strangely, no longer hurt. I touched one, expecting to feel blood, but remembered I was in spirit form.

Periodically, a bubble popped and I knew it was the air from a fish in the water, darting in search of food. Pine trees dotted the riverbank, watermarks showing the seasonal flooding from the snowmelt.

I bent down to touch a faded water line on the tree, sadness dominating my emotions. How many saplings had died during the floods, never to reach their true potential as a majestic pine?

Do not trouble yourself. The sound was neither male or female. I looked up, feeling as though the words had come from above me, mixed with the breath of the fresh pine needles. I stretched my hand up, following the thick base of the tree to the lowest branch, continuing until I could reach no further. *We give life to bring life. It is the way of our kind.*

I nodded, softly tracing the lines one last time. I remembered Kaga's stealth as he moved through the trees, a ghost blending in to the very limbs. He had been careful not to push or brush aside the branches, and treated even the undergrowth with gentle respect.

This is what the Indians revered—the Earth, with its living parts. They knew the smallest elements of life—a blade of grass—created the whole. They were a part of nature, but they did not attempt to change or disturb it.

I might as well have been blind and deaf for all I'd seen of the world before experiencing life in my spirit form.

The wonderment of the new world encompassed me as I followed alongside the river, unsure of what I was seeking.

The skin on my face was hot from the sun and the sound of the water made me yearn for a cold shower. I resisted the urge to laugh. How could I have physical sensations at all? I was a soul, a spirit, and shouldn't have physical senses, certainly not one with the human experiences of taste and feeling and wanting a shower.

I had no answers. The mystery remained with me as I walked. The rapids were downstream, south of where I stood. By my feet were eddies where the rambling current had gotten caught, the water trapped in an endless circular motion, going nowhere at the edge of the stream. The frustration of the fish in the bowl like area struck me: I watched as one struggled to free itself from the heavy bonds of the water while other fish were content to do nothing more than go around and around.

Next to this was a deep pool where a dense school of fish lounged, resting before their journey began again. The animals were healthy, directed and focused, the eyes of the leader sure, the others a respectful distance behind, waiting for the command.

I was thirsty, but afraid I'd frighten the underwater residents. I leaned over, seeing my reflection on the surface. What I saw surprised me. I had a physical body, complete with the same coloring and size that I knew. I thought I'd be a walking spirit, invisible and enlightened.

I pinched myself hard to make sure.

"That felt real," I said out loud. Laughter erupted around me, and I glanced left and right. The long, green moving grasses seemed to bob up and down as they danced in graceful, choreographed movements. I smiled and the blades whooshed back. *Fascinating!*

Unable to contain my attraction at the new world before me, I lowered myself, watching the glimmering fish. Colors bounced off the silver backs as they huddled together. Small units, families I supposed, formed clumps with one another. Mouths moved, open and closed, eyes darting, tails flipping. They were communicating, but I couldn't hear their words.

"I would like some water," I said softly to the leader. "Not much." The fish jolted when they heard my voice and I quickly said I meant no harm. "I'll stay at the top of the water. Not near you."

Fins twitched at my words, but when the leader held firm and didn't swim away, those closest slowed the rates of their tails. Cupping my hands together, I dipped them under the cool water. Sets of eyes glistened under the surface, and I supposed they were grateful I kept my word.

As the water covered my eyes, the liquid itself wasn't what I'd known my entire life. The very water felt alive, comprised of billions of particles of life. The cells that lived within the water, the amoebas, were bustling in their own universe of energy.

I repeated the action again, untroubled knowing these animals were on me. They drew life from the water and the skin on my body; itself food for their organism. We all helped one another in our own ways. Why had I not known this before?

Because I was so self-centered and angry at my father for all those years, I saw nothing else.

A bullet broke through the wonderment. The fish below me scattered at the sounds, and the grasses tilted over, lying on their side, away from the brutal object. Then another shot was fired, followed by a low, agonized groan. I glanced over. The bullet had lodged itself in a tree. It was the very pine who had spoken to me.

Instinctively, I dropped down. Additional bullets ricocheted then stopped. As I waited, a pulsing came up from the ground, under my fingers. I spread out my palms, pressing. Men? No. The short thumpings had a sequence, one, two, three, four. It was the pattern of an animal, not man. The trees nearby bristled and I felt anger. Now I heard the hard pounding of hooves and the shouting of two men, their vibrations also underneath my palms. I glanced up. A trail of dust moved towards the sky. They were coming directly to the water, chasing the animal on the hunt.

I searched for a place to hide. If the fish could see me it was likely the men could too.

A clump of large cedars stood downstream, wide enough around to mask me from the men, but too far for me to run without the risk of being seen. The pines dotting the landscape provided no safety, nor did I see holes in the ground for a subterranean escape.

The cadence of the beast running toward me increased, and I instinctively knew it was going to reach me far quicker than the horses. A wild horse? I pressed harder to the ground. Unlikely. This thudding was soft. If it wasn't a hoof, it was a paw, and paws usually had long, dagger like claws at the end.

I crouched low to the fish. "I'm coming in, but mean no harm. I must hide." In an instant, the sets of eyes blinked and the fish moved to the rim of the bank. I slid on my belly, taking a breath before dipping my face, then body under water like an alligator submerging itself, finding safety in its natural home. I couldn't recall breathing before this, inhaling air or going out of my lungs as I walked, but it didn't matter. My lungs hadn't yet started to feel the ache of needing air, so I lay on the bottom, wondering how long it would be before the men came and left.

Then I had another distraction. A shadow passed over me, blocking out the sun. The men? No, it moved differently, and had no sound. I was about to rise to the surface, when the face of an enormous cat lowered to the water's edge. Its claws rested over the edge of the bank, drops of saliva hitting the ground and the water. It was heaving with exertion, its breath misting the surface.

It looked left and right then dipped its tongue into the water. Even from below, I heard the rapid pounding of its heart, the strain on its lungs. Then I heard…something else. Other heartbeats, rapid and soft, pounding from within the massive animal. This was a female, and she was pregnant.

Fascination and fear gripped me as I watched the beast replenish itself. The survival of her family depended on escaping alive. She stopped lapping to glance around her. Her concentration was fierce, her focus total. Assured she was safe, she began again. Her tongue was out and it hung to the surface, resuming the scoop and curl motion that captured the liquid.

Then she saw me. The yellow of her eyes gleamed like incandescent glow sticks, specks of brown seemed to rest on the glassy surface. In a split second, she swiped under the water. The fish darted away but I wasn't so lucky. Her claw caught my check, ripping through the skin. I felt water rushing through the wound on my cheekbone and saw red spreading through the water, the current taking it the river. Her paw was raised for another swipe, her mouth wide, showing the whites of her eyeteeth, the snarl she emitted low and victorious.

Another bullet ricocheted and she dropped her paw on the ground, her shoulders hunched as she crouched low. I could hear the men's voices now; they were close. The cougar had been distracted by me and now she was in danger.

"She's nearby, I can tell you that," said one, his drawl thick, the sound of his voice ragged.

"I reckon," shouted the other. "Be careful now. Don't want her claw on my back."

The other laughed. "The horses will be jumpy if she gets close. Don't worry now. I want that skin."

They were hunting for sport, not survival.

The cougar was still, unmoved from her position. She was now like me, unable to cross the river, run or hide where the pursuers would not see. The trees would offer no protection from the penetrating metal of a bullet. Her cubs would surely die along with their mother.

The fish had scattered, finding refuge in the thick grasses alongside the riverbank. Those that couldn't fit had gone downstream. I searched the bottom for rocks. The men would have to get close for me to be effective, but if I could scare them away…

"Look here," called one. "Blood in the water. I told you my bullet hit its mark. Must be around the bend up there. Come on."

Lay still, I wished to the cat. *Don't be frightened.* The animal's eyes darted everywhere but at the water. I was not her biggest concern now. I repeated my comments but she registered nothing. I had no choice.

I slowly raised my head out of the water. She whipped back to me, her snarl menacing, the skin around her canines pulled back, all one and a half-inches of ivory death staring at me. I continued lifting until my chin rested at the surface.

"I will not let the men hurt you," I promised in my thoughts to her. She kept her teeth bared, but didn't strike. Her coat reflected the light from above, highlighting the multi-hued golden brown, tan and taupe mixed together, the effect mesmerizing. Nature had given the cougar a speckled line of black fur starting at her inner eye, curling up and over the crest of her forehead, along to her ear. The dramatic arch continued along her neck.

"These are for the men," I thought, carefully lifting rocks out of the water. "I'm going to make sure they don't follow you."

The magnificent cat growled. This time, I heard her as clearly as I'd heard the trees and grass. *You kill our kind. Why do you help me?* Her lips didn't move nor her teeth. Her growl was her language.

"We are not all alike. I don't want to kill you. I want to save you and the cubs inside you." The cat's tongue throttled inside, catching at the back of her throat. I knew of the cubs she was carrying, and it made her vulnerable and wary. "Stay still," I mentally pleaded with her. "Do not move and I'll do all I can to keep you safe." She said nothing, though her ears flattened, then lifted, twitching left and right as she sought for the sounds of the men. "Don't be alarmed when I shout. I must get their attention."

She responded with a single dip of her head and I ducked below the surface, swimming to the other side of the river. Hiding behind an outcropping of reeds, I lifted myself up, gratified the cougar remained in place. I started wailing, doing my best to imitate a dying animal. As I did so, I ground the two rocks together, hoping it sounded like the claws of a mountain lion in pain.

"I hear her!" cried one of the men triumphantly. "She's close!" The galloping neared and I dropped back down, waiting for the men to appear from behind a large outcropping of rocks at the tip of the bend. As soon as the horse's nose appeared, I took aim for the man's face and threw, hitting him on the side of the head. He toppled off the saddle, smacking the ground with a thud. I threw the second rock at the horse's leg. It hit its mark. The thick skin on the ankle cracked, and blood poured down, over the fur to the hoof. The animal took off in the other direction, back towards the mountains from where it had come.

Khee hee hee, wheezed the cougar from across the water. She had seen the entire thing. The second man rounded the corner, shooting his gun the moment he saw me. I pushed myself to the sandy bottom, the spits of bullets hitting the water around my head. I felt a sting in my left shoulder, knowing more blood was lifting to the surface. If I could bleed in this time, I supposed I could die. And I wasn't sure, but if my spirit died here, I suspected my body would die back in the cave.

The muffled orders of the man directing his horse in to the water were followed by vibrations of the massive hoofs. Ignoring my aching arm, I gathered more rocks, swam to the middle of the river and bolted up, hurling the stones at the man's face and the horse's body.

This rider was faster than I gave him credit for. He fired back, shattering the rocks mid-air. I dove back under, the image of the cowboy with a broad, dark hat charging towards me. I could not let him get near the cougar where she lay, hiding in the brushes.

My stomach scraped along the rocks of the river, and I felt the tearing of my pants peeling away like a fish being skinned alive. A sear of cold confirmed the rocks had cut me, how deep I'd find out later.

A green and silver dart raced in front of me, turned quickly and then swam alongside me, its tail twitching back and forth as it kept pace with me on the river.

I'm so sorry, I thought to the beautiful creature, its incandescent colors reflecting off the glossy rocks. Sorry I had taken one of their kind for myself, with no thought to killing a mother or a father or their offspring. It had been about me; I'd been hungry.

The creature looked at me with a knowing eye. *We are here to provide life*, the fish thought to me. The words, spoken without harshness or judgment, made me feel worse.

But I didn't mean to cause pain like the kind I am feeling now.

The fish's eyes appeared to stop and look at me once, the tail slowing, then flipping back and forth again. *You are like all creatures. You do what is natural until you learn there is a better way.*

There was a better way, I agreed, nodding slightly. I'd remember.

My right hand rammed in to a large boulder and I felt the crunch of the three fingers between my thumb and pinky. I lost focus and the swift current pushed me back downstream.

No! the voice said urgently. The brilliant fish swam right to my face, fins and tail twitching with parental encouragement. *It takes no special bravery to swim with the currents. You must swim against the current.*

I dug the tips of my toes in to the rock bed, lurching myself forward. My aquatic guide led me to the side of the stream, urging me to keep to the clumps of grass. Above me, I heard the rider curse, directing his horse back and forth, racing from one side to the next. The large animal struggled as it lost, then regained its footing. Then it hit a deep pool, forcing the horse to swim.

I took a chance and lifted my head. The man was now further upstream, several car lengths away. With luck, the cougar would be moving in the opposite direction.

Then I turned and saw her. *No! Go the other way!* I mentally shouted at the great cat. The cougar was stalking alongside the bank, the sinewy muscles moving up and down with each calculated stride. She meant to take him down. *He is not worth it! Not for food. Not worth dying over.*

I dove under the water, struggling to the other side, hoping to catch her before she took action. I felt the water changing course and guessed the horse and rider were coming towards me. With a massive kick of my legs I reached the shoreline, ready to jump up and put my body in the front of her if necessary.

The cougar dropped low, a deep rumbling within her audible even under the water. Her tail flicked back and forth, anticipation pumping up her adrenaline. Then she launched directly above me, her front legs extended to their length, the massive power of her hind quarters propelling her more than twenty feet through the air. With her claws extended, her ivory belly passed above me, the length of a small car. The man uttered no more than a shriek of fear when her claws reached his chest, hurtling him to the water. The horse raised and bolted to the bank, never looking back to its rider, who was still missing below the surface.

New spots of blood rose to the top. I dove towards the cougar, believing she held him underneath. But as I neared, she released her paws and swam effortlessly to the bank, gracefully bounding out in one leap. When I reached the spot where the man went under, I pushed my left arm through the water to feel for his body, hoping she'd missed his throat.

"Where is he?" I thought to her, talking out loud, still looking around.

She grumbled. *Look there*, purred her reply.

The man was downstream, struggling against the currents of the river, gargling and yelling enough to assure me he wasn't seriously injured. I imagined his boots full of water and his pride hurt.

She listened to me. She had left him alive with minor tears to his arms and chest.

The man made it to the water's edge, coughing. "Get her," he spat to his partner, who was now rousing from the knock to his head.

"What'd you say?" groaned his companion. He rubbed his ear and shook his head, disoriented with his surroundings.

The soaking cowboy cursed as he gripped the bank, crawling his way up and over. He stopped at the base of a tall pine tree, leaning against the trunk. The cougar was on the other side, once again lying in the thick reeds that covered her protectively with their stems. I dipped back under the water and was on the other side seconds later, cautiously emerging just enough to see and hear the men. One man rubbed his head, a bit of blood oozing out of his ear. He emitted a groan and violently heaved on the ground. A concussion, I guessed, hoping I hadn't caused any permanent damage.

"Aaahh never mind," said the wet cowboy unsympathetically. "You won't miss this," he said, reaching for the other man's gun. "She's still here, I'll betch you."

The cougar was now licking her paws, unaware of the man's focus. His head was down, the cylinder of the gun open as he searched for bullets. He muttered about a lazy partner and checked his friend's pockets for more ammunition.

I swam back to the other side as fast as I could, already thinking my command before I raised my head out of the water.

You have to leave now! She turned her massive head to me, then back around. She was like any female I'd ever known. She was going to do it in her own time, when she was good and ready, not when some insignificant male was telling her to.

The cowboy raised the gun to his eye. With this other arm, he steadied the revolver. "Gotcha," the man whispered, his word followed by a snap and a click of the cylinder closing back into place. "Damn!" he said. The barrel hadn't loaded.

"*Get down!*" I hissed to her. The cougar finished licking her paws, then stood to full height. The heavy weight in her belly caused it to drop several inches from her knees. She was close to bearing her cubs. I heard the click as the man drew back the hammer of the pistol. The next action was going to be a shot.

On instinct, I sprung up out of the water. The animal started, turning her fangs to me in an automatic defensive move, sinking her teeth in to my right shoulder. I felt the eye teeth cut through my skin and muscle, stopping only at the crunching of the bone. Because my body was still in motion, the flesh ripped open and my eyes blurred from the pain. With the full strength of my shoulder, I lifted my arm, even as her jaws remained clenched, raising my hand up just in time to place it front of her belly. I then laid my other hand on top, hoping the double protection of both hands would be enough to stop the bullet from penetrating her stomach. It was all I could offer her.

A flashing, searing pain of heat sliced through both my hands and I rammed my wounded shoulder into the cat's chest, pushing her out of the way. The back half of her body rotated slightly but it was enough. The bullet had gone clean through my palms and hit the ground in the distance.

The man screamed in fury as the cougar growled in rage. "Release me and get down!" I ordered her, my voice cracking. The tips of her teeth ground into my muscle. For a moment, she failed to grasp what had happened, questioning if she dare trust me. "Your cubs are safe but not for long. Do it!"

She responded then, opening her mouth wide, turning her head to mine, inches away. My tendons were shredded, and I guessed my motor skills and nerves connecting the fingers to my wrists were gone as well.

The animal attentively listened, crouching alongside me. The man was cursing in the background. Rapid-fire shots began, continuing until the chamber ran dry, though he kept clinking, willing more bullets to appear.

"Wait," I whispered. I leaned over on my right side, using the pressure against my knees to curl my fingers in to my palms. Blood gushed from my shoulder, stomach and legs, the sharp rocks having torn my clothes and much of my skin.

The cougar observed me in silence and I felt her assessing my condition. I couldn't run as fast as she could, but neither of us was faster than a bullet. She growled and rose on her haunches. She wanted to track him down and end it. Now she was the one protecting me.

"No," I said, shaking my head, my eyes wincing. "He'll kill you and them." I said, glancing down at her stomach. "I have an idea."

I rose, peering over the grasses, seeing the man on the bank was yet again distracted by loading more bullets in his tool of death. I took in a large inhale, closing my eyes and spoke on the exhale, letting my words flow with the air on the wind. It had to reach the closest trees.

"He means to hurt us," I said aloud the towering trees. "To kill the cougar's family. Please stop him."

The words were caught in the wind and went away, curling and looping in the air currents, across the water, towards the trees.

The cougar's tail twitched. She rotated her body around, her massive head inches from my own. Her breath was sweet, the smell of her fur coat musky. Our eyes met and we turned to watch the scene before us. I counted the seconds until the wind carrying my words reached a great cedar tree standing among the others.

The man was still leaning against the base, muttering about bullets, finding one in a shirt pocket and another in his trousers. He was interrupted when a large branch cracked, dropping on his knee. He yelped in fury, pushing it off his legs before continuing his search for ammunition. Next, a branch released on his bare head. The skin ripped, causing a trail of red liquid to wind down his face in a jagged pattern.

He looked up, this time with more concern and moved to his left.

The cougar wheezed with enjoyment.

The cowboy found what he was looking for and inserted the metal objects into the chamber. He snapped it shut and gave the chamber a spin with his thumb.

"He's preparing to fire," I whispered to my feline companion. "You should go." It was time for her to make an escape while she still could. Only one of us stood a chance of living. "I can't make it."

The dark pupils of her golden eyes narrowed and her head dipped slightly, along with her eyes. It was as though she were scolding me like an impatient child.

The man raised this gun, stopping abruptly at the elbow, as if it were stuck. He grimaced uncomfortably, a red flush shooting from his neck to his face. Veins protruded from exertion, but his chest didn't budge. Soon he kicked out his legs, trying to adjust his position, but he was stuck. The tree had let its strong sap flow, adhering to every point of the man's body.

"He's trying to get free," I told her, elation clear in my voice.

The cougar's snickering had a layer of revenge.

The man had no choice but to take off his shirt. Yet even as he did so, he made the mistake of touching the bark with his bare skin. He cursed as his shoulder stuck to the tree, then frantically began trying to unstick himself when a falling branch hit his shoulder, throwing him back. Panic overtook him as he attempted to free himself when a branch the circumference of my arm dropped on his head, silencing his scream. His neck gave out and his head lobbed forward. Only his back being glued to the tree kept him upright. The branch crunched over his forearms, pushing his limp palms open, the gun dropping to the ground.

I exhaled a *Thank you* on the wind. *We go now*. Then I turned to the cougar, pleading. "Before the other one comes."

She purred, her rumble deep and melodic. She extended her tongue and neared. Her wet nose pushed against my useless hands, and then again, more forcefully. It broke the grip of my curled fingers.

"But it hurts," I admitted, my voice breaking from the spikes of pain.

The black kills, she purred. She and her kind would know. The voice was feminine, but had the power and force of a male. She proceeded to run her rough tongue across my skin from the wrist to my fingertips. Again and again, she licked me, drawing out the black powder left over from the bullet until it was gone. Once the clear, clean red of my own blood came, she stopped, nudging my hands to turn over. She repeated her actions on the tops of my hands and then on my shoulder.

Now you will heal.

A heart sickness washed through my soul. To gain such wisdom, the creature had endured terrible experiences from man. Yet, the life-sustaining knowledge the cats passed among themselves, knowing their survival depended on such information.

"Leave now," I told her. "Keep your family safe."

The cat raised herself up, arching her back and craning her neck to survey the exposed landscape. It was time.

Her muzzle came close and she licked my cheek where she had slashed it open.

We will remember you, she purred. She then raised her paw towards the south, the direction the men had come. *Go that way*, she said. The next moment, she was gone, jogging off through the green grass. When she hit the brown plateau, her running against the ground kicked up the dust. The wind carried it back my direction and I watched her figure until she became indistinguishable against the land.

CHAPTER 11

A blast of hot air blew across the valley, sending invisible specks into my eyes, the dry sand like sharp pellets against my lids.

I blinked spasmodically. Searing heat scorched my shoulder, chest and arms; while the fingers of my right hand were completely immobile from hitting the rocks. From within the pain, words came:

Push *through* it, not *against* it.

I stood, thinking my leg strength would be unaffected by the loss of blood. It was a mistake. I staggered, stumbling forward, hitting a boulder with my right knee, throwing me onto my left hand. I felt another crunch. My left hand curled into my chest, my eyes blurred.

The men would be coming soon, and one had seen me. To stay was to guarantee death.

This way, rose a chorus from around my feet. I looked down, guessing the source of the suggestion. The request repeated itself and I moved in the direction of the louder voices.

My course forward was crooked with pain. Fearing another misstep, I kept my eyes on the ground, scanning for badger holes or dips. The grass bowed down, creating a path I could follow.

Yet the air was still. There was no wind to push down the grass. Behind me the blades lifted up, seemingly waving me goodbye, their brown like heads on green spikes. A few had a bit of white; the old men of the field, encouraging me forward. But in front, just an inch before my foot went down, the grasses lay flat.

You saved one of us. We will help you. This time the words swirled around me, floating on the wind.

My steps were slow, each lift of my leg a challenge. The wounds might be clean thanks to the cougar, but it didn't stop the loss of blood. I'm sure there was a path behind me with dots of red, turning black in the heat. Should anyone want to follow, it wouldn't be long before they caught up.

This way, encouraged another voice, this one masculine. It came from a clump of trees and I veered towards the sound. Both hands were now tight against my chest, the arms on top of one another. The grass changed to a blanket of hard, brown stubble. It crunched underneath my feet, the sound out of time with my ragged breathing.

Come to me, the voice rumbled. I focused on a massive cedar in the distance. It stood in front of green pines and white-barked elders, the limbs as thick as my thighs.

My lips refused to move, a dry, white layer of saliva mixed with blood having formed a cement-like surface.

I can't make it, I thought. The tree seemed to respond. Its lowest branches moved forward and back, resembling arms opening wide. In my previous life, I would have thought it was just the air lifting and moving the tree limbs.

My previous life. Time was immaterial. It felt like a different existence entirely.

The white alders joined in a group greeting, the green leaves flipping down and up, shimmering back and forth, a wave of welcome.

I hesitated. I didn't want the man to follow me here, to hurt something else.

We will warn you, sang an invisible chorus.

The voices and wind were my companions as I continued in a southeasterly direction, away from the heat of the setting sun, drawing nearer to the massive tree. Just as I got close, the tip of my foot caught one of the above-ground root and I fell forward. Unable to catch myself, my shoulder hit the bark. It felt oddly soft, like the fur on the back of a kitten's ear. Heat emanated from within, the sensation comforting. I closed my eyes, catching my breath.

A flash of metal and the inscription of words from a thousand years before filled the blackness.

Adversity lasts only a moment.

I forced myself to concentrate. When the pain stopped, the healing would begin. The trees were my watch guards, the air the messengers from every living creature in the life chain.

They should all hate me and my kind. Instead, they were giving me rest and protection.

In response to my thoughts, the bark extended wide against my cheek, enveloping my entire face. The curved branches, each with stems of long, draping, flat needles, moved up and down like a fan, shading my exposed face from the sun.

Why? I thought with as much clarity as I had.

I felt your energy.

The marvel of communicating with a living entity abruptly ended with a growl from my stomach. My energy waves probably sent the mice in the nearby field scrambling for cover.

Sorry about that. How was it even possible that I was here, in spirit form, but clearly within a physical body that could both die and experience hunger?

The branches shook, popping up and down, like the laughter shaking a rotund belly. Not long after, I heard the flapping of wings. A dart of brown and red sped towards me, landing on the nearest branch above. Just as I looked up, berries dropped down and I automatically opened my mouth.

First the tree…then the bird. Life was protecting life.

Overwhelming gratitude emanated from me, the visual of my appreciation escaping the walls of my skin. This is what the Indians know; living with the land, not on it. They weren't simply fighting for their individual survival but for all living creatures.

No wonder they hate us.

I turned my cheek from the soft surface and rolled to my back, slumping down the side of the cedar. I wanted to forget what I knew about history.

How can you help me when your own death is a possibility? I wondered, looking up at the branches, the agony of a thousand unspoken apologies from those who would kill it torturing me.

The great tree shuddered from the roots and I saw a green, electric current flowing from the base where I sat. It continued upwards, the energy of life extending from the Earth into the tree.

Become me, it said. *Then you will understand.*

I recalled a master who once tried to explain how the natural man—the kind he called unenlightened—put barriers between the light and enlightenment that comes with revelation. "Take it in you," was what my master often repeated. I didn't understand what he said, and he knew it, but assured me one day I would.

I closed my eyes, trying now to visualize what he meant by a barrier. It could be mental as much as physical.

Slowly, using all the stomach muscles I had, I lifted my back off the ground. Slower still, I separated my right hand and arm from below my left, the bicep muscle the only ones still working. Around the great trunk they went. My cheek, chest and arms were against the tree, like a little child hugging its mother.

Be me. Feel me. Let it go.

My eyes relaxed in the dark and I visualized the pain leaving, pushing down my neck, alongside the gash in my shoulder and into my lungs. I imagined each pocket filling to capacity, the air turning to sap, the blood vessels changing to the energy of the tree. In every way, trying to be the tree; my skin becoming cedar bark, my feet the roots, even the sounds I would make if my mouth and smile lines had sound.

When I opened my eyes, the world I'd been in was once again different. My legs were gone. My heart skipped a beat as I realized I wasn't me. I was the tree.

I'd been taken within.

As I looked out at the world, I was small and close to the ground, my stomach pushed flat to the surface, away from the ferocious winds that hit me like a battering ram. The barren land was covered with white, and I huddled against myself, crying silently in the midst of the lonely landscape. Springtime came and I had friends: Small alder trees dotted the land and proclaimed their intent to nourish and protect me. They would give me the necessary nutrients to help me grow so I could be strong for the forest.

My stomach lengthened and my arms extended, giving me power. Under the shade of my arms, I gave birth to life. Animals from above and below joined to scatter my offspring. The alders watched, joyfully accepting the new additions. As I grew, the ground moved further and further away. My roots numbered seven, the long, dark tentacles of life turning golden under the sun. The Earth praised me for watching over the land, the animals thanked me for giving shade, the birds loved me for providing shelter.

Then a man came. He was dark and wore skins and spoke to me quietly. He stroked my bark, asking me for permission to use my people for special tools to help catch fish and feed his kind. I gave him what he asked, moving a branch unused by the animals.

He prayed and offered me thanks, giving offerings of food and water before he carefully removed my branch. It hurt a little, but I was strong. I had many, many more branches.

Periodically, my man friend returned, asking for my help and honoring my people. My white barked friends grew as well, becoming fields upon fields throughout the land, providing a musical chorus in the spring that died down in the fall as their leaves replenished the ground. It was the death of the leaves that gave me the strength I needed for winter.

As I grew, I no longer bent from the wind, for it was submissive to me, moving around and through me, kindly releasing the heat through my upper reaches. The sun no longer bothered me but instead felt warm on my head and shoulders, cascading light through my many arms. My stomach was thick and full, my legs extending deep through the Earth, down, down, penetrating even the rock below.

As my trajectory continued, the leaves blowing on the wind told me of other men resembling my friend who also came with requests. The men were honorable and respectful, replenishing what they took, leaving my people intact. Years and decades went by, the land transforming before my eyes as the course of the river changed, the mountains shook and a valley was formed. Generations of animals moved through the valley: deer, elk, bear, mountain lions, long-horn sheep, calves and pups, growing up and in turn giving birth to their own. I saw a pack of three cubs following their mother through the grasses, and as they walked, the three grew to adolescence and adulthood, eventually separating and going their own way.

When I was full grown, I continued to increase in stature, my strength like a mountain, my influence felt on an entire region. I listened to the forests in other valleys and talked with the birds that rested on my limbs. The sky gave me news from places I'd never see, telling me of changing lands and people. My branches sagged at the stories of lands being burned and forests hewn down, but lifted when spring came and new plants sprung up.

One day, my sap bled at the impact of the first gun shots hitting my bark. I remained strong, pushing out the manmade evil with my life force. I welcomed the men and women who came to heal my wounds, comforting me, promising to protect the land and fight those who would harm me and the life around me.

And then I saw a young man save the life of a cougar, who I instantly recognized as one of the cubs who had passed before me years ago. The man was wounded, caring for nothing but others. I protected him, offering him safety and protection, just as I promised I would.

Then I was back in my own body.

My heart felt as though it were going to explode, and tears came to my eyes, causing my throat to constrict. A passion was within me, stronger than I'd felt for the one who drove me to fight against a room full of skilled opponents. It spread from my chest, consuming my senses. I wanted to spring out of my physically damaged body and take hold of the march of progress, somehow creating an invisible but real barrier to this world, so unique and threatened.

The surge of desire hit my fingers that still felt connected to the tree. They responded to my yearning, feeling like the prickling of skin during a thaw. Life was coming back to me…my own life, with the experiences of another. One far older and more significant than my own.

You understand.

I nodded my head, gently lifting my skin from the bark, peeling away my arms from the trunk.

It was excruciating.

"I don't know what I can do," I told the tree, looking around at the land before me. I was wounded and lacked an army of men or authority in the Government. I had a father who I couldn't trust, a sister who was incapacitated and my body was still stuck in a cave full of men who were wondering if I was going to come back alive. And who might kill me if I did.

"I don't know if I'm capable of stopping this," I concluded, despondent.

Maybe not here or in my lifetime, came the response. *But it will happen. Use your will. It is mightier than the highest mountain, more resilient than my thickest limb and stronger than my deepest root.*

I felt prickling then. First my fingers, then hand and arms. I struggled up from my knees, using my left elbow as a prop. My physical state was changing yet again. This time, I watched myself disintegrate, knowing I'd come together whole again, on the other side.

CHAPTER 12

Voices and images, muted and fuzzy, came in and out of my consciousness. Hot liquid burned my lips and moved down my throat. I gagged. Pressure on my shoulders, cheeks and hands caused me to involuntarily moan. A cold cloth was pressed to my forehead, and I rejected the ice slipped into my mouth. Soft fingertips pressed my lips together to keep in the moisture. I wanted to know what had happened. Was the cougar okay? Would my shoulder return to full capacity?

"His body heals fast," said a woman's voice. "Press this, here."

"Salia, why can't we use the orb? I bet I could get his fingers to turn it the right direction."

"No. The elders want him to heal naturally. His body and mind must—I don't know the word."

Mia offered up words to fill the gap. "Connect? Fuse? Bond?"

"As one. Go. I will stay. You must learn now from Kahinsula."

"But why? What's the point?"

"The elders have given you the...how do you say?"

"Task? Privilege?"

"As I have healing, Kahinsula has horses and weapons. You are to have each."

Mia hummed an appreciative response. Even in my blind, pained state, I could feel her sense of pride.

"How long until you think he will be well?" Mia asked.

"A half-moon." Two weeks? I groaned in frustration. A soft laugh filled the room.

"He doesn't like that answer," Mia remarked. "But that's good. It means his brain is working."

"Go now," the woman said. "I will stay." The soft padding of footsteps faded and my awareness dimmed.

"You cannot talk yet," said the woman Mia had called Salia. "But you can dream. Know this. The dreams you will have are real. It is part of a gift you have been given by living through the other side. Other dreams are visions. It is what may come to pass if you are one with your spirit. Sleep now. Your dreams will tell you all."

She replaced the cold pack with a warm cloth, the scent of lavender making me think of purple fields in bloom. My chest constricted, and I jerked. The healer hummed, as she alternated the cool and warm. She began singing in low notes, a melody without words. It was soothing and distracting, her hands lightly touching my skin, rubbing some kind of substance on me. I felt a hot liquid run down either side of my ribs, the pain ebbing.

"Now you sleep. Remember, your dreams will tell you all."

In the first dream, Mia was picking a yellow flower, brighter than gold, with a cushion center and long, thin leaves. A woman showed her how to spread the pedals. With delicate fingertips, Mia successfully picked out certain buds and crushed them into a powder form. A young girl came forward, the bruising on her arm mixing with her tears. Mia followed the woman's direction, mixing powder with water, gently spreading the mud-like result on the girl's forearm. It dried, along with her tears. It was obviously a healing herb, and Mia smiled, seeing the almost immediate results.

The sun set and rose many times, each day showing Mia in a new light. Her hair turned honey colored, with strands almost white from the sun, contrasting against her tan skin. She wore leather pants and a top with a draw string, easily lifting herself on a small horse, guiding it up and down the rocky terrain. Her horse bucked her off when a snake lunged, and she fell, hurting her arm. The horse stamped the snake, killing it.

The horse was skittish, but Mia stood firm and held eye contact, letting the horse knew she had the confidence to be the rider. It whinnied, bowing its head, allowing Mia to take the reins. She lifted herself up, riding through a blackened area when she stopped, dropping to the ground.

Mia used her knife to chip away at the rock beneath her, smiling when she held up a black rock. Holding it to the light, she grinned. Back in the safety of the rock, she showed the Lapuan and the others what she found. She used a piece of obsidian to crack the rock, exposing the diamonds. They were not impressed. Gold had worth, diamonds didn't. With each ride, Mia filled a satchel with gold and another with the black rocks. She was storing wealth.

The scene changed to Boncho showing Mia how to handle a spear with a sharpened rock at the end. He turned her palm upright, placed the back end on her shoulder, extended her left hand, her pointer finger as the guide. The first attempt didn't hit the mark, but as she practiced, the spear came closer to the middle, until finally, a bullseye. Then she was on a horse, throwing that same spear at different targets as she galloped through the forest.

In between being woken and fed by Salia, the dreams continued. Winema came among the tribe, meeting with the elders. Mia took part in these meetings, her clear voice and strong opinions facing down Lapuan. In each session, he spoke of continuing the fight against the white settlers, who had invaded the area. Mia advocated peace and reaching an agreement. She kept her strength, and during the conversations, their opposition to one another had turned in to a partnership focused on helping the tribe.

I saw Mia and Lapuan riding at dusk, with snakes coming out from the rocks, seeking the heat. Mia wasn't paying attention and her horse was bit by a large rattler. Lapuan threw a tomahawk to kill the snake before it struck her. All at once, snakes swarmed the area and he used a rope to lash them back as Mia jumped off the injured horse. The horse was left to die, the snakes surrounding the unfortunate animal.

Mia sat behind Lapuan during the ride back. Dark storm clouds had collected by the time they stopped at the edge of the settler territory. Silently, they watched my father and the officers. Mia's stomach clenched in anger, and Lapuan rumbled his hatred. They were unified in their mutual desire for revenge.

The next sunrise Mia went out for gold, waving to the sentry who stood guard at the cave opening. She returned empty handed. Muleo approached, seeking to understand what had happened. Her anger with our father had surged anew and her gift had stopped working.

"Your spirit is now blended with your body," Muleo explained. "You must be in harmony."

This infuriated Mia even more. I saw her cry in the darkness of night, huddled between the warmth of the hot stone and the comfort of the course blankets. She was resistant to forgiving our father, stubbornly telling herself she had enough gold and diamonds and didn't need the stupid gift of seeing what men wanted.

As Mia struggled with her internal emotional conflict, she continued to learn. Tribe members came into the caves with snake bikes, and she learned how to cut and suck out the venom. She was also shown pain management techniques.

A woman carefully demonstrated how to collect and wash a branch with thin, brown stems and red berries at the end. Mia was about to eat one and her hand was caught roughly by the woman.

"You will hurt," said the teacher, who emphasized how much by putting her hands on her stomach, then emulated throwing up. She counted five berries in her palm.

"This many will kill you."

Mia understood, watching the woman take a different berry, this one white with dark tips. They looked like little eyes on the end of a round marsh mellow.

"Watch," said the woman. She called to a dog and fed the berries to the animal. Within moments of eating the berries, the animals eyes were open, but its legs seemed to become paralyzed. Soon it had dropped to the ground, but all the while, the eyes were blinking and alert. The berries had a paralyzing effect.

Again, she counted. This time three. "Pain stops, then death, here," she demonstrated, tapping her heart.

"Heart attack," Mia said, nodding her head.

Mia and the woman walked to a field where a plant with draping, leaves drooped over, like a long-eared puppy. When Mia went to touch it, the woman's hand stopped her. Instead, the woman pinched her hard enough to make Mia yelp.

"Watch and feel."

The woman pressed the petal on her skin, and Mia's lip dropped with amazement.

"Salia, I don't feel anything. It's numb."

Salia nodded in agreement. The woman used her forefinger and thumb to pinch a corner of the petal, touching the tip to her tongue. She motioned for Mia to do the same.

Mia nodded, scrunching her nose. "It's numb too."

"A little is good. More, like this," she said, running her fingertip along the length of the pedal, "stops this," she said once again, pressing against the area of her heart. "It is called Wolfsbane. We use for killing wolves when they are many. Put it on the tips," said the woman, pointing to the sharp-edged spears.

"A humane death," Mia had said, approving.

Mia was learning and Cage along with her.

The dream dissolved when hot liquid touched my lips. A gentle hand lifted my head.

"You must wake and drink." It was Salia. She was trying to comfort me, I felt that. "Open," she encouraged. I tried, pulling my sticky lips apart, hating that my mind felt trapped in my body, my eyes unwilling to open and mouth unable to move. She pried my skin apart and I gagged slightly but was able to swallow.

"You have been teaching my sister to heal," I got out.

She nodded, pleased. "You saw this in your dreams? That is good. Yes, Mia learns very fast. Rest now."

In my next dream, Mia was on her horse, racing across a valley, a wide smile on her face, one that she wore when she'd won a competition. Kintpuash was behind her, his awareness of the surroundings high. When they reached a meadow by a lake, they dismounted, walking through the emerald green grasses, the nearby deer unaffected by their presence. Mia saw a canoe and ran ahead, asking if she could get in. They paddled to the center, Mia showing Kintpuash her swimming skills, those she'd learned in Girl Scouts. In the center of the lake, it was quiet, the heat cooling off with the setting sun, the fish starting to bite.

Mia's interest in him was clear, but he was focused on teaching, pointing to the hills, many dotted with the black obsidian. He was telling her it was an old, dormant volcano. When he was done, she added all that she knew about volcanoes from her history and geology classes, without revealing the future.

As the orange sky turned to red, the tip of the canoe hit the shore and Mia jumped into the water, pulling the craft forward onto the sandy beach. Kintpuash had been half up, ready to help when the jerk caught him off guard. He fell back in the water, unable to catch himself. Mia laughed while trying to lift him up and Kintpuash's returned her smile. It was full, broad and true.

She extended her hand and he tricked her, pulling her in the water with him. They play-tussled in the shallow water by the shore, a competitive thread flowing through their playful movements; him thinking he would easily subdue her, while she continued to surprise him with her boldness.

They stood, walking to the water's edge, when she pushed his back. Instead of falling forward into the water, he caught himself and spun low, in a move resembling one of my low sweep kicks. Kintpuash caught Mia's leg, lifting her up so quickly she was on her back in the water with a splash. His legs straddled her before she could rise, her two wrists in his grip, holding her still. He was steady, while she was triumphant, the proximity of their contact exactly what she had hoped for.

Even in my dreams, I felt Mia's desire. So did Kintpuash.

And yet I also felt his resistance. It wasn't physical, because he was captivated by her aggressive spirit. Her blond hair and freckles were a source of constant fascination. He was holding his emotions in for the sake of his tribe and because he knew her time here was only temporary.

One day she would leave, just like her father had before her. She was not a part of his tribe, and never would be. He needed a woman in his life, a partner, to bear and raise children. He was the son of the leader. When his father died, he would lead the tribe.

Kintpuah abruptly changed his grip and helped Mia out of the water.

"Wait," she called, hoping to understand what was happening…or not, between them.

"We must return."

"But…" she started, reaching for his arm. He stared at her with all the emotions he could not put to words.

"Come," he said, less severe. He had dropped her hand but now extended his once again. It was all he could give.

Mia had the maturity to understand more was going on than a simple rejection. Kintpuash was a warrior, not a teenage boy or a Prince she could manipulate. The choices of today meant whether a member of the tribe would live tomorrow.

She placed her hand in his and they walked to the horses. I watched her learning expand in her dreams, along with her heart. The infatuation with Kintpuash had been replaced with a yearning to observe him. She saw him leave at dusk to hunt, returning with a single elk which the men dressed. She watched him stand between two warriors with knives, dirty from a previous fight. Kintpuash demanded the Indian version of apologies and a compromise.

One thing I observed through all my dreams was Mia's unrelenting desire to get what she wanted. She approached Kaga asking to experience the fire of testing as I had done within the cave of the elders. He said no. Undaunted, Mia asked Muleo, and failing with him, she appealed to Kintpuash. The elders met, discussed her progress with the healing, horses and weapons, and took her back into the cave. For this, Winema, the translator, was present.

"If you die, your brother will not be here to save you," Muleo warned.

"I don't want to her to die," Lapuan said flatly. "She is to help us get her father."

Mia looked him in the eye. "I will do that and more, just as I promised. But you must let me try."

Lapuan held her eye, considering her promise and request. "If it will help us fight our enemies and get back our lands, I will allow it."

The peace pipe went around the room, and Mia inhaled strongly, but less than she'd done the first time when I'd been in the room with her. The male elders hummed and Muleo blew into the fire.

Mia continued to stare, but her body did not rise or change. The flames didn't explode or turn to green as they had with me. They changed to a deep red.

"It is an angry fire," rumbled Kaga.

Winema translated for him, and the fire grew ever more red with Mia's frustration.

"She does have strength, but not enough or the right kind," Muleo said.

Muleo leaned to Sconchin, who bowed his head. "Mia," said the chief. "The elders will put out the fire."

"No," she argued. "Give it more time."

"You cannot be with the spirits when your soul is angry," said Muleo.

"Of course I'm angry!" she retorted.

Kaga turned to her, his eyes steady and firm. "An evil spirit can do more harm than a good one."

"I'm *not* an evil spirit."

At this, Muleo leaned forward, his eyes turning cat yellow with his words. "But you may become one if you do not bridle yourself."

Boncho stood beside Mia as Winema took her place on the other side. They were to escort her out of the council of the elders.

CHAPTER 13

A soft shake woke me.

"It's time to change the bandages, Cage."

Fuzzy at first, I saw a shadow, then face come into focus. "Mia, give me the orb," I said, grateful my previously fused lips had loosened.

"Not allowed." Her voice carried a humorous lilt. If she thought I was dying, she'd be on the emotional edge, not cracking jokes. She must also be over the fire rejecting her—if that was even real, of course.

"What's happened since I've been out?"

"Well, I didn't go through the fire, which made me so angry I shot high and to the right, like an undirected missile, and I've learned what happens when you disobey or ignore their request. I don't particularly like being slapped."

"You got slapped?"

"Twice. Both times by women."

"What'd you do?"

"Once, I tried to find you in the caves when I was told to wait. I got lost and ended up on a river of ice, yelling for help. The other time I talked back to Kahinsula."

"You talked back to a woman who can speak to horses?"

She pinched my skin, but it didn't hurt. "Yes—wait, how'd you know that?"

"I've been having some crazy dreams, Mia."

"Me too! All that peoti stuff they smoke is seriously strong," she said with a laugh.

She then turned a bit serious. "You'd be utterly shocked to know that I've learned to be a tad more respectful here." She paused, lifting a cup to my lips. "Salia said that once you could speak, I needed to give you this drink then solid foods. No. No more questions right now. Drink."

Compared to the tar-like substance that I'd been given during the fifteenth century in China, this was like drinking air. Then there was the salmon. The rough texture of the meat melted softly in my mouth.

"The drink is going to put you out again, so I'll talk fast. And before you ask, it's been eight days so far. You have a few more to go. Salia guesses two."

I groaned at the length. "Tell me what happened when you woke up in the cave with the elders. Was I already taken out?"

"When I came to, I was in a cavern with girls my age. My old clothes were gone, replaced with this, if you can see it." I saw the light yellow leather shirt, which matched the one she'd worn in my dream. Mia proudly showed it off, pointing to the threaded stitching down the sides of the pant leg, the shirt open at the neck, a V with a draw string. "And these are better made than any tennis shoes I had back home," she complimented, lifting up her leg encased in well-oiled, dark brown leather boots with a reinforced sole, extending up to her mid-calf.

"You do look ready to ride a horse," I observed, my voice stronger, although I was already starting to feel groggy again.

She nodded enthusiastically. "Kahinsula taught me to ride, and now I can mount all of them, even the biggest one called Ghost Dancer. She says I learn fast, so Lapuan showed me how to throw a spear."

"And you can hit a mark while riding?"

She nodded, smiling. "You bet I can. I can also lasso a tree from about ten feet. Salia is teaching me to heal, so now I can remove snake venom, fix bruises and even kill someone if I want to. See, I don't even need your orb."

Horse riding and healing in eight days. The dreams were accurate.

"The acceleration capabilities of time travel still work."

"Don't take away from my greatness," she said without modesty. "But going back to your question, when they let me see you, I got a look at your chest, and I was so mad I went after Lapuan myself, thinking he'd done that to you. I kicked a rock at him and it hit his face. Then he lunged for me and Kintpuash stopped him. You should have seen it!" she was practically giggling. "That forced them to tell me what happened, so Winema translated. Of course, I didn't believe it at first, but after a while, you started speaking in your delirious state."

She stopped, gazing at me with inquisitive wonder.

"Did that really happen?" she asked, her voice filled with awe. "Your soul separating from your body?" I nodded. "Wow. Well, I stopped giving them trouble and didn't want to leave your side, but the tribal elders said, in so many words, that I was worth more with knowledge. Did you know some plants can make you get the symptoms of food poisoning or fevers or whatever, but then you heal on your own? There's even one that makes you have diarrhea, but you can recover from it too."

I didn't need my eyes open to see the broad smile on her face.

"Kahinsula is amazing. She taught me how to understand their eyes, feet, posturing, the different ways they stamp and direction they turn their heads. Of course, one time I got thrown when I was with Lapuan, but that was because a snake bit the horse."

As Mia described what Kahinsula had taught her, I visualized Mia petting the enormous animals, the wild, wary eyes watching her touch the coat, tentative at first, then with more confidence. I imagined the large, dark eyes of the animal losing the fear, the lids lifting with its comfort level.

"When Ghost Dancer nuzzled me, Kahinsula hummed." As Mia spoke, I could see the scene through her eyes. The large stallion had a white, diamond shaped patch that had moved up and down against Mia's face, the front paw scraping the ground.

"Then Ghost Dancer scratched the ground and Kahinsula whistled," Mia continued.

I saw how Mia had stood away, lowered her hand to her hip, then flicked her index finger to the right. The horse had turned, stopped, and Mia jumped up on its back.

"How is your arm?" she asked abruptly.

I rolled my shoulder around, feeling the muscles stretch and pull themselves out of dormancy. "Stiff and still sore.

Question, are your horse skills unique or can everyone talk to horses?"

"Command and direct, yes, communicate, no," Mia said triumphantly. "Not even Kintpuash or Lapuan can communicate like I can. Sure, they whistle and the horses come, but Kahinsula is like the horse whisperer and I'm her understudy."

"Do all the horses respond to you or just one?"

"It took a few days, but I can get most of them to listen to me now." She didn't have to say the words: she was thrilled to death she had two skills I lacked and couldn't replicate, even with the orb.

"That's really great Mia."

"Sure," she drawled. "I can hear the enthusiasm oozing from your voice."

"Trust me, the sentiment is legit. I just feel like my innards have been turned inside out."

My eyes felt heavy, the drink was definitely taking effect.

As I started to drowse, I visualized Mia laying on her stomach, looking down at a camp, with Kintpuash next to her.

"Did you go to the camp where Dad was with the Army?" I murmured, already half in my dream-state.

"I didn't personally go into the camp, but my idea for getting Dad back worked."

I saw Mia take some of the gold she had collected to Lapuan. The two of them, along with Kintpuash and Winema, went to General Canby and the exchange for my dad and gold was made.

"You traded gold for him?"

"Good guess."

It was no guess. By now, Salia's words were validated. *Dream, so you can see all.* I was seeing all, even before I was told.

"Tell me, do your gold finding skills work all the time?"

Her eyes snapped down. "Well…no, not really. I got mad and it stopped. Why do you bring that up?"

"When I was in China, the orb wouldn't work for me when I was mad. It was Gee who told me I had to clear my mind before it would let me heal anyone."

"Oh." Mia went from looking offended about her secret being discovered, to one who is happy to have a confidant. "That was exactly it! But in my case, it was Muleo who told me I was angry."

"So now we know, we are stuck in the mud when we are mad."

Mia laughed. "You're slurring Cage, but I liked the phrase, stuck in the mud. How about completely useless when we are mad?"

"That works too."

"But it's all okay now," she said quickly. "I can see diamonds and gold again, but I'm telling you, it's hard. I feel waves of fury about Dad that I have to subdue. I can't believe he tried to betray the tribe."

"You don't know that, Mia. What was he going to do when he was captured? Tell them the truth, then go wander in search of us, leading the army to their location? Come on." The drink had removed any filter of diplomacy I might have taken with her.

Mia said nothing, her silence the affirmation my words had merit.

I yawned. "Does Lapuan still want him tortured and dead?"

"Lapuan wants to fight the Army, settlers and Klamaths until everything is returned to what it was—"

"Which won't happen—"

"So, in the meantime," she paused and I heard her smiling at our back and forth bantering, "Dad is back in the familiar zone of the cave-equivalent of a dungeon, deep in the catacombs. The tribe doesn't trust him, and I don't like him, so he's stuck."

We had Dad back and I was nearly healed. We had time to get the artifacts, rocks and leave. Things could be worse.

"Are you sure the elders won't let me use the orb?" I pleaded.

She laughed at my whine. "Yes, but it wouldn't matter now anyway. You are healing quickly. Hey, maybe you can see what you look like if I help you up before you conk out again."

She gently lifted my shirt, the soft woven fabric catching on a wound. She gave a tug and it released.

"Oops. Sorry. That was a scab. Here," she said, placing her right hand under my back. The dim light was just enough for me to see my skin.

"Whoa," I said, looking at my chest and stomach. I traced a line that began just above my belly button, then moved below and around the side of my rib cage. Another line went up and over my chest, where it separated into multiple lines, like little mountains. Down and around it went, to the other side of my chest and ribcage.

Mia couldn't take it any longer. "What you can't see is the coloring. No, don't worry. It's not ugly. It's amazingly beautiful. While you were still in your state of delirium, Kaga added color."

"He tattooed me?"

She sighed. "Let me get us a better light. Lift yourself up higher if you can." I lifted up from my elbows, breathing shallow.

"Oh—wow," I said.

"You could say that."

The pattern below me was a cougar, the face on my lower left chest, the eyes directed at me, seeming to look up. A paw stretched out over my chest, the claws open, reaching. The animal's mouth was wide, its fangs bared, the aggressive posturing a mix of attack and protection. It was the same expression I'd seen on the cougar who'd bit me then saved my life.

Suddenly, all the anxious fear I had associated with the cougar and her cubs returned. The men, the killing of the trees and all I knew about the settlers made me want to be healed, *now*.

The grogginess that had been overtaking me was momentarily gone.

"Give me the orb," I demanded, the urgency in my voice real.

"Cage," she said soothingly, though I felt like she was mocking me. "I already told you, no. Most people are asleep right now anyway, especially with the amount of sedative I put in that drink. The answer is still no."

The sinking feeling moved down my shoulders to my lower back. Mia lowered me to the rug.

"You said a few more days?" I asked irritably.

"Just exercise patience, something that you could stand to develop. By the way, you didn't see it, but the wound on your shoulder has healed perfectly. Salia said there was no infection."

"The cougar…she bit me."

"Really? But she didn't kill you."

"I…saved her cubs," I managed to get out.

"You can tell me about it later. Heal so you can help us."

I didn't have a choice.

CHAPTER 14

My eyes were closed. Then why was I seeing General Canby?
Because I'm dreaming again.

The officer stood with three others. Two I recognized; they were the ones who'd been hunting the cougar. The third was in the same military uniform as the General but with fewer embellishments.

"But General," said the younger officer. "We already made an agreement with the Klamath Indians."

"They are only Indians," the man with the large cut on his head interjected. He was the who had gotten stuck to the tree in his zeal to kill the cougar, then me. The head wound from the falling branch was discolored around the edges, red blending with brown, the swollen tissue a sign of infection.

"Yes, Jones," affirmed the General, "and those Indians can still throw a spear with more accuracy than you or I can shoot. It would do us well to remember that as Private Olsen stated, we did make an agreement."

"They can be moved a hundred feet," muttered the man. "Five hundred. A thousand! They will never know the difference."

"Shows how little *you* know," the General emphasized with quiet but thinly veiled impatience. "They know every tree and branch that has been in their territory for hundreds of years. Don't be a fool."

Jones chewed and spat black slop. "Then we have to find a way to motivate them."

"Through peaceful means," the General emphasized. "I've got an assignment from the President of the United States, and that's to restore order and keep it that way. One way to do it is working with that man Fleener."

"What does he have that we care about?"

The General and his subordinate exchanged glances. "Go ahead Private Olsen." With a nod, the younger man dug into his pocket and lifted out golden rocks.

"Those," said the General. Jones' eyes grew wide, and even in his dream, Cage felt his blood run fast. "This is what we got for giving George Fleener to the Modoc tribe," General Canby continued.

"Why did they want a white man?" the other man standing with Jones asked.

"No idea. That's not my problem or concern. I'm going to use the gold as incentive to extend the direction of the settlements to the other pasture land, northward of the Modocs."

"Whose side are you on?" demanded Jones.

"The government's side, Mr. Jones, who, might I remind you, has the right to take away and give every square inch of land in the United States. Understand?" The man gnawed the inside of his lip in frustration. "Now, you and the settlers already have a good deal of land ceded by the Klamath tribe, which takes you to the edge of the lake. Today, you are demanding the river frontage. The Modoc have already moved miles down the river, giving up the best fishing holes. What are you going to do? Exterminate the entire population of natives?"

"The thought had occurred to me," he muttered.

"Go back to your settlement and tell your group that they will have to purchase land from the Indians with hard gold if they want it."

For a moment, the man named Jones looked confused. "What am I supposed to do? Tell the men, women and children to eat gold? We want the land. Places to raise crops."

"So do the Modocs."

"I don't care."

"Fine. Private, you may now put that gold away, as Mr. Jones here doesn't want either the gold or the land."

"No, wait. Wait just a minute," Jones backtracked. General Canby lowered his eyes, the contempt he felt for Jones evident. "You give me the gold, and I'll have one of my trusted soldiers take that gold and distribute it among our people."

"Really? How about you bring the heads of the families and I will pass it out myself. Wouldn't want any of these nuggets getting misplaced along the way, would we?"

Jones was caught in his guilt. "And what if they won't take it?"

"Then they prove themselves unfit to manage the lands in the first place, and the government will designate it as national lands, and no one can inhabit the area. Good to you?"

The man ground the heel of his boot into the powdered dirt.

"Fine, but I'm telling you this, if our settlements keep getting raided at night, we'll take matters into our own hands."

General Canby nodded to Private Olsen who put the gold away.

"The last time you did that, forty of your men died. How many more are you prepared to lose? A chicken here and there is a small revenge for displacing a people who have been here since before our kind came into this country." Jones started to argue and Canby held firm. "We aren't going to rush in and kill the tribe when you attacked them first. You'll be on your own, the death of your people on you, not the Indians."

Jones pushed his lips out, the scruff on his upper lip touching his nose. It twitched.

"It may not be us who attacks them."

The General touched the gun on his holster. "Don't even think about stirring up the Klamaths to do your dirty work. We already forced the two tribes to live together so you could get your property, and that's what started this mess in the first place."

"Don't tell me what I can and can't do," retorted the settler. "We have the right by virtue of our skin color to have any land we want."

"And you also have the right to be hanged or shot for going against an agreement signed by a General, that would be me, who is under the President of the United States. What's it going to be Jones? You going to work this out and live in peace or hang from a rope on a high tree?"

Jones said nothing. Instead, he tipped his hat and left with his companion.

I felt the slow and steady thumping within General Canby's chest. The interaction with the settlers had not increased his pulse one bit. He was objective and analytical, fair and methodical. He was asked to make peace in a land where every day was a struggle to survive.

"Sir, what are we going to do about Jones? You know he's going to go straight to the Klamaths. At least they were smart to give up their lands."

"No," disagreed the general. "They weren't smart. The chief saved lives in the short term, but both tribes are slowly starving. They don't have enough area to support their people, and that's why the raids are increasing."

"But sir," said the private, scratching his head. "If that's true, I hate to say it, but the Indians dying from starvation would have solved their problems."

"Son, I've been in a lot of wars and if I know one thing about human nature, it's the survival instinct. Mankind will do just about anything to live, and if that means taking food from their mother or baby, they'll do it." The younger man grimaced at his leader's words. "War is an ugly thing, and I'm afraid this is going to get worse."

General Canby raised his hand. A soldier in a faded, dirty uniform appeared. "I need you to send a pony express. We have only 250 troops. I want three thousand more out here at once."

"Three thousand?" exclaimed Private Olsen.

"With the combined members between the two tribes, we are greatly outnumbered. What we don't want, Private, is to have both turn on us and the settlers. It would be a bloodbath."

"With the way things are going, it might happen soon enough," predicted the Private.

"That's what I'm afraid of."

I was shaken awake and given more to eat and drink, this time by Salia. Between bites of food, I answered her questions about my health, eager to get back to sleep. I was learning more by dreaming than I ever could have from walking around.

She touched my wounds lightly. "The walls on this cave foretold that the one who goes through the fire emerges with dreams that will tell the past, the present and the future."

"The ones we had to walk by on the way down?" She confirmed with a nod they were the same. "Does everyone know that?"

"Yes. But the walls only speak to Kaga. He is the chronicler. That is his gift."

"What else does Kaga say?"

She touched my arms. "Your dreams will tell you all," she said with a slight smile.

"Then I should get back to sleep, right away." Her smile grew wider, and she was about to give me the drink that made me sleep when a figure came into the cave. It was Winema, a concerned look in her eyes.

"Hooker Jim is injured. Two others as well. A soldier and a Klamath captive." I visualized a Modoc I didn't recognize alongside Mia and two others. They were taking horses from the settlers to stop them from farming the country.

"Mia was on a raid?" I asked, already sitting up.

Winema stopped, then nodded. "Yes. Her purpose was to gather gold." I rolled my right shoulder, hearing the popping of muscles moving over bone. They helped me up and aided me in putting on some clothes. The material grazed the scar lines which stung, but was bearable. I guessed the scabs would be coming off soon.

Salia nimbly spread ointment on my skin then removed a pouch from her belt. She sprinkled a light mist of the fine particles on the wounded areas, including my shoulder. My skin went slightly numb, and I thought about my dream where Mia ground herbs into powder. This was one of them. It would have been so much easier with the orb, but no, I had to heal naturally.

When I stood, Winema caught me as I fell back, disoriented. Salia brought me a drink tasting like berries with some type or herbs in it. After a few minutes, the natural sugars took effect, and whatever else was in that cup had an energizing effect.

"We can go," I said.

Winema led me up the path at as fast a pace as I could handle, while Salia stayed behind. Periodically, a draft of cool air floated up from below us. There must be more than one underground river or lake in this area.

"Do the women use the ice to cook?"

"Yes," Winema answered. "Every day, the women cross the rock bridge from the tribal council area to the other side. Can you see those steps, over there?" I looked and noticed a path carved into the wall. "They use ice picks made from the black rock, then boil it over the fires. We can bath, cook and drink without leaving the caves."

"How do you make it through the year?"

"During the summer months, the women and young harvest seeds, nuts and berries. In the fall, the men catch fish and hunt, and those kills are dried. We also take wool from the wild sheep that are on the countryside. By the time the snow covers the ground, we have gathered enough provisions to live all winter. Kintpuash is wise. He moves us to different locations so we can never be tracked."

"It must be a lot of work, picking up your belongings and moving."

"We use animal skins to take our things along the rivers. Even the children can move large packs. The horses take the paths alongside the ice or walk on it."

"Winema, if you were to leave now, do you have enough food to survive?"

She glanced over her shoulder. "If we had to, yes."

"Cage!" It was my father's voice, startling me. I paused long enough to locate him within the darkness. He was alone in a natural crevasse, a warrior sitting guard, his spear upright. "You're alive."

"And walking," I replied, not altering my gate.

"Cage, can you stop long enough for me to tell you something?"

"Not now. People are injured."

"I'll be fast," he said quickly. "Cage, Mia doesn't believe me and the tribe doesn't trust me, but listen. I went to the clearing where I last saw an outpost camp of the Modocs.

They were gone, and the Army and the Klamaths were in their place. I had to improvise. What Mia told me you all saw; it was an act to get out of there. To save myself and get back, I used the only bargaining chip I had, which was gold. I suggested to the General that he give the gold to the settlers in exchange for returning some of the lands to the Modocs. The war need never happen!"

Dad's redemption for the loss of Nolina was going to come in the form of the lands being returned.

"No, Dad, the settlers don't want the gold."

He frowned, skeptical. "How could you possibly know that? You've been asleep and out of it for over a week from what Mia said, and…"

"Don't have the time to go through it, Dad. Trust me when I tell you, I saw it with my own eyes. General Canby made an offer to a guy by the name of Jones who tried to kill me. See this?" I untied the drawstring, dropping the shirt from my shoulder. "If he hadn't been dead set on killing, I wouldn't have gotten this."

"But how?"

"I can come back later and explain everything. Look, your intention to use the gold makes sense, but they want the land no matter what."

"You sound like you've had conversations with the General."

"Like I said, I was there. General Canby is trying to do the right thing, or at least it seems so, for now."

Walking away, I felt his confusion, skepticism and anger, not directed at me, but at himself. He'd thought he'd been ingenious and resourceful and learned his efforts hadn't played out the way he expected.

We reached the upper cavern where three men lay side by side on thatch rugs. Kaga came to me, offering my backpack.

Natural light shown down as an angular beam through crack in the rock, illuminating two of the men who moaned in pain. I felt a wave of energy in the area, unlike anything I'd felt before.

Must be the power of the orb getting ready to be used.

"I'm going to heal them all, correct?" I asked Kaga. He nodded. "Be prepared with those two," I suggested, knowing I could heal all of them at once. Boncho took his place on the other side of the Klamath warrior. I couldn't see the wounds on the other man.

"Private Olsen," I mumbled, unhappy that he was wounded.

Other members of the tribe were silently coming to the area. Lapaun looked over Kaga's shoulder, speaking rapidly in Modoc. The warrior watched me expectantly, waiting for a response. I had the ring on, but couldn't understand him.

Must have gotten adjusted while I was recuperating.

I fiddled with it, turning it as I had in the cavern with the elders. Nothing.

"Winema, I'm not sure what's happening. Can you please translate?"

"Lapuan says that you must heal Hooker Jim so he can go tonight on a raid with the war chief. He wants to take revenge for our injured warriors."

I gave up on the ring and removed the orb. The light was dim but it wasn't required for me to activate the object. I felt the now familiar indentions on the outside of the metal, knowing what tones were and where.

"What role does Hooker Jim have in the tribe?" I asked quietly, wishing I possessed Mia's depth of history.

"He leads all the raids for the Modocs. Hooker Jim is also Muleo's son-in-law." He didn't appear to be a member of the tribe, at least from his hair. It was cut short, above the ears like mine, and parted to the side.

I gently turned his head, trying to determine the source of the blood coming from his neck area. It was hard to see; his face was covered in plaster-like ash, a mix of white pumice and blood.

"Did he fall?"

"No. For his raids, he puts pumice ash on his face and the settlers can't tell if he is one of them or a Klamath Indian," Winema explained.

Moving was hard. The ointment and herb Salia had put on my right shoulder was working; it was losing feeling, the numbness was now extending down my forearm and hand.

I struggled to turn the knob to the right, expecting the flow of positive stimulation. *Nothing.* I rechecked the spindle.

Bats screeched overhead, and I briefly considered moving the man outside. No. That would take precious time and we didn't want a soulless zombie.

The numbness had now extended to my fingertips, making my right hand ineffective. I moved it to get a better grip on the orb and it fell on the ground.

"My hand has lost feeling," I explained to Winema. "That's it!" I realized. "I don't think it's working because I can't feel anything on my right side. Here, help me move this to my left." Winema came to my aid, putting the orb back on my lap. With my right hand disabled, I tried to hold the orb in place and turned the top half to the left.

"Ugh!" I groaned, my back arching up, writhing in pain. A fire spread through my veins with the speed of lightening, the existing wounds feeling ripped apart and torn. It was as traumatic as going through the fire.

As I yelled, a vein in Hooker Jim's neck shot forth blood, hitting my chest. The light was extinguished as clouds covered the opening above.

Both Boncho and Lapuan sprang forward, Boncho to help me and Lapuan to take the orb.

"No!" I yelled. "I did it the wrong way. Winema, help me hold it."

Her cool hands held down the orb. It took all my concentration to focus through the pain, purposefully turning the top half with my left hand. In a split second, the torment stopped and Hooker Jim's body went limp, the pulsing vein stopping its bloody spray. I felt a flush of warmth through my skin, from my head down through my cheeks. Energy flooded my organs, the yellow light travelling down the shafts of my arms, past my elbows and into my hands. Touch and sensation returned to my right hand, then my fingers. The pains along my chest turned itchy then almost as quickly, stopped. I visualized the last of the wounds going flat, the new skin causing the itch, and then a nano-second later the skin softened.

This had been my first experience with the painful powers of the orb and I had learned a vital piece of information. The orb needed functioning flesh to work.

My right hand and shoulder were no longer numb, and neither my shoulder nor stomach showed bruising. The skin was healthy and whole.

I felt for the ring on my right hand and immediately understood Hooker Jim, who was rubbing his throat.

"It is true," he said, his voice a whisper higher than the others. "He is the one." Hooker Jim sat up, rolling his head around, pointing to my chest. He hadn't been at the meeting of the elders that night but had most likely heard about the event.

I raised my shirt. In its healed form, it was a magnificent tattoo.

Hooker Jim leaned close, the inspection close. I felt him trying to comprehend all that might have occurred to leave this permanent imprint on my body.

A movement to my left. Private Olsen, the soldier I'd seen with General Canby in my dream, was running up the passage way. A *whoop whoop* was heard then a bonk! Boncho had thrown his tomahawk, the heavy, flat end hitting the base of the private's head. The man dropped, his body motionless.

"I didn't kill him," Boncho said with a smug pride. "His head will only hurt."

Instead of running away, the Klamath crouched, as though he were going to spring forward. Lapuan was closest. For a half a moment, I wondered if he were going to attack the Klamath I'd just healed.

As I put the orb away, the same current of energy I'd experienced before healing the men pushed through me. But it was odd; the energy felt negative, not positive.

Lapuan's knife was in his hand, crouching as he faced the Klamath Indian. The retreating warrior looked like he had no desire to escalate the situation. He was still backing away.

"No, Lapuan," cautioned Boncho. "We need him for the exchange."

"You might want to blindfold him then," I suggested, feeling healthy, rested and whole. "What he sees can be used against us."

"I can put his eyes out," offered Lapuan.

"No," I said forcefully.

"Lapuan," said Kaga. "Do not harm him."

"He needs to die. Why should we listen to this white man?" Lapuan demanded.

He was right. I had no place or standing in the tribe. This wasn't my affair.

I leaned toward Winema. "Do the tribes speak the same language?"

"We have enough overlap so we can generally understand one another," she whispered. It was a good guess the Klamath warrior knew what we were saying. No wonder he was motionless. I wouldn't want my eyes gouged out either.

Lapuan dropped his hand to his side, probably because he no longer saw the captive as a threat. The fiery color of aggression diminished.

I stepped toward the Indian, intent on checking his wounds. He shrunk from me and using his hands and feet he crawled away from me like a crab trying to escape a tidal wave. I waved my hands up and down, trying to calm him. He refused to let me close, pushing right up against the wall.

I'd inspired anger, sure, but fear of the kind he was displaying? Never. Then again, not everyone responded to healing in the same way. It had to be unnerving.

Suddenly Lapuan stood up, dropping his hand from his weapon. "Let us go now. We follow you."

I glanced between Kaga and Lapuan, checking my ears. Did Lapuan really mean it or was he going to turn on me?

Kaga nodded once, the indication Lapuan was indeed being serious.

"I need to check him." As I did so, Lapuan asked Winema about my dad.

"Is the father still in captivity?" he asked her. She responded that we had passed him on our way to here, and I ignored the rest of the conversation. With the Klamath captive healed and removed to the other corner, my attention moved to Private Olsen.

"How are you feeling?" I asked him in English.

"Odd," he said honestly.

"You've been through a lot."

"I thought I was dead," said the Private. The bullet hole to the right of his heart was evidence of a direct shot.

"You were, momentarily. Indian healing is miraculous, really."

The Private felt for the bullet hole in his chest that no longer existed and touched the back of his head. The man's eyes flicked to the others behind me, his countenance one of caution.

"No one can speak much English except the woman who you know," I said in an undertone. "If you talk low and fast, they won't understand."

"Who are you? Why are you here?" asked the Private. It had finally dawned on him that my presence in the midst of the Modocs was an anomaly. "Are you a settler who has defected?"

That gave me an idea. "Yes, actually. I am related to that man George Fleener. I'm trying to help the Modocs."

"Were you the one who provided the gold to us for his release?" he asked, understanding mixed with admiration. "Why use the Modocs and not come yourself?"

"You will learn soon enough," I said, my plan already in place. "The short version is the Indians have been through enough. They need peace."

He rubbed the base of his neck. "That's what my General says."

"He's right. Here. How's this?" I pressed on his chest area and he grunted an exhale.

"Good, but I don't think you or the General are going to make a difference," he told me. "I was on my way to deliver the gold to the settlers and was ambushed by a group of Klamaths. General Canby probably thinks I'm dead right now."

"Well, you certainly aren't," I said, patting his back. "Did they take the gold?"

"Sure they did, and once they had it, I got myself a bullet hole. The person who shot me is that Klamath warrior right there." He jerked his head. "The General was right. Jones got the Klamaths to do his dirty work for him. He was hiding in a tree."

I watched Olsen's face and felt his emotions. He was telling me the truth as he saw it. The next moment, I was in the scene of the battle myself. The Klamath warrior was hiding behind a large pine, lying in wait for Private Olsen who was meeting with Jones and a few other men. The private extended his hand and the sound of a gunshot rang out. Olsen dropped to the ground. Hooker Jim, my sister and several other Modocs were on horseback at the far side of the settler's camp. Jones and his group scattered, screaming obscenities, leaving Olsen to die in his blood. The Modoc warrior jumped down from the tree, just as Hooker Jim rode into the clearing. The warrior got off one shot, right to Hooker Jim's neck. He was already falling off the horse, but even in his wounded state, he ran right into the Klamath warrior, running him over.

Three men were laying on the ground when a crow swooped down, circling the men twice then left, dipping low over the Klamath before flying away.

"The General seems like a man who can be trusted," I said.

"How did you know that?"

"From what you tell me, is all. I've been here awhile, healing from my own interaction with a cougar." I showed him my shoulder. He whistled in amazement. "It wouldn't have happened except that idiot Jones was tracking the cougar who ran right into me while trying to escape."

The man's eyes grew wide. "You…are you the one that Jones said he tried to kill?"

I nodded. "I didn't need to kill Jones myself. A well-placed branch falling on his head was a better way to leave him alive and get out of there."

"Wow," he said. I figured Private Olsen couldn't have been much older than myself.

"Private, Jones is a bad one. The rest of the settlers might be honorable, but he's not." I turned to the others. "What now?"

"We must meet with the Council," answered Kaga.

"We should kill the Indian," said Lapuan, motioning to the Klamath still pressed against the wall.

"The elders will decide," Kaga affirmed. "To the cavern."

"Will the Private and the Klamath be safe?" I asked.

"They will be with your father," Boncho replied.

Then it was up for debate. Mental anguish was certainly a form of torture.

Once I knew Dad was back with the Modocs, my father's well-being hadn't been on my mind. The tribe seemed to apply the same principle with him as they had me and Mia: we were some good alive, but no good dead.

When Boncho approached, the Klamath warrior's eyes verged on terror, the very touch of another's hand causing him to shy away. Even the others noticed.

Referring to the Klamath, I said: "Maybe he's like this because I healed him," I conjectured. Having experienced it first hand *was* pretty weird

"He will see nothing but his own spirit soon," said Lapuan.

CHAPTER 15

"Are you hungry?" Winema asked me.

"Very," I replied.

As she led me through a new warren of passages, I felt confined, the earthen walls had become a dark prison, not a sanctuary.

"I *am* hungry, but I would really like to breathe in fresh air. Can I get out, even for a minute?"

Winema changed our course. Above me, a circle of orange was framed by hardened lava. It was the reflection of the setting sun. A fluttering of wings erupted, then there was a combustion of activity as a swarm of bats fled the cavern.

The next sensation was a smell that nearly overwhelmed me. *Bat guano.* The torches attached to the wall reflected off a sloped hill with glistening particles. It was moving, the scratching sounds coming from millions of creatures.

"What are they?" I asked.

"I don't know the word for it in your language," she said. With her permission, I removed a torch and leaned over the edge of the path. Cockroaches, millions of them, probably blind from being inside since the cave was formed, their sightless existence maintained by a never-ending supply of food.

A bat dropped down from above and was immediately attacked, the crunching sounds nauseating. Old or sick, the winged animals provided food for the insect scavengers.

I was grateful when we emerged into the cold night, the brilliant orange and reds dripping into the encroaching blackness like a painting. The warmth under my feet met with the cold which hit me at my waist; the beauty of the Earth and sky connecting.

"Incredible," I whispered, feeling grateful. I was whole again, endowed with new gifts, wondering what was next to come.

The red lava flow from the dream appeared in my mind's eye. Despite all that was going on around me, I was here for a mission, to get rocks and artifacts and then leave.

"Winema, lava flows exist all around this area. Is it possible that one is red?" It was colored black on the tapestry, but the terrain looked similar to what we had around here.

She raised an eyebrow at me inquisitively. "Yes. It is called the Burnt Lava Flow. It is shiny, black rock, but it burns red at certain times of the year."

"Is it important?"

"It is sacred. On a single day in the summertime, the sun shines down its energy on the Earth. In the evening, this turns to red energy. This is the sun's life force, bringing forth food for all in the valley."

"When does that happen next?"

Her lips twitched.

"The cougar chose you. Not me." Still, she lowered her voice. "The sun shines its energy down tomorrow night."

My pulse quickened. "How long does it take to get there?"

"Less than a quarter turn of the moon in the sky."

She brought me smoked salmon and cooked elk with ground huckleberries from their vast storage supplies, and I wondered about Jones and Peter, one man self-serving, the other seemingly wanting to exist with the native people.

"I was thinking about the two settlers," I said aloud to Winema. Her eyes lowered. "I'm sorry. I know you are married to one."

"He is a good man."

She sat down on the warm rock beside me. Children played as their mothers prepared the berries and meat. I felt their curiosity about my presence. A young boy ran to his mother, leaned to her and pointed at me. She looked up, nodding and smiled. His eyes widened, and he ran back to a group of friends. Their noise level increased.

"They know you are special," she confided.

"Does this…happen often?" I asked, glancing down at my chest.

"Once in a lifetime. The last was Muleo."

"Have no other warriors tried?"

"Every warrior, when he reaches the age of a sapling, goes to the Council of the Elders. None have been brought in to the fire as you were."

I wondered what that meant. It was still incomprehensible that my soul had lived in multiple bodies over a millennium, but then, science fiction novels held the concept of eternal souls. Heck, even the Bible referred to the eternal soul, so was it really that far-fetched that this version of me was one of many?

Hidden things come to light, and secret things are made clear.

A line from the ancient sword given to me by the master of weapons at the Imperial Palace. It had been one of the attributes of a seer: to see the past, the present, and things which are to come. It had been in context of gaining all the skills necessary to defeat the master of evil.

I could not see the past yet, but I was seeing the present through my dreams. The future was still dark for me. But perhaps one of the gifts acquired here would give me that power.

All gifts had to be earned, and as I had experienced, the cost was high.

"Do you mind telling me how you met a settler?"

"When I was a young girl," she began, "the settlers had already arrived. It was 1848 as you calculate it. They were not interested in Modoc territory and left our people alone. I played many summers down at the river which leads into Tule Lake. The birds rest there because it is very shallow."

I thought of the lake I'd seen upon our arrival, where I'd shot the cap gun. "Millions, dark as a cloud?" I asked.

"Yes, that is Tule Lake. There were boys down there, not many girls, and we played together as children. When I was fifteen summers, I fell in love, and my parents agreed to let us marry. They thought it would stop the white people from invading our lands."

"But it didn't."

"No. However, I learned the language and can help my people."

"Lapuan doesn't like it," I stated.

"Lapuan likes nothing since he lost Nolina. It was thirty seasons later that our chief ordered our warriors to attack a wagon train with families. Many died. That was the same summer that Nolina…"

"That she died?" I prompted.

"Yes. Things between the tribes became worse, then we were forced to share land."

"Winema, do you think we can stop the settlers?"

"No. The settlers have more people and guns especially combined with the soldiers."

"Then why keep trying?" I pressed. "You certainly can't go underground the rest of your lives. They will eventually stop Hooker Jim from raiding."

Her darks eyes grew strong and proud. "Because we *are* the land. We cannot be removed from it. It is us and we are it."

I thought of the big cedar that had saved me from Jones. It would die in its place, but until then, would continue to give life to those around.

"So, you will die here?"

She nodded her head.

Not interfering was a tenant of traveling through history, collecting only what I needed and then leaving, but Dad was right. With the right motivation, the settlers *might* be persuaded to compromise. If not for gold, something else. And if that failed, the tribe needed a back-up plan.

My heart increased its speed.

"Winema, who do I have to talk to in order to get me to some of the places in the area? I must visit them as quickly as possible. It is why I came."

"The Elders."

It all led back to the council. At the edge of the cave entrance, the outline of a figure against the darkening sky sat motionless. He was the sentry, alert for intruders.

"Is your tribe hoping the settlers will leave if things get bad enough?"

Regret and sadness were thick in her voice as she spoke.

"Yes. When the Klamaths first fought back, the settlers killed many of their people. Their chief agreed to give them the most fertile land in the valley. He thought they would share, like tribes did in the past. However, years went by and that wasn't enough. Hundreds came. They spread across the land, taking more.

"When the raiding started," continued Winema, "Kintpuash argued with the old chief. Scarface Charlie and Hooker Jim disagreed with Kintpuash and kept raiding. In revenge, the settlers waited for the right time, then massacred many Modocs, almost fifty near a river hole. Most were women and children. After that, the revenge killings on both sides increased, and finally, the soldiers were brought in. General Canby gathered the leaders of both tribes and made a treaty. It forced us to leave our territory and move by the river, but the Klamaths kept much of their homeland. In the beginning, it saved lives, but it forced both tribes to share a small space. That's when Captain Jack took over."

"Captain Jack?"

"It's what the army and settlers call Kintpuash. When he first met the soldiers, he learned they did not respect him because he was not the chief. He named himself Captain and took the name Jack from a young white settler he had met and respected. Before more blood was spilled, Kintpuash took the tribe away from the river where we were supposed to stay. He followed the water until it went underground. He is the only reason we are alive today."

Given the timeline she'd described, Kintpuash wouldn't have been more than seventeen or eighteen when all this was happening. Even now, he was probably no more than twenty three or four.

"Our first night here, my father took us to a sacred area. We were safe as we slept, and my dad said that the souls of the dead protected us. Is that land protected from both tribes?"

"Yes. Even the Klamaths do not violate that area of the dead. It is known as Medicine Lake. These tunnels flow to that lake in the south, but also to the north."

"How many days journey north, do you think? Underground."

She thought for a moment. "Two full days by horse." That was a long way. With a quick calculation, I guessed it would end up near or about Crater Lake.

A figure approached, calling to us. It was Boncho.

"It is time."

CHAPTER 16

Within the Council of Elders, Mia sat beside Lapuan. He observed me, the angry lines on his face less pronounced.

Maybe he'd already been sucking on the peace pipe.

Among the group were two additional individuals: Hooker Jim and another male with a massive scar on his face. It must be the war chief my father had mentioned in the glade, Scarface Charlie. His injury was deep and disfiguring, starting just below his nose on his right cheek, going straight down, then up, stopping just before his ear. It was as though someone had made a literal checkmark on his skin.

I much prefer the cougar on my chest.

I took the open seat beside Kaga. The fire was clicking and sparking.

Sconchin spoke. "The council has decided a celebration will be held for our warriors tonight. You and your sister will be honored."

"Thank you," I interjected, "but I have other things to discuss. I must get to the red lava flow tomorrow when the sun causes the rock color to change." My statement had come out of nowhere, and I watched more than one mouth turn down at the corners.

"How do you know about that?" asked Sconchin. In my peripheral vision, I saw Muleo's eyes turn yellow. He knew.

"It is on a map I have." Low hums around the room voiced an unspoken concern. "Is something wrong with me going there?"

Kaga put both hands on his knees. "There is evil when the lava burns red."

What could possibly live in and then come out of burning lava?

"I must go," I said, undeterred. "It is why I am here."

"You are going to get more rocks for the orb?" Mia asked me in Mandarin.

"Yes. Three images are on the map Bao drew for me."

"I will go with you," offered Lapuan in English.

Mia turned to him. "When did you learn Mandarin?" she was half-joking, but I cocked my head at her question.

Lapuan stared at her. He knew some English, but not much, and definitely not the word Mandarin.

"I think it was a good guess on his part," I said.

"Oh," she said, shrugging it off.

"In addition to the lava flow, we have Private Olsen and another captive," I said to the elders. "We also have my father. My plan is this. I will go to the army settlement with Winema, dressed as a settler, and to speak with the General. I will give him directions for another area the settlers can explore and potentially move to, along with more gold. In case they refuse, you begin packing your things, preparing to leave this area for safety."

Hooker Jim looked pleased. "Good. You talk to the General and I will raid."

"No," I said firmly, ignoring his frown. "You stop raiding for the next two days. At least until the peace treaty. We make it appear as though we are cooperating."

"Who told you about the peace treaty?" asked Scarface Charlie.

"I saw General Canby talk about it."

The room went quiet. They all knew I'd not been out of the cave in ten days.

"Are you trying to trick the General?" asked Lapuan, his opinion of me improved.

"No trick," I said directly. "I want to make sure the tribe is safe. That means leaving. Permanently."

The group talked of staying, and Hooker Jim and Scarface Charlie gradually convinced the majority of the elders to agree fighting was the best solution. On the other hand, Kintpuash argued for a peaceful resolution, and strangely, Lapuan took his side.

Mia asked for a translation and I gave it to her, growing angry as I did so. Their obstinacy and pride were going to kill the entire tribe.

At first, I thought the heat of my emotion was nothing more than my anger rising. It started to gather within my gut, expanding to my shoulders and my chest.

Then it became something more. The tickling sensation of the cougar on my chest was insistent, but I dared not look down or open my shirt. The feeling of protectiveness, fury and power consumed me, just as the mama cougar experienced when she tried to save her cubs.

Control what is within, said a voice, that wonderful, peaceful voice of love I'd not heard since the day of our arrival. It was my mother, her soft whisperings from the other side warning me.

The spirit animal inside me was responding to the situation. *The protective instinct.*

I pushed the spirit within back down, concentrating with all my might. Through the fire, I saw Muleo's yellow eyes watching me.

"During the peace treaty meeting," he began, his deep voice cutting off the others, "we will be asked to sign away the remainder of our lands or take a small portion and live in peace. No more fighting."

"And no more growth," said Scarface Charlie through his bared teeth. "Our people will starve to death. To kill us with guns would be better." The other elders in the group murmured in agreement. "Kintpuash, you know we can defeat the army. They have fewer men. We can outlast them."

"Yes, we have the men and the advantage here in our caves," agreed Kintpuash. "But to fight means some of our men will die. Cage cannot save everyone." A sense of admiration came from Mia towards Kintpuash, and I added mine. He did not want his people to die.

"You saw what he did," disagreed the war chief. "We take him with us. This will not stop. They will push us to extinction."

"Let me go to the settlers first, to try and speak with them," I proposed. "Show them where other good pieces of land exist."

Winema held up a hand.

"They will not listen. They do not want to move from this fertile land. My husband tells me that they would rather die than leave."

"Then you must go away from here," I said passionately. "The night before the peace treaty meeting, we can move most of the tribe out of there, through the underground tunnels. Those who want to stay can take their chances with the settlers."

"But Cage, if the peace treaty goes like the history books say…" Mia interrupted in Mandarin.

"If I get the right rocks, and there is an artifact here they can give me…."

"Seriously?" she asked, incredulous, still speaking in Mandarin. "You're just going to leave them here to get slaughtered?"

I gave her a hard look. "They can choose to stay here or leave. It's called free will, Mia."

"But what if the General dies and Kintpuash is tried for murder?"

I felt the red in her heart, the growing respect for Kintpuash on the verge of becoming love. *Real love.* Regretfully, it couldn't factor into my consideration now, just like my love for Bao wasn't a part of my decision making to leave her in China and letting fate take its course.

"Mia," I said with a bit more empathy in my voice. "What I'm trying to do is make sure Kintpuash attends the meeting and it ends peacefully, with no one dying. To accomplish that, I need motivation. That can only be provided with me showing them a place that's as wonderful to live as where they are now. Can you help me in doing that, please?"

She pulled in her lips, wanting to fight me but knowing this was out of even my hands. She reluctantly agreed.

Mia nodded. "What do you need me to do?"

I told her about Crater Lake. "You help Kahinsula with the horses and tell the council all you know about the land northward, where the people can live in safety."

"Crater Lake is like this area," she said to the group, with Winema translating, forcing an enthusiasm I know she didn't entirely feel. It was going to be a hard journey ahead, and they would leave behind all they'd ever known. "It is high, the lake about the same size as Medicine Lake, clear and deep with an island in the center," she said, her eyes brightening slightly with real feeling as she touched her thumbs and forefingers together. "You will be very safe."

"Safe from who? The settlers? We could kill them overnight," said Scarface Charlie.

I took a breath.

"That might have been true a few days ago, but you cannot kill the three thousand soldiers the General has requested." I took in the shock from the group. "They are coming to force the relocation of this tribe. If you do not accept their terms, you will have to leave or they will kill you. Those who are not killed…" I hesitated.

Kaga spoke. "What will happen?"

"You will be forced to walk across the country. Very few will make the journey alive."

His eyes were dark but believing. "You have seen this?"

"Yes."

"What of the Klamaths?" asked Lapuan.

"The Klamaths have not broken the first agreement, they have stayed on their lands. They do not intend to break the treaty that will be signed. The tribe will stay by the lake and keep some of the land."

Even after hearing the future, the war chief was undaunted.

"I want to fight," he maintained. It was Hooker Jim who now vacillated. I sensed his emotions for his woman and a son. To fight and lose meant to risk all he loved. Even his father-in-law, Muleo, was in jeopardy.

"There is another way," Lapuan said, staring at the elders, then tipping his head to me and my sister.

Sconchin and I locked eyes. By now, we were as much a part of the tribe as their own people, honored to the point of having sacred gifts bestowed. But we lacked one thing. Their skin color.

"Leave us," Sconchin requested.

At least this time, no warriors rose to escort us out.

"I guess they finally trust us," I muttered to Mia, disgruntled.

"Not enough to include us in their biggest decision."

We were up the path, and crossing the river of ice when Mia stopped.

"Do you think it will work?" she asked me.

"I don't know. It's like the Kintpuash we know wants peace, but in the history books, he showed up and killed General Canby. What made him do that?"

"Who knows?" she questioned with bitterness. "It could have been self-defense. We know how the government changes history when it suits them. He's not a cold-blooded killer. Not like Pulamon."

"Or Lapuan," I added.

"Yeah, but even he seems to have mellowed since we arrived here," she said, gliding her hand along the rail as she walked.

"Isn't that the truth? Clearly you two spent a lot of time together while I was healing. Your influence might have rubbed off on him."

"Did he tell you that?"

"What? That you rubbed off on him?" I asked, realizing I'd said too much.

Mia elbowed me. "How did you know I spent time with him?"

"I just figured you must have because I had several dreams about it."

She huffed a response. "I'm serious. There was something in the stuff we smoked. But then, you are my twin. It could be in our DNA."

I decided not to share with her the knowledge of this new attribute I'd acquired. I needed her help not her competitive spirit.

"Mia," I put my hand on her arm, drawing her to a halt. "You do realize that once I get the right rock and artifact, we need to leave?"

"Yes, and you know that I meant what I told you before. You can't just abandon them at such a critical time. You didn't do that with Bao. You figured out a way to save her, and the Emperor and Empress."

"That was different."

"No," she challenged. "You made a different choice. You aren't romantically involved with anyone here so you don't care."

"Mia, you aren't seeing the larger picture of our mission. You're only seeing the here and now."

"Mission?" she asked incredulously. "Are you kidding me? We are going through time, taking what we want, saving people and changing lives, but when it doesn't suit you, then it's forbidden? So hypocritical," she spat. "Just like Dad."

She jerked her arm free.

"It is the only way, Mia."

"Wrong. You are always spouting off about doing the right thing, no matter the cost. It's not the right thing for you to go to the red lava flow tomorrow, and then say—hey, thanks for showing me everything. Here's our father. We're out of here."

"I need you, Mia. Kintpuash can't even let himself be in a real relationship with you because he knows it's impossible."

She drew back further. "And how do you know that? Another dream?" she demanded.

"Yes," I responded coldly. "You and he were on the lake. I felt all the love you have for him. And you know what Mia? I felt his too. Does that make you feel better? But when he pulled you up, and you called after him, I felt his love ebb because he knows you are not from this time, that you can't stay. He needs a partner Mia. Someone who will be here to have his children. Are you prepared to do that?"

Emotions fell across her face like curtains dropping on a stage.

"You're cold and callous, Cage, no different than Lapuan. All the while you were recovering, I was getting to know these people. The young girls, the mothers and grandmas, the toothless men and toddlers who would fall in the dirt and smile."

"What are you saying, then? You want to stay here?" She hesitated, a split second too long. "Mia," I said gently. "You aren't meant to be here anymore than I was meant to stay in China."

"Who says I can't?" she said with a crack in her voice. She gripped the hand rail, looking down over the ice. Her forthcoming loss of Kintpuash's companionship was inevitable. She was asking me to change her destiny.

"I can't do this on my own."

"Why not?" she challenged. "You do everything else on your own."

"Do you think any of this was constructed by me, for my own selfish desires to have growing powers just so I can piss you off? Do you think I enjoy making hard decisions, having nothing but faith in the visions I've been shown, putting my life in danger every time I turn around?"

She scrunched her lips to the side.

"Look, I respect your feelings for Kintpuash and I'm sorry for you, because I know from personal experience it's going to hurt to leave. But Mia," I said, touching her shoulder, "there are evil people everywhere, some just waiting to be tapped. If you stay here, and I leave, you really think I'll succeed?" Mia remained quiet. "Neither do I. I'll die and your mortal life will end here, among the Modocs. The end."

In the half-light, I felt the ache of sorrow growing within her. She was valued and appreciated here. The strongest, bravest, most handsome warrior was her equal. They had become partners in a sense, without the physical intimacy or game-playing she'd had in the past. It was exactly what she needed, but before now, didn't know how much she wanted it.

"Can you do it?" I asked softly.

Her eyes were glassy. I wrapped her in my arms, and she cried in the crook of my neck.

She was still in my arms when Boncho found us. She wiped the tears from her eyes, giving me a flat-lipped nod.

"The Elders have decided," Boncho said.

We returned to the cave, sitting in the vacant spots we'd left. Sconchin waited until we were settled to speak. The men wore a look of complete solidarity. Winema's face was expressionless, unlike her emotions, which were flowing as quickly as a stream; glass on the top but a torrent underneath.

"Cage, we will allow you to go the settlers with Winema. You will take Private Olsen with you as a sign of good faith. Hooker Jim will raid as planned."

"But—" I started to say. The old chief stopped me with a glance.

"You are allowed to go to the burnt lava flow tomorrow night. The next day, we will sign the peace treaty and give back the Klamath prisoner and turn over Private Olsen."

It was a compromise, although it didn't include the most important part. I translated for Mia.

"And what of my father?" asked my sister.

"You said you wanted him drug across rattlesnakes," reminded Sconchin. "Do you still want that?"

Mia considered the question once translated. "Do what you want with him, but I ask that you let me prepare your women and children to leave this place."

"You are willing to sacrifice him for our people?" asked Lapuan.

Mia stared at the man, the last of her innocence replaced with strength of character. "You have my word."

Winema translated, but it was unnecessary. Everyone in the room felt her conviction.

The men looked at one another.

"We have a ceremony this evening," said Sconchin. "You and your sister will be a part of it. You must prepare."

Kaga caught my eye.

"What do Mia and I do until then?" I asked him.

For the first time, Kaga gave me a smile. "You get dressed."

An hour later, I wore a sunrise orange leather top, the front laced together with a leather strap. At the bottom, an eagle's feather was attached with a small arrow carved from obsidian hanging beside it. My leather pants were deep tan, the color of the clay in the surrounding areas. My slippers were soft leather on the sides, thick on the bottom, multiple layers of hide stitched together.

Mia wore a leather dress, with braided tassels hanging below her exposed collarbone, past her chest. A belt with inlaid red stones accentuated her narrow waist. Below this was a painted mural of a river meandering through trees with animals above and below dotting the hemline. Her blond hair was pulled to one side, an intricate knot and braid wrapped at the end with multi-colored twine of some sort.

We silently followed Winema from the corridor to an area which opened up wide into an enormous cavern. I felt the heat at the same moment I saw the entire population of the tribe. Men, women and children sat on rows of stone. I guessed there must be three hundred people.

Was this all that was left of a once proud tribe?

Another rush of anger moved up from the warm rock below me, heating my soul.

Control what is within. I again calmed my inner cougar.

As I gazed at the children, I thought of those who were slaughtered during the invasion by the Prince of Yan. In the process, many died. Yet he became a great Emperor who accomplished incredible things for China. What would occur if the tribe were saved from slaughter or relocation?

We were directed to sit on flattened rocks on the left side of the underground amphitheater. The elders of the tribe, and all the warriors who weren't standing by the doors as sentry, were seated in the front two rows. The low, pure sounds of reverent humming began, silencing the cavern.

"I will translate for you," I whispered to Mia.

"Members of the tribe," Muleo began. "Chief Sconchin has asked us to gather to honor two among us. This man," Muleo said, gesturing to me, "went through the flames and emerged alive, and with the sign. Cage, stand up and show the people."

I did so. I unwound the leather strap that held my shirt together. Opening it wide, I took it off entirely, dropping it to the floor. Gasps of awe filled the room.

Shoulders back and wide, I shared the permanent evidence of enduring my experience.

A thread of heat began under my right shoulder blade, starting at the tip of the cougar's ear. It raced over its head, then separated at the neck, down the paws and claws. Over my chest and around my stomach, then up again on the left hand side of my chest to the cougar's broad chest.

Those sitting closest to me drew back, but one curious boy stepped forward, fascinated. He stretched out his fingers and was called back sharply by his mother. His wondrous eyes caught mine and I smiled. What could it hurt?

I nodded my approval, and he touched the skin. A growl echoed through the room, and it shocked me and the little boy. We looked at one another, his father pulling him back protectively.

The growling continued, and I felt a stirring in my stomach, as though the beast were literally moving within me. I didn't think I could control this. It literally wanted to get out of me.

"Call her now," requested Muleo.

Her?? *The thing inside me was a she*? Of course. The big cat I'd saved with was a female, and a mother at that.

I thought of the beautiful beast. A snarl filled the cavern, the deep growl rolling along the curved rock, behind and over the occupants. My chest reverberated with the sensation, which continued until the sound died out.

Protective and caring. Fierce and loyal. Relentless.

"Look," whispered the boy.

The rumbling among the elders confirmed what I had guessed. A cougar spirit resided within me. The entire tribe had felt the power and my control.

"Is it safe?" asked Lapuan, curiously.

I translated for Mia, who smiled and nodded at Lapuan.

"Safe and strong," she said smugly. "Males give up. Females fight to the death."

Lapuan's admiration was now plain to see. "Yes, they will." He'd spoken in heavily accented English.

"I guess everyone's English has really improved," Mia observed, causing Boncho to chuckle.

Sconchin raised his arm. "We made an oath that if Cage survived the fire, he and his sister would be set free. He has saved three of our warriors from death. First, he saved Kintpuash from Pulamon. Then he saved Boncho's life. And today, Hooker Jim lives because of him. For Cage, we give him the crystal of the lake."

A growl rumbled within me.

"That is a powerful object," said a male voice from the crowd I didn't recognize. It wasn't on the paper that Bao gave me. It was possible she missed it in her rush to copy the tapestry. Or…perhaps it wasn't on there to begin with.

"Does he not deserve it?" asked Sconchin, looking for the source of the comment. "If a member of the tribe disagrees, let him talk now."

The silence was deafening.

And so Muleo rose, placing a braided rope around my neck. At the end was a rough stone, about twice the size a cashew nut, purple amethyst in color, with a low clarity, as though clouds existed within the rock. "The rope unites the elements within the crystal, drawing upon the powers of the Earth," he confided in an almost inaudible voice. "The wearer of the crystal has the power to command the land."

Once he took his place, Sconchin spoke again. "The woman, Mia, has healed our sick and wounded. She also found gold to trade to free George, her promise to Lapuan fulfilled. She used her skills to gather much gold for our use in bartering with the soldiers and the army. She earned the right to learn of healing powers and about horses. She has provided value to the tribe. Tonight, she receives the gift of tongues. Come," he beckoned.

Mia looked around for a moment then approached the old chief. He removed a feather from his hair, placed it in her lap, and closed his eyes, his lips moving, but heard by no one.

Half way through, Mia's lips parted in wonder.

"Did you understand me?" he asked.

"Yes. Every word."

"This is your blessing from the tribe. You will take it with you until you die."

Well that was awesome. No more translation required from me. At the same time, I was bummed out. I had to use the ring.

A drum beat sounded and a group of teenage girls left, returning with trays of food carried within hollowed branches. They started at the end of the rows, the members taking pieces of fruits, berries and meats. The formal part of the ceremony over, the tribal members ate and talked and laughed and the children were encouraged to play.

Kaga came to my side, kneeling. "Is this what you seek?" He was referring to the necklace.

"I don't recognize this from the tapestry," I told him, but described the other items Boa had drawn.

"No, we do not have things like that."

Then all I need are the rocks. I glanced at Mia, who had likely guessed my thoughts.

"Tomorrow evening, the burnt lava flow," Kaga said.

"I told you," interjected the war chief, who had been listening. "The dead landscape is evil. It is from a time in our history when the land was covered with serpents," he explained.

"More than you have now?" she asked. "They like the warmth of the rock, and tomorrow night it will be glowing red with extra heat."

"How often does this happen? Once in a generation?" I asked, my mind not on the rocks, but something far more critical.

"Yes. The serpents take over the land."

A riddle then. How to get a rock from the flow while it's red and covered with poisonous snakes.

CHAPTER 17

I was dressed in clothes belonging to Winema's husband, Frank. We were roughly the same height, but not weight. The pants kept slipping off my narrow hips and dropping to my thighs. With my shoes on, a little tight, I held up his pants and found Boncho.

"Can I use some rope?"

"Why?" Boncho wanted to know.

I opened my palm and the pants dropped down to my knees.

Boncho chuckled. It *was* funny. He cut a piece of rope and gave it to me. Once I had my pants on tight, Winema held out a hat. She told me her husband was from Kentucky, and he fell in love with her because of her hair.

"Your hair?" I asked, staring at it. Long and parted in the middle, it had natural waves that weren't curls, but flat ridges, as though someone took an iron to the middle sections and crinked it.

"It's red-tinted," she explained, drawing a torch close. Sure enough, her dark hair had a red shimmer. I hadn't known that was even possible with black-haired people.

"What does Winema mean?" She put the torch aside, hiding her face. "Is it bad?"

"No. It means woman-chief. The name was given to me as a young woman."

"Cage," interrupted Mia who had come up. She was dressed in leather pants and top, a thick, woven vest of black tied in the front. "Winema won't tell you this, but she saved a group of children who were caught under the cascades in a canoe." Winema, stood straight and tall, but wore a look of modesty as though her actions were nothing out of the ordinary.

"Impressive," I said, somehow unsurprised. Her role had been valuable to this point. It was going to be vital in the near future.

"Mia, do you think we could pass for husband and wife?" Mia ewwed out a teasing groan, but enthusiastically agreed to the ploy. "Can you work quickly with some of the men to gather what you need?"

She nodded and in a moment was off with Winema to get the picks required to chip the stones out of the ground. An hour later, Hooker Jim had assembled his group for the raid.

"We will go when you are meeting with the settlers," he told me as Lapuan and Boncho looked on. Scarface Charlie was staying behind with Kintpuash. I found him speaking to Kaga.

"Kintpuash, if you are going to be moving the tribe anyway, then…" I glanced at Kaga, looking for support,

"Can't you prepare to move anywhere, not just along the river line?"

Kintpuash's pupils were wide in the dim light, his face grim. "I follow the elders."

"So, you do intend to sign the peace treaty, without violence?" I felt him assessing me, as though I were implying he should take a different course. "What I mean is that you will go, read and listen, sign and then leave, correct?"

After another moment of curiosity, he nodded a yes. "Winema will be present to translate. Boncho and Hooker Jim will be with me."

That was good. Finding Mia chipping away at the rock I knelt by her.

"Tell me where to hammer. I want to get going." She pointed and I pounded, quickly unearthing the valuable gems.

"Mia, I wonder if you might be right after all, if history was rewritten. I felt Kintpuash's emotions. He has no inclination or even thought to go in and murder anyone. He is focused exclusively on preserving his people."

"Well," she said, grunting with effort as the pick cut into the frozen ice. "The Germans tried to write out the Holocaust early on until they couldn't. Why not this?"

We deposited the diamonds into a small sack that I put on my belt. Hoping to save time, I asked Mia if she still had the massive gold nugget she'd found the first day of our arrival.

"I was kind of hoping to save that for our return trip." I grimaced. "It's okay. I'd given some of the smaller chunks for Dad's return and was able to save for something *really* important," she added, the sarcasm thick. "It's in my fanny pack. I'll get it." I met her at the animal cavern. Kahinsula and Winema were already by their horses.

Mia and I were going to be on the same horse, and I could see she naturally thought I would take the reins.

"No way," I said, laughing. "China showed me I can barely stay on one for a few hours. As it is, I probably won't be able to walk afterward."

As if agreeing, the horse stomped as I neared.

"She knows you are uncomfortable," Mia told me, her knowledgeable manner making me grin. Mia hummed, stroking the chestnut-colored main of the female. The animal settled down, bowing its nose to my sister.

"Can you mount?" I did, but it wasn't easy or graceful. The other women laughed.

"Don't do that in front of the settlers," Kahinsula counseled.

Mia easily mounted in front of me, up and over. Kahinsula and Winema each had a horse, with small packs on the saddles.

Kintpuash walked over, touching the nose of Mia's horse.

"Return to us," he said to her. I felt the current of feeling extending to my sister and knew those words meant more to her than a thousand compliments about her hair and looks.

She nodded and used the reins to direct the horse forward. In seconds, we emerged from the darkness into the light of the stars. The sentry moved aside, and once Winema was out of the cave, he went back to his position. Kahinsula kept the horses to a slow gait through the lava beds, then started a trot when we hit the hard soil. The pace never hit a full gallop.

"Why aren't we going faster?" I asked Mia.

"Horses can run at high speeds but not for very long. The rider saves the horse's energy just in case. Like now."

In the distance, I saw campfires and white tents. Scattered across the land were small farmhouses, built of wood and clay.

It wasn't long before we were sitting in the small room of the home Winema shared with her husband Frank. It was unusual living arrangement, she explained on the journey over, but it worked for the situation, her going back and forth between the two locations as desired.

The fireplace burned bright. Two men were with us, Frank, Winema's husband, and Alfred Meacham, the negotiator sent by the government to lead the treaty meeting. The man had a high, balding forehead that curved out like an overhand on a rock, the eyebrows hanging from the edge, darkening his eyes. His full mustache blended to his beard which ended at his hairline. Winema sat quietly beside her husband, her translation skills unnecessary, but her watchful eyes assessing all.

Meacham's eyes flicked back and forth between me and Mia. "You two are out here all by yourselves?" he inquired.

"Yes, moving through to the Crater Lake area," I answered.

"Cage," Mia said, touching his arm lightly, the way a wife would to gain a man's attention. "Mr. Meacham is legendary for his work on behalf of the Indians, isn't that so, Mr. Meacham?"

He raised a bushy eyebrow. "I wouldn't say legendary, but I have been witness to the injustices toward the Indians."

"May I tell my husband a bit more? You can correct me if I'm mistaken." He nodded, clearly perplexed but willing to humor her.

"Mr. Meacham's parents objected to slavery and so moved from North Carolina to Indiana. When he was hired to help two tribes move a hundred miles away, he saw their grief and sorrow. Isn't that right?" He dropped his chin in confirmation, eyes fixed on my sister. "He already recommended to the Council for Indian Affairs that they listen and address the valid complaints of the Modocs because the Klamaths have been harassing them." She paused, looking at him again. "And they ignored you, didn't they?"

"Unfortunately."

"And that's why he's here this week. To fix what is broken. Oh, and perhaps most important, he's a Methodist minister and requested to help the clergy instead of the military."

"I believe faith and God get us a lot further than guns and bullets."

Winema's husband coughed over the last words, as though in his opinion the use of guns was sometimes necessary. "Young lady, you are exceptionally well informed for a settler from California."

"One must be aware of the surroundings before one moves, don't you agree?" Mia was playing the role of settler as well as she had the Empress's attendant.

We had met the men, and now we needed to deliver our incentive and leave. Only two days until the peace treaty meeting.

"Mr. Meacham, Mr. Riddle," I began. "My wife and I are like yourself; sympathetic Americans who are believers in a great being above. It was more than fate that brought us here today. Recently, we were blessed to come into an inheritance of great worth. We brought it with us to help us as we start out, but when we became lost, and then were found by Winema and Kahinsula, we took it as a sign from God. We discussed it on the way here, and we would like to help you, by giving you part of our inheritance."

Frank and Alfred exchanged looks.

"Mia?"

She opened her pack and the uneven block of gold. She balanced it in her hand, lifting it up and down.

"That's quite a rock you have there," remarked Frank.

"We hope that some of the settlers, maybe all, will use it to go to land that is further north, where we are going."

Alfred's skeptical manner returned. "Are you trying to buy them out so you can have the land yourself?"

"Do we look like two people who are going to come in and drive out the Indians?" Mia asked incredulously.

"Sir," I cut in calmly. "To my wife's point, we have no desire to stay here longer than another day or two, and then we will be on our way. We are seeking land not already occupied, if such exists."

"And you want nothing in return for this?" asked Frank.

"As my husband said, this is our inheritance that we are giving to you. Nothing is expected, we ask for only one thing.

We want to ensure that you give the Modoc fair treatment during the peace negotiations that are coming up, because they have been so unjustly treated by the Klamaths and now by the government. Can you do that?" Mia turned to me, and I felt her appreciation that she'd been given the chance to control the conversation.

"Yes," I nodded, giving her an appropriately supportive smile first. "Can you do that?"

Alfred Meachan pushed back in his chair, the shadow of his eyes receding as he lifted his chin.

"I have made it my mission to God and this country to see the wrong's righted. I intend to do all that is in my power to see the Modoc nation restored."

I glanced at Mia and she nodded.

"Good, because I have one more thing for you." I started to untie the bulging pouch at my belt. "It is common knowledge that the Modocs and Klamaths take turns raiding each other's camps, as well as land belonging to the settlers. They do this because they are starving. The settlers are overfishing and over hunting the area. So, we are giving this to you, since you are a man of God. Perhaps you can find a way to go down to the closest city and purchase food and supplies. This should be enough for several years."

On the wooden table, I tipped the end of the sack, opening it wider. The chunks of dark rock came out, the little glints of light within.

"Do you have a hammer or an ax?" Frank reached down by the fireplace and retrieved a mid-size ax, the metal end heavy and sharp. I turned it over, using the dull end.

"Watch carefully." I held the rock, careful of my fingers, and smashed the side of a rock. The black fell off. Again and again I did so.

"Well, I'll be…" said Frank. "It's a diamond."

"A diamond jeweler out of New York would likely do a better job, but you get the point."

"There could be millions of dollars here," said Alfred in a hushed tone. "More money than the state of California."

"Not quite," I tempered, "but enough to cover the settlers and the needs of both tribes until you can reestablish peace in the land."

I cupped my hand, scooping the raw gems back into the pouch. Tying the draw string, I pushed it to the other side of the table, beside the fist-size gold chunk.

"Sir, can I trust you will do the right thing with this inheritance?"

Alfred stood. "Young man, you have my word."

Kahinsula had stayed outside with the horses during the short meeting. The animals were restless when we approached, their large eyes wary.

"Something disturbs them," Mia told me as we neared them.

Frank and Meachan stood on the small porch with Winema, who was staying there overnight. The three watched us mount.

"If you're going to last out in the wild, you better learn how to mount a horse," joked Frank. I agreed, already waving when a shot rang out. The horses jolted, trying to break free from the reins. Frank and Alfred dropped to their knees, Frank's hand on his holster.

"Mia, go!" Kahinsula yelled and Mia kicked the horse's flanks. I held on, grateful for Mia's skill. Another shot rang out, the whir of a bullet close but missing its mark.

Mia issued a command and the horse broke into a full gallop, darting through the branches that lashed at us. We had just crossed from the wet, moist line of the valley into the higher desert land when a massive shove pushed me off the horse. The last thing I remember was my head hitting rock.

CHAPTER 18

"Well, now, isn't this interesting? I reckon I know this young man. I outta fix him right here, when no one else can see."

"No! Jones, you can't! Pulamon said he was coming from the Riddle home. That man Meacham is with him. The peace negotiator. You don't know what they said, or what's happening."

"Ah, it won't matter. The stupid meeting is going to come and go and nothin' will change. We're gonna drive these natives out of here, especially the Modocs."

"You better be careful what you say," cautioned his friend. "The next person Pulamon could slice up is you."

"Me and him are on the same side, Pete."

"Jones," said the man, his voice much lower. "I think Pulamon wants us dead as much as the Modocs."

"Ha, shows how much you know," said Jones. "Here, we need to get rid of this body."

"A nice mess you got us in now," griped Pete. "Why did you go and have Pulamon shoot a white man anyway?"

"How was I supposed to know it was this man? He was meant to shoot than blimey raider, Hooker Jim, who hit our camp an hour ago. But I'm just as happy he got this one. You don't recognize him, do you?"

"Uh-uh."

"That day we were hunting the cougar, about two weeks back. Remember the blood we saw in the river, and the head that poked up?"

A pause followed the comment. "You think he's the one?"

"Positive. I had him in the sights of my barrel when that stinking tree fell on my head, or I would have put a bullet between his eyes for sure. There's one way to be sure it's him though." I felt the pain of the rocks through the leather shirt, grateful for the strong material.

"Mother of Mary..." uttered the man named Pete. "That doesn't look like a bullet wound." I felt finger tips running along the skin of my shoulder.

"Look around. I know I hit him with my shot." The rest of the shirt came off and both men cursed.

"Have you ever seen something like that before?" Pete asked.

"Never. Not even on an Indian."

"What does that mean?"

"I don't know and I don't care. Lookee here." My right hand was raised and stretched. It was dropped, then the other was raised. "I told you. My shot went clean through both hands as he raised them to defend himself. He lived and has the scars to prove I made my mark."

"Jones," said the man, his voice sounding nervous. "Where are you going to get rid of this man so he won't be found? We don't have the tools or the time to go back and get some and dig a shallow grave."

"You have a point. Ohhhh, wait, I know the perfect place to leave him, dead or alive. The wash, on the low planes, just before lava flow begins."

"Why there?"

"If he's dead, he won't mind the snakes using the last of the warmth in his body. And if he happens to wake up, then his death will be slow and painful, suffering just as I did during our last encounter. And if they don't get him, the coyotes will."

The other man grunted.

"Here. Help me get him on the horse. We'll dump him and be back before anyone notices we're gone."

"What about Pulamon? Does he know he shot the wrong person?"

"Oh, that crazy native thinks that this man is related to someone he hates, probably a cousin or something. He said it was a spirit of fate that gave him the chance to get revenge."

"What in the world is he talking about?"

"Eh, some old grievance that started before the settlers came but ended up with someone he loved dying. Here, let's do this. One…two…"

I felt my body lifted up and dropped onto the saddle of a horse. I wasn't unconscious, but my body wasn't operating in line with my brain. I must be paralyzed.

At least this way, my death would be fast. My body would fade, and Mia would be able to stay with the Modocs. My only hope now was that the valuables we'd given Alfred Meacham would create a new history. One that included a white woman named Mia Fleener marrying a warrior named Kintpuash.

At some point, I'd fallen asleep.

In my dream, I watched Kahinsula make a bird call as she neared the sentry outside the cave entrance, who cupped his mouth in turn, alerting others of their arrival. She continued riding down into the cold blackness, with Mia a nose-length behind. Kahinsula slowed as he lifted his hand.

"Where is Cage?" asked Kintpuash.

"He was attacked," Mia answered breathlessly. "I saw him. It was Pulamon."

Kintpuash called out and Boncho came running. The men were gathering their weapons, preparing to ride in search of me.

"I'm coming," Mia announced. Kintpuash ignored her, moving up the corridor with the other warriors. "Hey," she said, grabbing his arm. "He's my brother and I can help."

"You will stay here." His eyes were cold and voice hard. He yelled and a sentry appeared at the mouth of the cave. Kahinsula stood by Mia, her countenance firm.

"Are you going to babysit me?" Mia asked bitterly.

"You are to remain with us, safe, while they find your brother." The older woman was unbending, leaving Mia frustrated. After the men disappeared, Kahinsula spoke with more compassion.

"Your brother has the cougar spirit. He will return to us."

"Right, but as what? A person or a ghost?" she asked, worry overlapping her bitterness.

As I lay in my comatose state, I dreamt a sentry walked through the corridors, taking his time as he passed the wall of pictograms that had moved when I'd walked by the first time.

In the light, I saw it was Lapuan. He'd not gone on the recovery mission for my body.

Lapuan traced his fingertips along the wall, pausing at the woman under the water. He walked slowly, the crease of his eyes deepening when he laid three fingers atop wavy lines. The snake-like images were moving towards a figure on the ground, tongues out, ready to strike. A frown appeared on Lapuan's face when he looked at a stone dangling from the end of a rope. His hand lingered on it for several seconds. It was the same necklace that hung around my neck.

Beyond that, mounds resembling massive chimneys were in groups, the tops open and dark inside. Lapuan ended his inspection of the wall, retreating to the men's cavern.

The dream ended and I woke to the feeling of my body being moved.

"Pete, here, this is perfect." The two dumped me on sand, which was a blessing. The oddity of my mind working within an unresponsive body meant I could hear the crunches and movement and still felt pain, despite not being able to do anything about it.

Blessedly, in this case, the sand was a soft pillow.

And this is where I'll die.

"Too bad he's not awake to feel what's going to happen next. Wish I could see it."

"Jones, you are still sore he stopped you from getting the cougar. Not sure being poisoned to death is the same thing."

"You're not going to last in this territory being soft like that." I heard and felt the kick at my foot, a parting shot at a frustratingly unresponsive man.

"I just don't think it's normal retribution Jones. Pulamon was meant to kill one of the Klamaths. This guy has just been in the wrong place at the wrong time on two occasions now."

"Yep, and this'll be the last."

I heard a hiss, followed by Jones cursing.

"Perfect timing. They need warmth and are going to find him quickly."

"Hurry, Jones. I hear more of them!"

The creaking of a stirrup and the leather groaning from the weight of men was followed by a low, "*Hee-yah!*" and then the soft pounding of hoofs on the ground quickly faded away.

I waited, presuming it was still dark. My eyes had been affected along with the rest of my body, entombed like a living mummy.

But it didn't take much of a working brain to know that the poisonous creatures Jones was talking about were snakes. I felt the ground move with soft vibrations and had a visual of snakes moving sideways along the sand, being drawn to my warm body like the glow bug to a light.

"*He is warm, but not dead,*" said one.

"*Look!*" hissed another.

I sensed, rather than felt, living things line on either side of my body, coiled at the bottom, the middle and top sections straight up, peering onto my chest.

Whether it was real or a dream, I didn't know. They were staring at the cougar on my chest.

"*He is safe to us*," proclaimed a third reptile.

The vibrations increased around my paralyzed body. Up and over my feet, on top and up my lower legs, knees, my thighs, neck, stomach and chest. The feeling continued along my cheeks. Anywhere my skin was exposed, the vibrations touched. Then the sensation decreased, it was as if the volume had been turned down on the stereo.

Then came the pulsing.

Why had my mind continued to operate? Was this what it meant to be in a coma, where the mind functioned but the body didn't?

Having the orb wouldn't help even if it were laying beside me. I couldn't speak, so communicating with Mia or anyone else who found me would be useless. They'd assume I was dead, but then be perplexed at my breathing and heartrate.

A lot of good getting the cougar had done me or the ring, which was now useless, and who knew what the stone around my neck was for.

The slow pulsing continued, and I felt the energy of hundreds of snakes around and on top of me, using my heat for overnight warmth.

Call her.

It couldn't be. Mother? What am I supposed to do without a working body?

Call her so she can help you. She is within you. You have felt her. She will come.

The teenager in me started a thread of complaint, of my sufferings and the burden of my role in this journey, but it was cut short. The kind, loving tone replaced with a firm, parental tone.

Use what you have been given so you can receive more.

In other words, it was my choice to go forward. Somewhere, in her comment, was the opening for me to do nothing, die, and be done with it all.

No. I wouldn't do that. When I was delirious with frostbite on the torture wall in China and not when I was being burnt alive within the fires to encounter the cougar. I wasn't going to do that now.

Become what you need to be, in order to live, and survive.

Another riddle. *But mother…!* I mentally cried, wanting more.

Silence. She'd given me wisdom and then she'd left.

Visualizing the cougar on my chest, a replica of the one I'd saved when in spirit mode, I called to her.

Come to me. I need you.

I kept repeating those words until fatigue overcame me, and slept.

CHAPTER 19

In my dream, Boncho, Kintpuash and Hooker Jim were at a full gallop heading to Winema's home. Kintpuash dismounted, and before he could knock on the front door Frank was there, gun in hand, Winema behind him.

"Cage has been taken and is injured," he said angrily. Winema started to translate, continuing as Kintpuash told of Mia's return, where the attack took place and Cage's fall.

"The shots started as they left here," Frank said, putting down his gun. "Who did this?"

"We don't know. We go to find him." Frank and Winema shared concerned looks.

"It could have been one of us," Frank admitted. "Someone in the settlement who doesn't want the peace process to happen, or the Klamaths, trying to get back at the Modocs. We will help find him. He is a good man who brought us valuables to move the settlers in a different direction so you could get back some of your land back."

Kintpuash shook his head.

"No. You stay. We need the peace man Mia said is vital. Protect him. No matter what the cost. He must not be injured. He must be at the peace meeting. Agree?"

Frank put out his hand to the warrior. "Agreed."

As Lapuan and his two men rode into the area where I'd last been seen, I dreamt that Mia was plotting her escape. She had her horse by the reins.

"You cannot leave." Kahinsula was by her side, dressed in riding gear.

"They aren't back and you aren't his twin. I can find him." Kahinsula repeated that Mia couldn't leave, and Mia clicked her tongue at the horse who cantered up to her. "You will have to shoot me then."

Kahinsula waited a moment, then clicked to her horse as well. Soon, they were making their way through the maze of the lava flow. Periodically, Kahinsula slowed, leaned over her horse, and made a decision on the direction. She reached the point where I'd fallen, and dismounted. It was dark, sunset still hours away.

"No blood," said the horsewoman. "No walking."

"What does that mean?"

"Here." The woman pointed down. "Boots." The deep lines in the ground were from the back heel of a boot.

"You mean they dragged him somewhere?" Kahinsula nodded. The woman glanced up at the night sky.

"We must return until the sun rises. There are many animals out at night. The horses will bolt." Mia knew there was nothing left to be done. Her attempt at containing her worry and fears was unsuccessful. Tears mixed with the wind as they sped back to the safety of the cave.

A rough tongue moved along my cheek. I knew instantly what had done it, and wanted to smile in appreciation, but my mouth refused to follow my command.

"You came," I thought.

I was across the valley, in the hills with my cubs.

Now those cubs were alone, without their mother. She should not have come. "I don't want them harmed," I thought to her.

The cougar's wet nose touched my ear. *They are in the den, sleeping and safe.*

If they were asleep, it must still be dark, and the men would be back at their camp, unable to fire on this beautiful creature.

"I have you in me," I thought to her.

We will always be one.

Where are the snakes? I hadn't moved an inch, and the snakes were at ease.

"Why aren't they biting you?"

The same reason they haven't hurt you. You have my imprint. You will not harm them, or me.

"But I am stuck in my body," I thought to her. "I might as well be dead."

Another wheeze and a nudge, the understanding affection a parent who knows a child has much to learn.

With my spirit, you can go into other living things.

What does that mean? I wondered. I couldn't endure moving through flames each and every time I wanted to have the out-of-body-in-the-spirit experience.

She lay down beside me, the rapid pumping of her heart moving through my skin and bones.

Your spirit is one with the land. You can move your spirit into other beings to serve your needs.

"Even when my body is unresponsive, like it is now?"

Yes. You are chosen among your people. Once, when I was a cub, my elder told of a man who had a bird on his chest. His spirit could fly with the eagles, but the man was killed and his body eaten.

A coyote howled in the distance. First one, then another, the sounds filling the valley.

They will come for your body and I won't be able to prevent them from eating it once the snakes leave. You must learn to move your spirit.

"But what do I practice on?" I thought anxiously. "The snakes??"

I will wake one.

A hiss came next. The distinct feeling of grumpy annoyance filled me. The rattler moved slowly at first, its knocking a warning to those against additional irritation.

"Can I move my spirit into you?" I mentally asked. "I won't be long."

The rattling continued, as though the snake were considering my offer.

"Now what?" I thought to the cougar.

Throw your spirit.

I thought back to the massive cedar tree, who had given me shelter when I was wounded, who had injured Jones when he was preparing to shoot me. I had wanted to see its life, and the tree taught me how, I'd just forgotten.

I mentally closed my eyes, focusing on becoming the spirit within the animal, as I had with the tree.

Slowly, the darkness became light, and although I knew my physical body to be dormant on the sand by the cougar, I felt a brightness that at first, I thought was in my mind, but then knew it was different. It was my spirit, floating up and out of me as it had in within the fire. This time, it was moving to the snake.

It hurt, moving out of my body and into another form.

Gradually, the black faded and I started to see shades of red. My vision was based upon levels of heat. *Amazing*! That's how snakes knew what to strike at, even in the dark.

My shoulders moved back and forth as I looked down at the man on the ground and the female cougar beside him. All my family were sleeping on and around the man.

That man was me, and I am the snake. We were sharing the same physical body, but I had the clear understanding that I was the one in control of the body while in it.

"I won't harm you," I thought. Then to the cougar, I thought: "I am here in the snake."

I go now to your people and will bring them back thought the cougar.

"No!" I silently shouted. "Not the white settlers. You must go to my friends, the Modocs, who live in the lava beds."

The ones who live underground and hide from others. Yes, I know them. They are friends of the earth.

"Should I stay in this form?" I thought to her.

You must practice while I am gone.

She rose and trotted off in the direction of the lava beds. It wouldn't be long. I only hoped the sentry would know that she was on a mission for a friend.

As I swayed back and forth, I told my physical host I would be leaving it. "Then I will try to come back." The snake hissed its acceptance, and I focused on entering my body laying on the sand. Quicker this time, I felt my soul dissipate and then reenter my body. After a few moments of rest, I imagined my entry into the waiting snake, and I threw my soul forward once again. It hurt less and was faster.

Back and forth I went, the speed increasing in direct correlation to the pain reduction. As I continued the practice, I contemplated the possibilities. Could I do this only with animals or with all living things? And I knew I could die in this animal form, just as I could die in the arid landscape. Yes, this was real life and death.

Uneven pounding on the ground caused me to arch my reptilian back. My human body was still immobile and showed no signs of healing. The community of reptiles stirred on my body, the scales dark but visible in the fading moonlight. Sunrise was close now, maybe in an hour.

Soft padding accompanied the hard stomping, and I instinctively shrunk down.

Sharing the mind and body with an animal was a bit disconcerting. My physical instincts took over as my human mind tried to keep up.

No wonder the reptiles have been able to survive for so long. They react before we can even think of what to do.

The horses stopped at the edge of the wash while the cougar came up to me. I could see Mia and Kahinsula waiting. The cougar sat beside my body.

They have come, she thought.

I moved my shoulders back and forth, swaying, but it didn't capture their attention. I immediately threw my spirit back into my body, hoping I'd be mobile again. But my body didn't move any more than it had the entire night. Quickly, I threw myself back into the snake and rose up high to see the riders.

"What's that snake doing?" Mia said out loud.

I sprang up.

Mia made the motion to dismount, but Kahinsula put her hand out. "I don't know, but your brother is covered with snakes."

I leapt up again, then a third time.

"Wait," answered Kahinsula, observing. "Something is at work here. Cougars do not rest with snakes, and snakes do not jump up. They only attack."

"There is one snake, sitting right on Cage's chest, looking directly at us."

"Talk to it."

"I can't believe I'm doing this," Mia muttered. She waved to me and I crouched low, then pushed straight up again. "No way." I immediately slithered off myself and went to the sand. It only took seconds to send her a message in the sand.

Mia

I had written it with my body.

"Unbelievable," was all she could get out.

"It is because he is a spirit warrior. He called the cougar to get us. He is now in the body of the snake."

Mia's mouth had gone slack, staring between me and Kahinsula. The cougar snarled, turning her head.

Someone comes. You must hurry.

"Why is the cougar growling?"

Kahinsula looked around. "She senses danger."

"Cage," Mia said, "if you can hear me, you have to tell us what to do. How do we get the snakes off you? And are you going to remain in the body of the snake?"

I slithered my way through the sand.

Horse, I wrote.

"You're going to come into the horse?"

Yes.

"But we don't know how to get the snakes off."

The sun, I wrote.

"Yes. See there." Kahinsula pointed to the horizon. It would warm the ground, drawing the snakes to the heat. "It will be close," she murmured.

I went back the cougar. "Thank you," I thought.

I will come if you call again. The majestic cat nuzzled my cheek one last time and trotted towards the rising sun, back to her cubs.

I ventured near the two horses, wondering if one was better than the other. Probably my sister's.

"May I enter you?" I asked her horse.

I am willing. It took a few moments, but the feeling of being a reptile was replaced by standing on four legs, the weight of my sister upon my back like a feather resting on a hand. The snake immediately went back to my body, and I neighed strongly.

"Does...that mean you are in this horse?" Mia asked tentatively. I stomped my feet, lifted my head up and down. She laughed. "This is so awesome. I get to lead you around for once in my life." I jerked the harness left and right, increasing her laughter.

Kahinsula wasn't joining in the fun.

"Trouble comes. See there." I looked, seeing dirt rising in the distance along with the sun. Three horses, ridden by two white men and a dark-faced Indian. I guessed who they were, but without being in the snake body had no way to communicate.

I neighed and stomped again. "What does that mean Cage? Do you know them?" I stomped the ground. "Did they harm you?' I stomped again, harder.

"They are returning to see if he's alive," Kahinsula guessed. I surely wouldn't be if the sun didn't arrive before they did.

As the first rays of light hit the ground, the awakening was gradual, moving to the rock that turned from cold black to matte. In my form, I could literally see the colors of the rock changing underneath, the warmth of red extending along the earthen floor until it finally hit the sand. The speed of the heat quickened in the soft surface, covering the wash like a wave. It reached my head first, waking the serpents, who twitched and hissed. In my spirit state, I could see the warmth flowing under my body increasing faster than the sun above.

I willed it to go faster. The dust clouds were nearing.

Finally, the sun had crossed the entirety of the wash and the snakes had moved off my body, looking for a warmer source.

"Now," Kahinsula commanded. We rode close and my rider dismounted.

"He's heavy," Mia complained. Mia clicked and tapped me, and I bent down on the forelegs. "You're the best bro," she said with humor. I bumped her with my head, practically knocking her over. "You be nice or I'll leave you here."

While she spoke, Kahinsula lifted the legs of my body. Once Mia had a grip under my armpits, they heaved and launched me on the saddle.

When Mia mounted, I slowly extended my long legs to full height. I heard a call and immediately reacted. My ears flattened and I increased my speed. The power and exhilaration of this body was incredible. I felt a slight prick and veered to the right as the other horse passed me.

My body jerked when a *whooof* went off to my right. Just as soon, another *whooof* sounded to my left. I kept racing forward as the whoofs came with more frequency, until Mia cried out, pulling on the reigns.

To the left and right, I saw shoots of ash erupting from chimneys taller than my head. The plumes went straight into the sky. Mia had stopped me full, leaving the reins loose. I watched the ash spread into the sky like an upside bullhorn. Around us were many more of these cylinders of mud.

"Mia!" called Kahinsula, and we rode on. The jerky movement of the horse moved my physical body, dropping my arms over the side of my horse body, like Raggedy Ann.

Full onward we rode with no more distractions, the sun hitting our backs just as we reached the edge of the lava bed.

The sentry called down and men ran up to us as I stopped where I knew I was supposed to.

This horse was well-trained. I didn't even have to think.

"Muleo and Salia," Mia called out before Kahinsula could speak. "He can't move."

Kahinsula spoke with the men, but without my ring, I couldn't understand what was said. My body was gently lifted and taken out of my line of site, down into the darkness.

Well, that's going to be hard to get back in.

Kahinsula called for Kaga and Muleo, who came while I was drinking water from a stone trough. When I turned, they waited expectantly. I walked forward, bowed my head, and dropped to one knee.

"It is true," Kaga said reverently.

"Yes, he is the spirit warrior," Kahinsula said.

"He was in a snake and wrote my name in the sand. The cougar was with him the entire time," Mia explained.

"He needs his human form healed. We must go," said Muleo.

With the sound of a click, I knew to follow the men.

Although my physical shape had changed, my mind had been awake almost constantly for over twenty-four hours. The horse may not want to sleep, but I found myself becoming drowsy with mental fatigue.

When we arrived in the cavern where my body lay, I went beside my human form, kneeling. Without being directed, I dropped on all fours, then lay down with a sigh, relieved that at least I was back in the safety of the Modoc tribe.

"He's tired," said Mia.

"Salia. Mia. We must heal his body," said Muleo.

I closed my eyes, hoping for the best but expecting the worst.

CHAPTER 20

"Well, where is he?" growled Jones. Pete shook his head and Pulamon scoured the area, searching for clues. He dropped down on one knee and pointed.

"Taken."

The other two watched as the Indian lifted his arm in the direction of the lava beds.

"You should have killed him when you had the chance," accused Jones. Pulamon put his hand on his tomahawk. "But you will get that chance again. The meeting is tomorrow."

Pulamon mounted his horse. "The Modocs will die."

"I know you want them all dead," said Pete, "but why?"

The warrior paused, his face contorted with anger. "Didn't I tell you?" butted in Jones. "They were enemies since the beginning of time, but a boy from the Modoc and a girl from the Klamaths fell in love, years ago. They had a baby, and the Modoc warrior wanted the family to be together. It was Pulamon's grandpa, the chief, that forbade them to leave. They defied her tribe and went to live with the Modocs. That baby girl is now that translator woman, Toby."

"Winema," corrected Pulamon with a growl.

"Then what's the problem? She is doing the Army and us a service with the Modoc."

"The problem is that Winema's mother had a sister, much younger than herself. She too, ran off with a Modoc, Lapuan."

"Okay, I'm still not putting together why Pulamon is so mad."

"Pulamon had been promised the sister's daughter to wife, Winema's cousin. He demanded that Nolina be returned to his tribe and to him. Captain Jack, the leader of the Modoc tribe refused. He knew Lapuan, his warrior, and Nolina were in love. Nolina begged Captain Jack to stay with Lapuan, leaving her tribe behind. Long story short, Captain Jack agreed, even though it meant the two tribes would be at war."

Pete scrunched his face. "Captain Jack did the right thing, I think. They were in love."

Jack scoffed. "Not for long. Within the year, Nolina died. Some sort of sickness."

"But…" began Pete, casting a wary gaze at the warrior who had been listening to the explanation. "She's dead. No one gets her."

"That don't matter. Pulamon blames Captain Jack for it all, and will never forgive the tribe. He wants vengeance. As long as he breathes, he will do anything in his power to bring blood and death to that tribe."

The three turned and rode from the area, watched by three other horsemen: Kintpuash, Boncho and Hooker Jim. They too had been to the army camp and the Klamath settlement but hadn't found Cage. Kintpuash had tracked the horses back to the wash, finding their adversaries first.

When the way was clear, he led the men to the wash and traced the activity, just as Pulamon had done. Without a word, he launched on his horse and raced toward to the lava beds.

"Cage," Mia said, patting my head once, waking me from my dream. I gave the horse's equivalent of a groan. She then touched my massive jowl muscle. "Muleo says you must move out of the horse's body now, to see if the healing we did worked. Can you do that?"

I opened my eyes and gazed up at her. The horse loved her touch; the tips of her nails scratching the hair, digging in to the muscles, massaging the fibers. An appreciative groan came out that had nothing to do with my spirit but everything to do with the bonding between rider and horse.

Lifting my enormous head was as effortless as breathing. I saw my still body on the ground beside me, face down on my stomach.

Why stomach? The next moment, I was inside my own skin again.

It hurt my neck, actually, the position squishing my face.

"Well, this is uncomfortable," I grumbled. Mia whooped with joy and I heard the familiar grunt-chuckle from Boncho. I hadn't expected to hear a sound. "What'd you do to fix me?"

"Can you move?" Mia asked.

"Carefully," advised Salia.

Hands helped me turn over on my back. The group was assembled: Muleo, Boncho and Kintpuash, even Lapuan.

"You had a large bulge on the back of your neck. Salia knew what plant to put on it, and then the men stood around you, chanting and praying for your recovery."

"The spirits heard us and answered," said Muleo reverently.

"Thank you," I said to Salia, then Muleo and the others. I opened and closed my fingers and moved my head. It all felt in order…stiff, but even that had become a familiar sensation.

"Feels strange to be back in human form. Did this take a long time?" I wondered, immediately concerned about all the time that had been lost.

"No," Mia answered. "It's not even noon, the day before the peace treaty."

I started to raise myself up, using my hand and elbow. "You're still going?' I asked the men.

"Yes," answered Kintpuash. "We must settle the dispute."

"I reject it," said Lapuan with force.

"But yesterday you wanted to go." He looked at me like I was crazy. I looked at Mia, who seemed just as surprised by his change in attitude.

"I know about Nolina," I told him. "All of it. Her running away from the Klamath tribe to be with you." Turning, I spoke to Kintpuash. "I also know why Pulamon hates you. You wouldn't make Nolina return because she loved Lapuan. You and Pulamon were good friends before this happened, but that is over. Kintpuash, he will never stop hunting your tribe. As long as he lives, he will try to kill you.

Every last one of you. And if he can't do it on his own, the settlers will help out."

The red aura of hate around Lapuan softened to an amber. The direct approach with Lapuan had worked—to a degree.

"Who told you this?" Hooker Jim demanded.

"I heard the settlers talking. They know," I said, standing up to my full height. "They are using Pulamon's hatred to stir up more trouble between the two tribes. Don't you see, Kintpuash? It will never end. You must prepare to leave here." I looked at the others for support but found none.

"Nothing has changed since I was gone?" I asked Mia in Mandarin.

"No, except Muleo and Hooker Jim have been meeting a lot with Kintpuash. I think they are discussing what to say and do at the council. And it seems as if Hooker Jim is now saying we need peace and Lapuan has gone back to wanting war."

"An odd role reversal," I murmured to her.

"Peace won't come until Pulamon is gone," I said in English.

"Do you propose killing Pulamon?" asked Lapuan. Perhaps for the first time, Lapuan was realizing he wasn't the only person who suffered when Nolina died.

"Not unless he tries to kill me first. Tonight, I must go to the lava flow when it turns red."

Kintpuash nodded. "I will take you."

I ate and slept in the cavern, the experience blessedly peaceful. No dreams entered my unconscious. When I woke,

I wondered if it was because my mind was simply so happy to be back in human form, it too, needed a break.

I got lost in the maze of corridors, being misled by the echoes of voices I thought were around the corner, but ultimately was a dead end. A kind, elderly man guided me back to the main pathway and from there, I found myself walking beside the wall that came alive.

Without a time constraint, I examined the carved figures. The woman who had been below the surface did not appear, and the images resembling snakes didn't move. But…

The snakes had slept on me. I thought it had been for warmth, and maybe it was. Or, as they had said, I had the imprint of the cougar upon me and wouldn't hurt them. But the rock on the necklace in the carved stone, it appeared the snakes were going towards it, compelled in some way.

I traced the chimney-like figures. They resembled the vertical mounds that I'd thought were formed by ants. These didn't show ash coming out from the top, but perhaps the carver of this image didn't know their capabilities.

My fingers were on the rock at my neck before I thought about it. Instinctively, I paused, thinking back to the spontaneous eruption of the plumes.

My spirit had been in the horse, incapable of commanding anything other than the animal's body. The rock had been around my neck…somehow, when I was thrown over the body, my fingers must have crinkled around it.

That had to be the connection. As with the ring, I'd had to direct it to the person or group for the amazing capabilities to take effect. For the translation aspect to work, touch had been required to activate it. And now this rock had the ability to command the land, as Muleo said. No wonder someone in the tribe hadn't been happy when it was given to a person not of Modoc heritage.

Gratified I'd figured it out, I kept walking then paused, feeling the sensation of being watched. An eagle, carved into the rock caught my attention. Its white head, yellow-rimmed eyes and sharp beak came alive at my gaze. Its pupils narrowed, the fierce, hunting gaze of a bird of prey preparing to attack. A snarl turned to a growl and I glanced around, almost expecting to see a cougar next to me. I felt the vibration inside me then saw a motion on the rock. A cougar launched at the bird while it dove down, then up, backflapping its wings, claws stretched out, as if to gouge the eyes of the cat.

"Cage!" yelled a voice. It was Kaga. The figures stopped mid-fight. The cougar's claws were outstretched, ready to slice the bird in two, but a quick aerial maneuver allowed the bird to escape.

"Yes?" I asked.

He came to me and gazed at the rock wall of pictographs before us.

"Salia said you have been dreaming." I nodded, gazing back at the wall. "That is the past, and the present. This," Kaga pointed, drawing his fingers to the wall but not touching it, "is the future."

Okay, so a bird and a cougar will fight. Got that part. My odds were on the cougar, unless the bird flew off. When the pictograph had come to life, on my first walk down, a woman had raised her hand up then down beneath the surface. What was that all about? She didn't resemble Mia, or my mother.

"These will happen within this life?" I asked.

"The images revealed will occur in the life of the person who sees them."

That would be me.

"It is time to prepare for our journey."

"Now? You said it wasn't far away."

"It's not, but the snakes are out. We must go through the glass mountain."

Two more days and we would be gone. I went to find Mia, looking in the women's cavern first.

"She is with your father," offered Salia.

A sentry stood with his torch, moving aside when he recognized me. *The privileges of the scar on my chest.*

"Family reunion?" I called out as I approached.

"Hardly," Mia said, walking beside me as she left the cave.

"How'd that go, Dad?" I asked my father when Mia was out of hearing.

"As well as it looked. She told me I was going to be given back to the settlers or the Army, and I could stay if I wanted."

I folded my arms. "Coming with us wasn't an option?"

"Not one she mentioned. It's pretty clear I'm persona non-grata. It was like: 'best of luck to you,' and then she left."

"Mia is pretty good at making her point."

"So, what do you think?" he asked.

"About what?"

"Coming with you."

"Honestly, Dad, I hadn't thought about it at all. It's out of my hands."

"That's what Mia said, but I wasn't sure you'd go along with it."

"Did you really expect otherwise? You essentially told me your plan to give yourself up so we could survive in the glade. Then you took off. Ironically, your life was definitely extended when the Klamaths took you instead of Lapuan or you'd have been dead two weeks ago." He acknowledged the truth of it. "What makes you think that they will let you go and come with us, assuming we make it out of here?"

"They trust you. You have both healed or saved their people. You could ask."

It was an interesting dilemma I faced. Typically, when situations were dangerous, my stomach clenched. If I was headed in the right direction, I'd feel calm and peaceful. Here, with Dad, I felt absolutely nothing.

It matters not.

Three words inscribed on the ancient sword.

"How could it not matter?" I said to myself.

"What? Me?"

I shook my head. "You coming with us or staying here? Look, I don't mean to be rude or disrespectful, but I don't know if your presence matters."

"That saddens me, yes. Offends me, no. In truth, it might be easier if I wasn't with you."

"Don't go having a pity party," I told him, a twinge of guilt coming through.

"I'm not asking for your sympathy. I'm agreeing with you."

Boncho called for me and I yelled back.

"What are you going to do?" I asked. "Would you choose the settlers or the Modocs, if they'd let you live, that is."

He chuckled. "The Modocs have no reason to want to keep me among them. I'm a reminder of a bad memory and have no real skills for their tribe. The Army will eventually leave the area, and I'm not going to sign up to be a soldier. The Klamaths would just as soon kill any white man that uses the food from the land to feed them. That leaves becoming a settler."

I had a visual of my dad in trousers, digging into the hard soil with a hat shading his face. It would be hard work and his body was past his prime.

"You think you could handle that life?"

"Good question, Cage. I may have the chance to figure that out."

"Look, Dad, this whole experience has been hard. I was pissed at you for three years, the entire time we were in Washington. It took me two months of living in China and you almost getting killed to get past your lies, and basically ignoring us while you went through your own grief with mom. I've mostly moved beyond it because we have there here and now to worry about. But that's me. You are starting at ground zero with Mia," I continued, feeling the relief that accompanied getting emotional deadweight off my shoulders. "We arrive here and the first thing she has to deal with is humiliation."

"How so?"

I put my hand on a hip, the other running through my hair.

"Dad, she consistently defended you, relentlessly getting on me for not giving you the benefit of the doubt. That was blind trust and devotion…"

"And innocence," he quietly added.

"Exactly. You tore that away from her, so then she gets the double whammy of knowing that I was right the entire time."

"That I was the flake. The loser."

"Yeah, pretty much. But on the plus side of your life, you displayed moments of greatness in China, and I'm being serious when I say that. Times when you showed you had two balls and were willing to use them. For us, for our lives. That was good, and that was strong. But here, all she's seen from you is weakness, an inability to do the right thing for the tribe, and then you were with the enemy."

"And she thinks I'm betraying you, and us. But Cage," he said emphatically. "I have tried explaining and she won't listen."

"Do you really blame her?"

He shook his head, dropping it in shame. "No." When he raised his eyes to meet mine, they were glassy. "Do you think she's ever going to forgive me?"

Honesty sometimes hurts, and this wasn't going to feel good.

"Dad, I don't know what you can do that will hurry up a process that's going to take time. You blew her trust. You blew mine. The only thing that's going to build it back up is a lot of time, and actions. Not words. We've both had enough of that."

Kaga yelled to me; he had my backpack and the group was ready to leave.

"Good luck, with whatever you are doing."

"Thanks. See you when I get back." I'd already turned when he called my name. "How am I supposed to change my relationship with either one of you when I'm down here in a cave and not even around you two?"

"Use the same philosophy you applied when you left us for extended periods of time: you'll have to figure that one out on your own."

CHAPTER 21

Kintpuash led the ride with Hooker Jim behind me. Boncho had chosen to stay behind, his presence near Mia telling me more of his concern for her than anything he could have said. Without her request, I wouldn't have saved his life, and he was eternally grateful.

Hooker Jim was focused and showed no emotion whatsoever. I felt no adrenaline coursing through him or tension of any kind. Raiding was second nature, the notion of stealing from those who had stolen his land fair and reasonable.

"Has the crystal worked for you yet?" he asked.

"I haven't had a chance to use it. What does it do?"

"It can raise the lava, change the land and call the serpents."

I looked back over my shoulder. "Really? Can anyone who wears the crystal do this?"

"No one has been allowed to wear the crystal since the last spirit warrior died," Hooker Jim said with obvious irritation.

"When was that?"

"Fifty-two seasons ago."

It meant that another chosen family made it this far and failed at the very end. The person died, and the crystal returned to the tribe.

"Do you know what happened?" I asked, vitally interested in any clues to help me avoid the same terrible fate.

"The legend is that the man who had an eagle on his chest was killed when a snake bit his leg, before the bird could take off. Other snakes attacked and bird was poisoned."

"You mean the spirit was in the eagle?"

"Yes. The eagle died while the spirit was in him. The spirit didn't have the chance to go back to his human form. The human body never moved again, and died. He was burned in the fire so his body and soul could be reunited."

Really glad I asked.

We crested a bluff and I felt a wall of heat that repelled me backwards. I turned my head at the same time as the horse, both of us wanting to escape the burning.

"It is over there," Kintpuash said. At the edge of the flaxen brown plateau, where it met with the black lava, an individual flow was turning colors with the setting sun.

If it was this hot so far away, there was no way we were going to be able to get near enough for me to pick up a rock.

Not in human form, the thought came to me. But then what? It would burn a snake or a cougar. The only thing it couldn't hurt were the feet of a hard hoofed animal, like a mountain goat.

Or an eagle.

I looked up and around. It wasn't like these animals were simply waiting around for me to throw my spirit into their bodies. There had to be another way.

"Come," said Kintpuash.

Down the plateau and through a narrow valley formed by an ancient river we rode. On the other side, the ground changed to black shards of obsidian. It was a good sign for me, but it challenged the horses. Their hooves slipped continually on the slick black surface, making the ascent a nerve-racking experience. I let go of the reins. Having been inside one, I knew my holding him back would only hurt his efforts, not help.

When I relinquished control to the horse, I felt for Kintpuash's state of mind. He was wary, but confident in his ability to get us closer to the source of the heat. There was caring for my sister, but it was subservient to his first priority. He wanted peace, he wanted a family, and he knew that could not be found with Mia.

From Hooker Jim, I felt nothing. Revenge wasn't in Hooker Jim's heart, nor was killing the other tribe. His emotions were...almost non-existent. Hooker Jim was shut down inside, as though he were removed entirely from the situation. *How could that be?* He was planning on attending the peace meeting with Kintpuash to serve as protector, along with Boncho. Kintpush's trusted warriors, who had saved his life and, in turn, I had saved theirs.

Reaching my arm around, I removed the backpack and placed it on my lap. The climb was slippery, but slow and steady. As long as I leaned forward and kept my balance in the center, I was in no danger of falling.

I removed the orb, replacing the top half as I examined the inside, needing to refamiliarize myself with the patterns on the hollowed out parts. Two of the five were filled, leaving me three to work with.

I replaced the lid and screwed it on tight just as my horse slipped. I cursed under my breath, calling for the others to stop. I struggled to get the bridle, losing the orb in the dark shale.

"What is it?" asked Hooker Jim.

"My orb. It's fallen." He joined my search as Kintpuash kept watch for any one of the three groups who were after us; the Army, settlers or the Klamaths. "There it is!" I exclaimed in panic. It was rolling back down the hill, from where we'd come.

I slithered down as fast as I could, but the ball was picking up speed. Uncertain I had any other option, I did a Superman launch into the air, hoping to land on the object before it went even further. The force of my landing bounced black shards in all directions, lifting the ball straight up in the air. I rotated on my back, the ball coming down within my hands. My head connected with another rock, hard.

Not again.

This time, I didn't hesitate. I turned the top half a quarter to the right, immediately healing my injury.

"And then some," I uttered. Whether it was a slight vision improvement or a play of the setting light, I saw that it wasn't just black obsidian that lay around me. Some pieces were green.

In that moment, recollections from our first childhood visit to this area with Dad came back to me. He'd come here to research certain types of volcanic rocks only found in this mountain range and in Mexico. They were the color of green. Green obsidian.

I held the orb close to my chest, scrambling along the ground and picking up two pieces or rock. They had striations similar to the black obsidian, but whereas that was opaque, the emerald was translucent, the thin edges nearly see-through.

Kintpuash called to me, but I remained in place, rubbing my thumb over the surface of the green object. My pulse slowed and I knew it was going to be alright. We'd get what we needed and continue on our journey.

I scrambled back up the hill and turned my back to the men. Angling the orb in the fading light, I opened it up, looking for distinct characteristics.

Please, please let this be the one. In fact, maybe I didn't need to go to the red lava flow at all.

There they were. Curved lines within the empty cavity of the orb. This was different than the straight indents of the black obsidian.

The first rock was too big, but I slipped it in my pants, pulling out the second piece of green obsidian. It was slightly larger as well, but I took a piece of black rock and nicked off the edge.

Perfect.

I turned down the top, wanting to activate it then and there, but knew we were nearly out of time.

The backpack in place, I half-ran, half-crawled back up to my horse.

The horizon and the red lava flow now met. Strangely, the heat was less intense than it had been moments before. Dark masses of snakes were making their way to the lava run.

"Look," pointed Hooker Jim. It was like the reptiles were going to Noah's ark, organized and directed.

On the horse, I watched and waited, hoping for inspiration. I was positive the red rock was what I sought, the feeling of confidence and calm reassuring me.

I pondered the next obstacle in front of me.

Control the land. Muleo's words floated up with the ebbing heat. Yes, that is what Muleo and Kaga said, but what did that mean?

I purposefully touched the crystal hanging around my neck with my thumb and forefinger. *Controlling the land.* There were no chimney-like ant hills around and spraying ash wasn't what I required.

Just one piece. I thought about the hot flow, trying to recall all I knew about the types of red volcanic rock. Dad had said it was unique because it was formed before it had pushed out of the earth.

I continued touching the crystal, wondering if the powers already within me activated certain elements of the crystal unavailable to others. Perhaps…

"Stay here," I commanded the two of them. "And don't leave until I speak to you again, no matter what."

I urged the horse forward, getting as near to the snakes as I could before the horse stopped, unwilling to get closer. I held the rock within my fingers, issuing my request to the red flow in front of me.

First came a gurgling, the underground acknowledgement of my silent request. Next was the cracking sound that metal gives when it cools, right at the point when it's chipped off and molded into something useful. The horses stamped, their ability to sense shifts in the Earth coming seconds before small air pockets occurred in the red flow before us. Quarter-size nuggets shot up from the static ground, high up into the air.

At that moment, I closed my eyes and threw myself into the nearest rattlesnake. I hissed, immediately looking up to the sky, anticipating where the rocks would fall. They were going up and coming down in all directions. I'd failed to give specific direction as to their destination.

I threw myself into the snake in front of me, moving forward as fast as I could, toward the first landfall of rock. Again and again I went in and out of the reptiles, getting even closer.

Then I realized the falling rock would land on my head, smashing me. I hissed a warning to those around me to scatter. The rock landed with a clean strike on the ground, bouncing once then coming to a stop.

"Kick it to me," I said to the nearest king rattler. He flicked it with his tail, hissing after he struck it, the heat of the rock singeing his scales. It came a foot closer to my position.

"Again," I requested. The snake nearest whipped it hard, shooting it within striking distance. It must still be extraordinarily hot because that reptile too, hissed with annoyance.

"Follow me with your tails," I requested. I had to get the rock closer to the horse.

I slithered as fast as I could, creating a trail that the snakes could use to hit the stone. Finally, the last snake gave a whack and the rock landed at the foot of my horse. Focusing on my statue-like body still sitting upright on the horse, I threw my spirit back into myself.

I shook my head, moving my shoulders, opening and closing my mouth. After being in snake form, it felt good to have my arms and legs again.

Dropping off the horse, I retrieved the rock. Hooker Jim raised his hands, and I thought he was issuing the Modoc version of a thank you. I followed his lead.

"Thank you," I said quietly to the snakes, expecting a calm response.

A rattler went straight for me, the fangs already extended. A tomahawk sheared its mouth in half, taking two others with it as the body rammed into those behind.

"Cage! Hurry!" yelled Kintpuash, who had thrown the weapon.

I leapt on the horse and we charged out of the area, the snakes rising up behind us in force.

When we finally slowed, I asked Kintpuash what had happened. "It was as they were told to attack."

"It was the evil Kaga described."

Hooker Jim rode alongside me. "You escaped what the man with the eagle did not."

If that were the litmus test of success, then yes, I'd succeeded one more the trap of death.

Now, if the future was truly inscribed upon the rock wall, I had the death of a woman to look forward to, along with a fight between a cougar and an eagle.

How could we make it through the peace treaty tomorrow night and have all these things happen as well?

CHAPTER 22

As soon as we returned to the cavern, I jogged to the holding area, searching for my father.

"I have something for you." I said, grabbing the torch. "Hold this." I dropped the backpack and removed the orb.

"A gun to shoot myself with?"

"Hardly."

He took the stone from my hand, lifting it to the light. "I needed this, thanks."

"Dad, I'm not giving it to you," I clarified. "I'm hoping you can tell me about it."

"I will, and happily so, because it immediately made me feel calm." He rolled it in the light. "Green obsidian is known as the chakra, the balancing stone. It's found only in the Sierra Madre mountains here—"

"And in Mexico," I interrupted. "I remembered that from our trip when we were young."

"Right," he said. "It's known as the heart chakra. It brings the mind, body and spirit into a state of natural harmony."

"So, it's a physical thing blended with emotions," I said impatiently.

"Here, hold the rock for a minute so you can relax and listen. The feeling will stay with me for a few minutes."

I took it with more annoyance than real interest, and immediately felt like I'd stepped into a hot bath. Totally relaxed.

"See?" he questioned. "If a person is angry, it will calm him or her down, like it just did with you. If you are tense, it will soften the edges. Did you have a reaction when you first held it?"

I remembered my experience at Glass Mountain. I had been full of adrenalized anxiety, but attributed my feelings of relief to finding a rock that fit within the orb, not the rock itself.

"I didn't think they were connected," I readily admitted. "What do you think it will do once it's in the orb"

"I can only guess. This heart chakra literally draws out the negativity of the person holding it, from the inside out."

"I have one other rock that fits within the orb." I removed one of the two salmon colored chunks I'd gotten from the red lava flow.

"Oh, now this is unique. It's a rhyolite, which occur in volcanic plugs or dikes. Where'd you find this?" I told him about the lava flow that had changed colors. It was on the other side of the glass mountain, where I got the emerald obsidian. "I've never heard of a change that happens only once a generation."

We passed the piece back and forth. "I don't notice a change in my mood, do you?"

"Nothing."

"In simple scientific terms, this type of lava is a vesicular pumice. Well," he paused, scratching his cheek. "There's only been a few instances of this type of flow in the 20th century, but one of the attributes of this rock is it's highly explosive, and the deposits can combust." The rhyolite's flat surface was porous. "Not too close to the rock," Dad, said as he drew the flame away, making it hard to see. "I've never seen the combustion in action but know that it can be extremely volatile. It's typically used as a base in explosives."

"Can you point the torch in the orb?" I requested.

"That one," Dad offered. "Same texture as the inside of that crevasse."

He was right. The patterns were an identical match. "Only one rock to go," he said, a wistful tone in his voice. "I'm sorry I won't be there to see it."

"Look Dad," I began, reattaching the top half and putting the orb away. "All that I said to you before is still true, and won't go away for a while, and yes, it's going to take work to become a constructive, happy family unit again, but that doesn't mean you aren't going to be coming. I mean, if you're not around, how can things ever improve?"

"It's a moot point. Mia doesn't want me."

"True," I acknowledged, "but what has running away gotten you in the past? Nothing, other than Nolina's death, although that was accidental. You can't avoid it by staying here, even if she doesn't want you around."

"You want me to face this, with you?"

I didn't feel like I actually needed him, but it would be nice to have another male around. He *had* been useful. "I see no reason to purposefully have you stay here."

"Mia isn't on board with that."

"Mia isn't going to have a say in it."

The sounds of movement were occurring up in the tunnel.

"Can you tell me what's happening?"

I exhaled, hoping a little of the green pumice was still in my system. "The tribe is preparing for the meeting tomorrow with the peace delegation, members from both tribes and the U.S Army. The lead negotiator is Alfred Meacham, who seems like a decent guy."

"What else? I've watched Mia stomping up and down like a caged lioness."

"She and I want to get the tribe prepared to move, just in case the meeting goes badly—"

"Which it will—"

"So say the history books. If I've done my job, and they listen to me, maybe not."

"And then what?"

"I guess we'll see tomorrow. Thanks for the insight on the rocks. Dad," I paused. "I really would like you to come. We're all the family we have left, you know?"

Up the tunnel, I found Mia with Salia. Despite the decision of the council to stay in the tunnels until after the meeting, Salia was quietly and efficiently assembling dried herbs, placing the dozens of dried flowers into marked sacks. Beyond her, I saw young adults closing up sacks, presumably with salted meals in them.

"Careful of that one," Salia cautioned my sister. "It causes..." and then she pointed to her butt. "Bad and painful."

"My timing is good then," I cracked. The women turned and Mia gave me a solemn wink.

"Cage, Kaga knows what we're doing," Mia said in an undertone. "Most of the food has been bundled, and Kahinsula had the kids stack and rope the food for the horses. The rugs, blankets and anything that wasn't being used is also rolled and ready to go. You think it's going to go badly, don't you?"

"I'm hoping for the best, but as Dad always used to say, expecting the worst."

She touched my hand, moving me away from Salia. I glanced up the path, watching Kintpuash speak with Scarface Charlie.

"Be prepared for tomorrow night," I asked, giving her a quick hug.

"You got it."

Lapuan was gently putting the bridle over his horse's head and adjusting the strap. He swayed as I watched, then shook his head.

"Are you feeling well?" I asked him. His black eyelashes dropped.

"Yes," he answered, his voice hard.

"It's just that for the last day, you were—I thought you had changed your mind about the tribe and what should be done."

"I wasn't myself," he answered, pulling the leather tight. He patted the horse, then left.

As I made my way through the tunnels, tension filled the air, the anticipation of what could be mixed with hope and fear.

"You need to sleep," Kintpuash said when he saw me, gesturing to the men's sleeping quarters. A few warriors looked up from their tasks: sharpening the spears or honing the tomahawks. Others were inspecting the rifles, weapons seized from the settlers. The popping and echoing sound of shots being fired well down in a deep cavern were muffled. No doubt they were practicing their aim.

"Kintpuash, do you know the area which we spoke of? The lake with the island in the center?" He nodded and I continued, ready to tell him more, but I felt a slight hesitation that prevented my words from coming out. Now wasn't the time to tell him he might be captured and those in control might torture him to reveal where his people had gone. I may yet be able to alter that part of history.

"If you aren't going to sleep, perhaps you should practice," he suggested. I caught his tone, half challenging and half teasing.

"Do you mean I need target practice?" I asked, my own competitive spirit rising up. "Sure. Bring it on."

He smiled, calling out to his men. Soon, a circle of his finest warriors was assembled. The men looked at one another, their feet already light on the ground, moving in anticipation.

"Weapons?" I asked. "All of them," I said.

"But he is the spirit warrior," said one. "We cannot win."

"Maybe not," I replied. "But you can improve."

"Use this," Kintpuash said, throwing me a spear. "Begin," he commanded his group.

The room had emptied except in the entryway, which was full of watchful eyes, the young men who were there to witness the forthcoming test of skills.

The whooping of a tomahawk was the split-second warning I had before I leaned to my left, lifting up the staff of the sword, and capturing the blade on the wood. I peeled it off, flipping the tomahawk upside down, putting it between my hip and leather pants. A murmur from the young boys told me I'd done well, but it was hardly a feat of grand proportions.

A spear came directly towards me, which I deftly countered by spinning my own in front, my left hand on the bottom of the staff, my right on the top, capturing the horizontal shaft, rotating it upright. I then had a spear in each hand. They were light and maneuverable, the circumference easily managed within my grip. I twirled both on either side of me, just as I would do two Jong-bongs. The only difference between this and the traditional martial arts version was the absence of a ribbon on the non-threatening end.

"Now!" I commanded, wanting more. The answer was knives and razor sharp obsidian pieces much like Chinese stars.

The weapons of war were centuries and continents apart, but men of all ages knew how to create killing tools of all kinds.

Bam! Bam!...one after another, I intercepted the deadly tools with the spears. The slicing of air currents caused me to drop low, avoiding another spear as two warriors crouched and leapt. I put my left hand on the ground, still clutching the spear, and kicked with both legs, directly into the man's chest, hard enough to launch him in the air but not to break his ribcage. The other warrior took advantage of my legs being up to use a long knife, slicing under my side. I barely missed being skinned alive by arching up, dropping my legs and pushing from my left hand. Landing on my feet, I faced five warriors, each with machete-like long knifes in their hands.

One rushed me, weapon raised high. With the flat of my palm, I hit his ribcage, the force causing his arm to fall. Smacking down his forearm, I took the weapon, tripping him as I spun, pushing up the flat part of the blade from another warrior as it sliced diagonally at my neck. I kneed his mid-section, collapsing his stomach as he exhaled, dropping the weapon to the ground. I put my toe under the machete at mid-point and flipped it up to the air, catching it with my left hand.

Falling back, I twirled the two weapons in my hands, the fan-like experience creating a draft of wind.

"That doesn't work against a gun," said Lapuan.

"Try me," I challenged. He smiled, and I expected him to be thrilled to finally have the chance to kill me with no repercussions.

He put the rifle to his shoulder and fired. The clang off the broadside of my blade hit the wall of rock. As he reloaded, I spun, going through a twelve-step blade movement series designed for either bullet or blade. "He moves like a leaf on the wind," said a youthful voice.

The cock of a gun came again and I turned. This time, the bullet nicked the end of the blade, breaking off a piece of metal. Expecting more, I continued rotating until I saw Lapuan put his rifle over his shoulder.

I held my weapons in a ready position, as I sensed his mood. He wasn't relinquishing the fight, he was saving it for later. I looked around. The other men in the area didn't want to fight me either. They wanted me to lead them.

I flipped over the blades, extending them to Kintpuash. He was their warrior chief, not me.

"Kintpuash, what is it you want me to do?"

"Come with me to the peace meeting tomorrow. With you, I know we can succeed."

Oh, man. There was no record of yet another settler at the meeting. And what if Jones were there? That would cause a whole new set of issues.

He frowned, taking my silence for disagreement.

"The men who tried to kill me," I told him. "They might recognize me and think it's a trap." His countenance changed at my words. "I can't risk a fight breaking out at the meeting."

"Agreed." He looked up at the dark ceiling, then down at me. "You can attend in spirit form."

"I…" started to say I couldn't, but of course I could. "I'll go with you, waiting nearby."

It seemed like the perfect plan.

CHAPTER 23

The dinner was more of the incredible salmon and elk, and the myriad of berries and dried apricots were supplemented with potatoes, courtesy of the settlers, although the women in the tribe didn't know what to do with them.

"That's one good thing they've brought," said Mia, who showed the women how to slice, peel and dish them before boiling the vegetable in the earthen pots. When cooled, the women mashed the potatoes with their hands and sprinkled with dried rosemary and chives.

The entire tribe retired early that evening and the women were up before dawn making breakfast. This time, Mia used potatoes to make hash browns, which made some of the kids crinkle their noses.

"Think they liked the mashed version more," I said dryly. She laughed and fed the rest of the potatoes to the horses, who inhaled the food.

Kintpuash ate little, preoccupied with the day to come. The peace treaty meeting was to be held at 5 p.m. Every adult male over the age of thirteen quietly worked on their weapons, while the women remained in their own areas.

"It is always like this before a fight," Kahinsula confided to Mia and myself. We were in the stables, the nearly fifty horses kept there requiring attention. They had all the water and food needed to sustain their lives, but they were restless.

"They are feeling the energy of the men, aren't they?" Mia asked the horsewoman, who rubbed down a white and tan mare.

"Yes. They sense a battle is coming."

During a morning meeting, it had been decided I would wait with Boncho just outside the Army settlement. Lapuan, Hooker Jim and Muleo would attend the peace meeting with Kintpuash. Muleo wasn't originally going to be going, but Sconchin had insisted an elder be present.

"Do you recall how long the peace treaty meeting lasted?" I asked Mia. She had no idea, that part of history overshadowed by the events.

"What animal do you think you'll inhabit?" she asked me.

Kintpuash raised his hand and interrupted, shaking his head. He didn't want them to talk about it further.

"He overheard me?" Mia asked in Mandarin. I glanced at her without a word. That would be a yes.

I bent down, talking under my breath. "You can see how he feels about it."

"But why?"

I looked up, intensely focused. "Because he's trying to protect you. It's what we men do."

It took her a moment to digest my look and words. It was a frustrating compliment. If he didn't care for her, what she knew wouldn't require secrecy.

"Ok," she confirmed, her tone appropriately adjusted. "You have your task, and I have mine." A hint of frustration crept back in; she always wanted her way, but at least the emotion was balanced with her increased skills and level of responsibility, and the feeling Kintpuash had for her.

"Here, I want you to experience something," I said to her. "Don't leave." I jogged to the men's area then back, returning with the second green obsidian in my hand.

"You're unhappy and rightfully so, correct?" I asked her. She stared at me in frustration. "And let's add to that worried and fearful about me and Kintpuash."

"And the rest of the tribe. Are you doing this to make me upset again, because I was just calming down?"

I smirked. "Yes, and for good reason." Mia put a hand on her hip, lips flatlined with irritation. I grabbed her hand and flipped it over. "Feel this."

Mia started to give me a retort and stopped before the first word was out. Her mouth was still open as she stared wide-eyed at me, as though a jolt of lightening had caused an intervention. She then looked down at the rock.

"It's called green obsidian," I offered before she asked. "In our time, Dad said it's popularly known as the heart chakra. It takes negative energy and turns it into good."

"I was ready to smack you…" she said with false passion, raising an open fist. I lowered it with a grateful expression.

"And now you love me more than life itself, or at least Kintpuash?"

She smiled genuinely. "Let's not get crazy."

"It's one of the rocks now in the orb, and don't ask me what it's going to do because I have no clue. Do you want to hold onto this one while I'm gone? Might make you feel more at ease."

She looked down at her pants then back at me. "I really love these leather outfits, but they don't believe in pockets. Oh, wait!" She went to the herb area and came back with a small satchel, the type she'd used for the gold and diamonds. "Perfect."

"I'm not sure if it works as well if it's not being held in your hand. You'll have to figure that out for yourself."

Mia's face grew somber.

"Cage, please. Be careful."

She gave me a fierce hug and I left to join the men. It wasn't long before we were on our horses, riding to the peace negotiation meeting.

We were on the edge of the settlement, looking through the trees to the lush, green valley where the newcomers had built their homes. The tips of the leaves were just now turning yellow, the color of fall. The Klamath Indian had his hands tied behind his back and was laying across the front of Hooker Jim's horse, his mouth gagged with a piece of rope. Private Olsen lay in the same position on Lapuan's horse, both men to be given over at the start of the meeting.

"Do you still want to do this?" I asked Kintpuash in an undertone. I wasn't referring to the meeting itself, and he knew it.

"Yes," he said firmly. "It is the only way." I nodded, and he led our group to a densely wooded patch nearest the settlement without being seen. No one else knew about our plan, and we felt it best that way. Kintpuash wanted it kept a secret for purposes of his pride and his position as the young leader. I wanted it secret for my own safety.

"Are you ready?" I asked quietly. He nodded. The others waited for Kintpuash to give the signal to follow him. "Here we go."

In the blink of an eye, my spirit left my body and entered Kintpuash. I was now on his horse, within him, feeling his emotions, hearing his thoughts and knowing his past and present.

I was sharing his body but his spirit was still there, submerging itself to my control.

The experience was at odds when my body was overtaken with another evil spirit. Then, he desired complete dominion over my mind, to kill me from within. Here, I was cohabitating and guiding with a willing participant.

I gave Boncho the command to stay with Cage, referring to myself in the third person. I looked at my spirit-less figure. It was motionless on the horse, watching without moving.

When Kintpuash had approached me the night before, when the others were asleep, I'd initially rejected the idea.

"It's the only way," Kintpuash told me. He was concerned that the others, especially Hooker Jim, wanted to fight. They didn't support a peace agreement. This way, he, Kintpuash, couldn't be dissuaded from doing the right thing under pressure from his spiritual guide.

"You are worried Muleo will try and convince you to do something against the elders?"

"What he says, I follow," Kintpuash said simply. At the time, I didn't understand how the opinion of any one person could sway Kintpuash. Now, in his body, I got it intimately. Disrespecting an elder through an act of disobedience was the equivalent of killing someone. It wasn't done, under any circumstances. However, I, being an outsider, was not bound to the obligations of a tribal member.

Hooker Jim, Lapuan and Muleo, ignorant of our plan, waited.

"We go," I said, my voice not my own, but that of Kintpuash.

We rode towards the home of Frank Riddle in silence and without guns. This was a meeting where all parties left every weapon behind.

My shoulders raised with regret, wishing I'd kept the green obsidian not in the orb for myself. Having a clear and calm head was what I needed, now more than ever.

On the porch, Frank Riddle and Winema stood side by side. She would be translating for the men. Alfred Meacham stood beside Frank, his face blank, not welcoming, nor fearful. Beside him, were General Canby and Pulamon, with two other warriors representing the Klamath tribe. To the left of the building were a dozen soldiers. Like us, they were without weapons, at least none we could see.

"I'm sorry if you are uncomfortable," I said to Private Olsen.

"You speak pretty good English," he said through jolts. Crap. I'd forgotten that's why we had Winema to translate.

Well, it would give me a distinct advantage in case the men were being dishonest.

"Do me a favor and don't tell our people about being healed," I requested.

He scoffed. "They wouldn't believe me if I did, but it will make good telling to my grandchildren, assuming I live that long. Too bad our people won't learn the healing from you. They'd have a much better life."

When we reached the porch, the three of us dismounted. I purposely gave over the physical attributes of my host body to Kintpuash, as I had with the horse. It was a wise choice. Up, over and down, as if I'd been doing it all my life. Which, as Kintpuash, I had.

I untied the private's hands, lifting him by the waist, easing him down. He walked towards his General, giving him a handshake.

"I'm alright," he told the group of men. Hooker Jim had placed the Klamath warrior on the ground, but his hands were still tied.

"Free him," I told Hooker Jim, feeling the sentiment echoed by Kintpuash. Hooker Jim turned a shade darker, the coloring moving up his short hair.

Why had Hooker Jim adopted the look of the settlers? I wondered. Cutting his hair short, abandoning the traditional headpieces and other elements of the Modocs. It had made sense at first, but I wondered if there was more to it than trying to outwit the adversary.

"Come in," said Meacham, who had extended his hand.

I walked straight up to him. "You are the peace negotiator, Alfred Meacham," I said, my heavily accented

English raising eyebrows. "I am Captain Jack, but you may call me Kintpuash."

The man raised his dark eyebrows. Yes, I was well-spoken, and yes, I was going to command respect from this man, and everyone else.

"Your man is unharmed, as is the Klamath." The Klamath warrior had walked to his two tribe members, stepping aside from Pulamon, who had scowled at the sight of him. The former captive might have been better off back in the safety of the Modoc cave, for he had failed in his killing assignment.

"General Canby," introduced the other man.

Now I had a dilemma. I didn't know Modoc, negating the need for Winema to translate, at least for me. It was a gaping hole in our plan which would have interesting historical consequences. *Oh well.* At least she'd translate for the others as necessary.

"You will find we healed your man," I said in English.

The general turned to Olsen, skeptical. "They healed you?"

"As good as new, Sir."

"Let's go inside then."

We sat around the rectangular table, our delegation of four on one side, Pulamon and his two men on the other. Private Olsen and Frank were on one end, with a Reverend who'd been asked to attend and sat at the corner. General Canby and Meacham sat at either end. Once we'd taken our places, two sentries came to the front door, and Winema translated for General Canby. He told us that the sentries were armed, in case the group was attacked.

"I will begin," said Meacham. "There are those who do not want a treaty to occur," Meacham said to Winema, who translated.

I was glad I could understand English, because Winema struggled to keep up with the words regarding the constitution, the rights of the tribes, the lands that were being offered, and glossing over what was taken away. I could have disputed every paragraph Meacham was reading, but it wouldn't have made a difference. The settlers had made their case to authorities, and were getting their way.

It was exactly what had been written in the history books. When Meacham was done, Pulamon asked about his territories.

"You will have the land at the southern end of the lake," began Meacham. "Approximately three hundred acres."

I knew from history that the Klamath and Modoc tribes had over a million acres prior to the arrival of the settlers. Neither Pulamon nor either tribe for that matter had any concept of the size of an acre. To think that this space would be expected to house and feed a thousand people was absurd.

The former Methodist minister went through the offering to the Modocs. The southern region of Tule Lake, their ancestral homeland.

"You have gathered reeds from the lake to make your canoes, your moccasins and all your carrying goods," said Meacham, the words intended to make us feel comfortable.

"But we can't live on reeds to eat," I said in response. "Our people are starving, and we are being forced to share an area that is one third the size it was before, and with the Klamath, who are trying to kill us at every turn." As the white men exchanged looks at my words, I stared hard at Pulamon. While I understood his reasons for wanting to hurt the tribe, he needed to move on. Everyone had lost someone they loved, myself included.

"Winema, can you translate that for the others?"

When she did, Pulamon started half out of his chair towards me. The General gripped his arm.

"Easy," Canby said. Pulamon sat back down, his look of hatred never leaving my face.

"This is not about the two tribes getting along with one another," reminded Meacham. "It is about coexisting with the settlers. Might I state that there is another solution. A bad one, but it must be mentioned." The peace negotiator gave Winema time to catch up on the translation. "If one, or both tribes, do not agree to this document and sign, then the U.S. Army will remove, by force, those parties. You have no choice but to get along."

When Pulamon heard this, he faced the Meacham. "To where?"

"Across this entire country. It will be forty days journey by horse," Meacham answered, his face immobile.

I wanted my adversary to understand what it was really like. "Pulamon, what they are proposing in not like here. It is a different climate. Flat, high and dry. No water. It only has farming. No hunting or fishing. Both our tribes will die anyway." His eyes narrowed and he pushed out his lips. "Neither of us should have to leave," I said intensely. "It is the settlers who must give up ground."

"Now wait just a minute—" started the General.

"Sir," broke in Private Olsen. "They healed me and the other Klamath, and they had no reason to do so. Let Kintpuash talk."

When the private's words were translated, they had an impact on Pulamon. He inclined his head, and the General gave motioned for me to proceed. I spoke of lands northward, near Crater Lake. I ended by referencing the earlier conversation between myself, Mia and Meacham.

"We helped two of your kind who are moving to Crater Lake. The couple from California. That area is open. It is safe. The settlers would have much more land than they do here. Cannot that be considered?"

Pulamon folded his arms and nodded. It made sense.

"Well…" said Meacham, hesitating.

"Well, what?" prompted the General. "Can you take this to the settlers and ask them if they will move?"

Meacham laid his hands on the table, arms straight, as though he were going to give a sermon.

"Gentleman, leaders, I have tried speaking with the settlers. I gave the gold that young couple offered to us to provide the settlers with incentives to leave. The men have refused. They said they would fight for their right to stay."

It didn't take my spirit being in Kintpuash's form to feel his growing fury at the response. I saw Pulamon's face contort with resentment. Strangely, Hooker Jim was neutral, as if accepting what he now knew to be the reality of the situation.

"You are expecting us to give over all our lands, die at your hands, or be forced from here to make way for you?" I asked. I felt totally and completely blended with Kintpuash.

Across the table, Pulamon agreed with me, nodding his head. We had been at war because of the shedding of blood in the past, but were now being reunited in the grief of our future. Our tribes were going to be decimated no matter what we did.

"Then we will retreat to the river, and live within the land that no one wants," I said. "We will not be a burden to the Klamath tribe and won't cause conflict to the settlers."

The jowls on General Canby's face lifted at my words, and Pulamon dropped his arms. I wasn't going to cause conflict. We, the Modoc tribe, were going to live in peace in this new environment.

"What I demand is that we are not moved further and that the settlers do not rid the land of the trees, which serve as food, shelter and protection for our people. Without the trees, this land will die, and the settlers will die themselves."

After hearing the translation, the men agreed it was reasonable. Pulamon nodded vigorously, as did his warriors. Only the Reverend now opposed me.

"How can I say that we won't ever want more land?" he asked, tilting his head. "We will increase in number. The land is endless. God would want it this way."

"God isn't overseeing this meeting, Reverend," said the General. "The government of the United States of American is."

The Reverend crossed his arms over his chest, casting disparaging looks at both Muleo and Pulamon. Both men were fierce in their own ways, and to them, the Reverend only saw rough, wild men of the land, not refined, church going men of God.

"Doesn't the good book of the Bible teach that God loves all men, of all color, equally?" I asked him, staring him straight in the eye.

"Well…you don't know the good book."

"I know that God respects all persons, or does your good book tell you that he only respects one color, not all?"

The Reverend cleared his throat and the Private coughed in his hand, the insult clear to the entire group. Winema hadn't stopped translating, and I could see that I'd nearly won Pulamon over with my verbal sparring.

The Reverend was about to say something when his head dropped, as though it lost neck strength. When he lifted it up, his countenance had been humbled.

"You are absolutely correct my friend. Jesus the Lord God loves all his children. That is why I am here."

Winema paused before she spoke, looking at him and then me.

"I'm glad you are doing what's right for your people," was my reply, when really, I was pleased I'd slapped his prideful, prejudiced heart down a few notches.

Hooker Jim stiffened noticeably at the man's words. He had a decent grasp of the English language, but Winema's translations must have set him off, for he leaned into Muleo's ear, whispering intensely.

"Do you need to counsel?" asked Meacham.

"No," answered Hooker Jim curtly.

"Fine. I'll write this down."

Alfred Meacham took the piece of paper in front of him, and spoke as he wrote, using my words verbatim. He initialed the document and then slid it to General Canby, who also read and initialed it.

"On behalf of the United States Government, I am giving this my authorized signature." He turned to me with a proud expression on his face. "Sir, I am grateful for your cooperation in this matter. Your tribe will thank you."

I nodded. "Now may I please see that document as well?" He shared a shocked look with Private Olsen, along with Frank and Meacham. Without a word, he slid it over to me.

I read it. Meacham had been honest. He'd written down my words precisely.

"What do you see?" asked Private Olsen.

I turned it around and shoved it toward him. "I can see that the person who wrote this document failed to capitalize the state of California, and that Tule Lake is spelled t-o-o-l, like the tool, instead of the actual lake."

Winema laughed a little when she translated, and Meacham who scowled.

Private inspected the document, coughing with embarrassment. "I'm sorry, Sir. He's right."

"It's time for your signatures," said Meacham, passing the paper and pen to the Reverend.

"I'll be signing this on behalf of the settlers," he said. "I'm the only one they trust to do so on their behalf." Then the document came to me.

This was it. The reason why we were here, and it was almost over. No death. No hanging. Mia may not be with Kintpuash, but he would live a long, full life, and his tribe would never be forced out of the area, dying on their long march to Oklahoma.

"Let me see this," demanded Hooker Jim.

"What are you doing?" asked Winema in Modoc. "You can't read that."

"Be quiet," he said. I looked at Winema, as shocked as I felt Kintpuash to be. Muleo touched his son-in-law's shoulder in a gesture of patience, but he was brushed off.

Before I could stop him, Hooker Jim took the piece of paper and tore it up.

"What are you doing?" I yelled at the same time Lapuan hammer locked his neck. The next instant, Hooker Jim went limp and Muleo grabbed one half of the document, ripping it again. "No!" I yelled. What was going on? It was if something was making my people go crazy.

Oh, no....it couldn't be. Once he ripped it in two, Muleo's head sunk on the table, and Private Olsen turned to his left, putting his hands around Pulamon's neck, trying to strangle him. In a flash, the warrior gripped the Private's hands together and threw him over his shoulder, near the fire. The noise and confusion cause the sentries to burst into the room, rifles drawn, but they didn't know who to shoot at. The Private was rubbing his head, as though he had no idea how he landed across the room.

"You are a destroyer!" Pulamon shouted at Hooker Jim. Because he had no weapon of his own, he yanked the rifle out of nearest sentry's hand and lifted it up.

"Stop!" yelled the General, trying to intervene, but I was quicker. I ripped the rifle from the closest sentry and with the end, whipped it up, catching the end of Pulamon's firearm. A shot went off as it twirled up, hitting the ceiling. While it was still up in the air, Pulamon sunk to the floor, as though he'd had a seizure. It was the General who caught the rifle and pointed it at me.

All at once, I knew. Ubel was in the General. In a split second flash of recollection, I thought through the inconsistencies of various people. First, the Klamath Indian I'd seen in my dream, who'd been on the ground when a bird had swooped low. As a captive, the Klamath had come into the Modoc's cave. He'd been near Lapuan when he lost his energy, while Lapuan's personality had changed from wanting to fight the settlers to encouraging the peace meeting. He came here, to the meeting, and gone first into the Reverend, who stirred up trouble. When that didn't work, he jumped into Hooker Jim, who tore the document, then Muleo who ripped it again. He wanted us to die, and when being in the private failed as well, Ubel invaded General Canby's body so he could make sure it happened.

General Canby's firearm was aimed at my head. I dodged just as the bullet fired, my own instinct for self-preservation taking over.

If I could kill Ubel's spirit now, while in physical form, he couldn't jump to anyone else. It would be over.

I shot the rifle, straight into the chest of General Canby. He gasp, and dropped, the single shot sealing his fate in history.

"Go!" shouted Lapuan. He shoved me towards the door. I'd killed one man and a spirit, I realized in a daze.

Lord, forgive me, I prayed. The sentries were yelling for reinforcements, the soldiers already coming into the area. Pulamon was out the door with his men, running towards their horses. Seeing their warriors unscathed, the Klamaths made no motion to stop us from mounting our own horses. At the edge of the clearing, men were riding into the area. They were settlers who had heard the gunshots.

"He's dead!" shouted a solder. "The General has been killed! The Reverend has been shot also!"

The cries of murder filled the clearing as our horses ran at full speed to meet Boncho and my physical body. I threw my spirit into my physical self as the horses barely slowed down. Instantly, I took the reins of my horse and the four of us rode at full-speed back to the caves. Hooker Jim and Muleo were left behind.

The ride through the dark was breathless and painful. My soul hurt with the knowledge I'd killed a good man. Even in China, I'd not taken the life of a person; that had been left to zombies, dragons and six-armed statues that I'd brought to life. Being one step removed from killing had made it palpable.

Kintpuash called out to the sentry, a cry unlike any I'd heard before. The tribe was going to be attacked. The horses dove underground, men and women already in motion.

CHAPTER 24

Running through the cave, Kintpuash commanded all but three dozen warriors to prepare to leave. Kahinsula worked with the young men to ready the horse while Mia ran to the family quarters. I heard her meet Salia in the corridor.

"I put all the herbs in the bag," Salia told her quietly.

"You aren't coming?" Mia asked.

"I cannot. Muleo hasn't returned, and if our men go in to battle, they will need me."

Mia touched her arm. "But who will heal the sick?"

"I have trained others. Go now. They need you."

Salia glanced at me and I confirmed that Hooker Jim and Muleo had remained behind, why, I didn't know.

"You are right, the warriors might need you," I said to Salia.

They prepared themselves for battle, my jaw clenched in self-recrimination. I hadn't wanted to kill anyone, but *He* had gone inside the General and had to die. But I had killed him, not Kintpuash.

Right now, however, I had another issue. Kintpuash was not doing as history had written.

"You can't ride out to meet the settlers," I said passionately. "We have to lure them in one end so the women and children can go out another."

"No. We keep them away from here."

Kaga stood by his side, watching me.

"That won't work," I argued. "If you do, more will die. Kaga…" I said, looking at him for support.

"Kintpuash, Cage knows the future."

Kintpuash stared, waiting.

"You will be fighting them off for two months, but then…" I said, unwilling to continue.

"You have been in me and we are one," he said harshly. "Tell me."

I nodded regretfully. "Hooker Jim, right now, has the evil spirit within him. He will betray you to save his own life. Once the soldiers break the siege, you will be hanged."

Kintpuash's black eyes went vacant as he saw the truth in my expression.

"We must save those who we can," I maintained. "Anyone not out of the tunnels will be forced to journey east, and all but fifty will die." I paused, my chest feeling crushed. "I'm so sorry. I tried to change history, but it would not let me."

Kaga put his arm on my shoulder. "History cannot be changed. Only the future."

Kintpuash stood tall and proud. If death were his future, he was going to face it.

"What shall we do?"

"We draw them in through the tunnels…" Rapidly, I explained the strategy that had been coming to me over the last few days. "Jones hates me for saving the cougar and wounding him. He will follow me all the way here." The warriors would be placed at entry points, splitting up their group. I would lead the remaining men through one of the fifty-foot chimney drops. It will take them time to navigate the rope ladder. Once there, the torches will go out. It would take them hours or days to find their way out, if they ever could.

"They'll be trapped in their own tomb," I finished.

"What do you want us to do with your father?" asked Kintpuash.

In the commotion, I hadn't even thought of him. "It is your choice. He can leave with the women or stay and fight with you."

Kintpuash nodded once and called for his men, telling them the plan. Once it was agreed upon, I found Mia. She listened and confirmed her role.

"I'm going to head them straight up the valley," she explained, "keeping to what I remember of the freeway. Do you think we'll return before it ends with Kintpuash?"

"I don't know."

"Cage," she said, and I knew what she wanted before she asked.

"Go. He's up in the tunnel."

She jogged out of sight, and I went through the caverns and enclaves. Salia and the other women had worked tirelessly to prepare the tribe. Many of the areas were bare, the food and household goods collected and gathered into central areas. Kahinsula had the young women leading the horses, with the teen boys strapping the goods onto the animals. The elderly and young would ride, the fit walk.

"Why aren't they moving?" I asked Kahinsula, jerking my head to a group of grey-haired elders as I hefted a sack onto a horse.

"They are refusing."

"Can't Sconchin make them leave?"

She placed another sack on a horse and I latched it tight. "They choose to stay, saving the food for the young of the tribe. They know they will slow down the group."

That was true, I thought dispassionately. Good for them, making the sacrifices for the good of the tribe.

"Hurry," Kahinsula encouraged, gesturing for the pregnant women and those with infants first. She loaded them up, three and four to a single horse, made easier without a heavy saddle. When a dozen horses were ready, Kintpuash appeared with Mia. He assessed the animals and those on horseback. He went to each animal, whispering. I couldn't hear his words but felt his devotion and admiration for the animals, sensing his request for their safety and protection.

Yes, they would listen, just as the plants of the land had done so with his forefathers.

A seasoned warrior was at the front of the line, his horse impatient. He waited for the signal from his leader. Kintpuash nodded. It was time. In a simple gesture of affection, Mia kissed his cheek, her eyes full of tears. Kinptuash's arms pulled her into him, his lips on hers, lifting her off the ground. The room seemed to go quiet, showing respect for what all that was and more than couldn't be.

He set her down, and she turned to her horse, hiding her tears. Once on, she kept her back to him, clicking to propel the horse forward. Mia was honoring Kintpuash—and loving him—by helping save his people.

The warrior gave the command and the line began moving while Kahinsula kept loading up additional horses and people.

I gave one last look at my sister's back and the people who were leaving this place. They would never return.

When I rejoined the men, Lapuan and Kintpuash were together.

"Kintpuash, do you think you could get me a bat?" He looked at me like I was crazy, and I could see that for once, his mind and heart were elsewhere. They were on my sister. I looked at Lapuan.

"Are you going to fly within?" Lapuan asked.

"To lure and catch our enemies. Yes."

His eyes glimmered. He called out for a fishing net and soon had one in his hand.

"Kintpuash, you prepare the others, I'll work with Lapuan." The men agreed.

"Come," said Lapuan.

We ran, ducking and dodging the stalactites dropping from the ceiling, as we ran deeper in the earth. The overwhelming ammonia stench of guano made me want to vomit.

"Watch." Lapuan gave a tremendous whistle, followed by a clattering of rocks hitting the ceiling. Thousands of bats screeched and scattered, swarming the area. He hurled his net in the air.

I hope he gets me a good one.

Lapuan pulled the net down, struggling to maintain the bats inside. He looked at me with the respect a person gives to a friend who is going to jump from a bridge down into the freezing river below. Admiration, but glad it was someone else doing the act.

"Stay with my body," I asked him. He nodded seriously. "And you will have to let all of them free, because you won't know which one I'm in." At this, he nodded again. "And don't kill me when I return."

"Go," he growled, his snarl a half-smile.

The next moment, I was nearly blind, but my senses were on hyperdrive. I knew the distance between me and everything else, living and non. I flew straight up, spiraling, lifting and dipping around, over and under the obstacles in my way.

This was the best! I thought the snake was cool, and the horse powerful, but this…

Out of the cave I flew, shooting as fast as a rocket. Just for fun, I rotated circles in the sky, spinning with a rotation only possible in my dreams.

This. Was. The. Best.

I felt the equivalent of smug laughter. The bat spirit completely agreed with me. It did have the greatest life. Eating bugs. Hanging upside down in a cave the size of the world. The bat inside me projected its superiority and I chuckled. Every animal thought it had the best set of attributes.

Ignoring the others around me, I flew over the lava beds straight to the Army settlement. This was a weird experience, because I had speed and stealth, but no eyesight!

I know where it is, the bat silently communicated. It retrieved food from the fruit the settlers left out, as well as scraps in the field. The smoke from the soldiers' camp burned at night, hurting its nose.

Right into the Army camp the bat flew, hovering above the men who argued. Private Olsen told Jones he was next in command, but not authorized to go into battle. Jones demanded assistance, but Olsen was adamant. He wasn't going to face a court martial for starting a fight without proper authorization. In frustration, twenty of the men from the settlement had gathered, intent on hunting down Kintpuash and driving the Modocs from the area. But they had one problem; they needed directions.

"Winema, you tell Pulamon we need him to lead us," Jones ordered. Frank, her husband, reluctantly agreed with Jones. "You help us on this, Pulamon," continued Jones, as Winema translated, "and we will let your people have the entire southern rim of the lake, which I'll make sure is renamed as the Klamath Lake, in honor of your people."

"I'm not going to kill the Modocs," Pulamon replied.

Jones cursed. "After what they did in there? Wasn't them taking your woman enough?" Pulamon started to walk to his horse, raising his hand for the others to follow. "Okay, okay. No killing. You lead us and we will do the rest."

I flew down, flapping my silent wings as I paused mid-air. Could I capture Pulamon's attention?

"Pulamon, you do this for us, and we will leave you alone. I promise," Jones said.

"Then put it on paper." It was the strong voice of Alfred Meacham with a white bandage on his arm. Winema's heroic efforts had saved him when the gun fired, grazing his arm instead of hitting his chest. "You put it on paper, and then I'll endorse him going with you. Otherwise, you are on your own, and I'll report back to the authorities that you are using one tribe for your own purposes."

Cursing and orders followed. In due time, Jones had scribbled his commitment on paper, and Meacham reviewed it.

"Sign," Meacham ordered. Jones did, followed by Meacham himself. "Pulamon?" The Indian hesitated only a moment and then wrote his signature on the document.

"Let's mount!" Jones yelled.

I flew directly to Pulamon. The instant he was on his horse, I hovered straight in front of him, eye level. He watched me as I tried to convey all with my eyes that I could not with my mind. The next moment, I landed on his arm and threw myself into his body.

"We cannot let Jones kill the Modoc tribe," I thought him. "He will not honor his word. He will kill your tribe next."

Pulamon's spirit was quiet at first, then it spoke to me. *I understand and agree.*

"Cage will lead you," I thought to Pulamon. "Follow him and you will be protected."

I threw myself out his body and back into the bat. Lifting up, I flapped in front of him for another second, to make sure we were as one, then I flew up and away.

We had to prepare our decoy.

CHAPTER 25

Back into the cave I flew, skimming the surface of the ceiling, knowing the route to Lapuan was clear. He stood fixed in place near my human body. I landed on his shoulder, thanking the bat for the use of its body.

You have treated us well. We will be here to help you.

The next instant, I opened my eyes. It took a moment to adjust to light and clarity of vision, but seeing the bat, I stroked the soft black fur on its chest. It gave a squeak, then vanished into the darkness.

"I know their plan," I said to Lapuan. We ran to the others, talking on the way. Lapuan would have the men scatter and be ready, the goal to incapacitate, not kill.

I retrieved my backpack, slipping it over my shoulders. After we pulled this off, I didn't know when, or if, I'd be coming back to this underground world.

Lapuan leapt onto his horse, extending his hand to me. I didn't hesitate, his strength easily hefting me behind him. The clanging of the hooves on the rock were magnified by the six others who rode behind us. Out the entrance we went, and one by one, the others left to their own stations. We rode to the very edge of the lava bed, leaving the last warrior on his horse, then continued through the dry, rocky terrain with the odd formations.

"Are you well?" Lapuan asked me.

"Yes, but tired," I admitted. One downside of throwing my spirit was the drain on my energy level. It no longer hurt, but it was as though a little of my soul were being left behind in each animal or person. My internal battery needed to be recharged, but I wasn't sure if this occurred by sleeping or simply being housed in my own physical frame for a period of time.

"There," Kintpuash pointed. Only a sliver of orange remained in the sky that hovered on the very edge of darkness. The moon had already risen, the grey orb showing the rising dust of the enemy.

"I'm ready," I said, knowing it would take every bit of energy I possessed to outrun and outsmart Jones and his men. Hopefully, Pulamon would act predictably.

I dismounted, getting in to position. Kintpuash rode back to the primary entrance as I looked to the first warrior, who was in position and waiting. Anyone who didn't fall for the decoys would eventually chase me into the tunnel of ice.

When the men were halfway through the field, the riders came into focus. Pulamon was in the lead, with Jones behind him, the two Klamath's flanking the settlers. They were headed for me, the direction I wanted.

Pulamon's arm raised, and the v-like formation turned.

No! That was the wrong way. It would lead them around the lava beds, in the general direction of the outcropping where Mia and Kahinsula would emerge.

I cursed myself for not keeping Mia's bag of tricks with me, especially the cap gun, which would be vital right now, a sound to grab their attention.

My whistle alerted the nearest Modoc warrior and I gestured. He fired, the noise changing the course of the riders. They turned, coming toward me.

The orb was already in my hands as I pondered the rocks. The only one that made any sense at all was the salmon colored rhyolite. I had no idea if it was going to work as I intended, but Dad's information was enough to make me give it a try.

I rotated the top to the right. Nothing happened…for about two seconds. Below me, the horse started to dance, as though his hooves were hot. The next instant he jolted, turning about face without my prompting.

Cries of war echoed across the narrow valley, with Pulamon leading the charge up the hill. I was already at the next rise when I heard Jones shout for a halt. The heat from the ground had caused them to stop. The ground was too hot to proceed in a direct line. Jones had no choice but to split up the group. He directed ten to go one way, towards a visible Modoc warrior. He and the others followed Pulamon towards me.

I kicked the horse into motion. He kept on the soft path between the lava rocks while I struggled to turn the top of the orb the other direction, but it jostled so much I was afraid I would drop it. I pushed it between my legs, now in jeopardy of the plan failing because I'd misjudged how hard it was to ride a horse and hold an object in my hand. I gained an immediate appreciation for Mia and her riding-spear-throwing skills. I didn't possess them.

By now, the other Modoc decoys had shot their rifles, siphoning off small groups of settlers who saw victory within their grasp. Pulamon, Jones and their small group were still after me.

"Hee-yah!" I hissed, encouraging the horse through the area of land with the chimneys. Holding the reins with my left hand, the orb jostled, and I leaned forward, keeping it in place with my stomach as I touched the crystal around my neck.

Whoof! Whoof! Off went the chimneys behind me, shooting plumes of ash into the sky. I glanced back, over my right shoulder, watching the horses dodge through the chimneys like balls in a pinball machine.

Closer, just a little closer.

The whistle of a bullet went by my left ear, missing me but nicking my horse. He reared up and off I went, tumbling to the ground.

I rolled, hitting my left shoulder, the orb clanking against a rock. An explosion threw lava mortars into the air, slowing the riders but not deterring them. Jones yelled in victory as he saw me scramble to my feet, his rifle already drawn. I had no doubt he could fire and ride, unlike myself.

Dropping and rolling until I was behind a boulder, I counted the seconds.

Four….three…two… I leaned around the rock, pointing the ring at the nearing group. The horses froze first, the riders toppling off, their own positions freezing. Pulamon was stiff and straight, Jones' rifled was aimed and ready, while the others had tight grips on the horses' reigns. Thuds and breaks meant some of the men would either be completely knocked out or suffering from broken bones.

I scoured the area for the orb, finding it in the soft sand. The spindle was intact, as were the rocks inside. The explosion had proved Dad's theory of the rhyolite, and I was left wondering if it was luck, fate or something else that turned the spindle directly over it.

I put the orb away and the backpack over my shoulders, pounding the ground with my feet. Pulamon needed to see my tracks, or he wouldn't find the correct entry point.

A bird call confirmed Mia and Kahinsula had left the cave. Soon they would be miles away.

I ran faster. A spear to my right was a warning shot, undoubtedly thrown by Pulamon. The men had gained ground on me, and he could have hit me if he wanted.

Seeing my entrance a football field in the distance, I yelled to the sentry and the man disappeared, but not before he was clearly seen.

"Get them!" Jones yelled to his men. "Tell the others—where are they?!" he screamed in frustration. The other men were nowhere to be seen. "Forget them! You two, go there!" His remaining company veered right, while Pulamon and his two warriors, Jones, Pete and another settler followed me.

I purposefully fell, grunting in pain, as though I'd broken a bone. A shriek of impending victory came from Jones. I waited at the top of the chimney shoot, holding onto the rope placed there by Kintpuash. It was a long drop, fifty feet into the pitch black.

Pulamon had dismounted and ran towards me. I caught his eye, nodded, then dropped in to the hole.

The rope burned my palms as I descended, and I felt more than one tear on the back of my shirt as I rammed into jutting lava rock. Shadows and yells above confirmed the men were coming down.

When I reached solid ground, my knees buckled. I was practically jerked up by Boncho. He had a rifle and the yarn retrieved from the women's sewing area. He'd wrapped a piece of yarn to the spool, holding the trigger very carefully.

"I will wait for your signal."

He left and I waited as Pulamon landed in front of me.

"Fake an injury," I suggested before jogging further down the tunnel. I hid in the dark, watching Pulamon grimace in silence, holding his ankle and falling on his side. When the others were gathered, they hesitated.

"Go around him!" Jones commanded, grabbing a torch. I loudly moaned in pain, the sound of one trying to escape.

"He's close," hissed Jones. "I bet they are all here, hiding like sheep. Go!"

I avoided the dangerous hanging stalactites, passing through the deserted women's quarters. I heard ragged breathing and a wail as someone hit a suspended cone. I smiled. That was going to be the least of their injuries. Behind me, the fleet footed Klamath warriors had nearly caught up. One gave a cry of victory. I ran across the thin lava bridge, waiting in the dark on the other side. The men were in a line, the Klamaths in the front, with Jones and his men behind him. They slowed down, seeing the ice below, sensing the danger. I moaned again, and the single file group moved slowly, holding tightly to the wooden rail.

When they were mid-point over the frozen lake, I whistled once. One crack, then another occurred, the sounds of the wood rail breaking. With a clean jerk, the railing was ripped off. The men teetered, one losing his balance. His screams shot up and down the empty chambers as he fell onto the solid ice below. He landed with a thud, dead.

"One down," I shouted in a challenge, adding a pain-filled cough to give Jones incentive.

"I'll kill you yet!" Jones promised. He crouched low, watching the two warriors in front of him.

He might not do so well without light. I whistled twice, and the whirling of tomahawks were heard a split second before the Klamath at the front of the line lost his torch. It whipped out of his hand, the force knocking him off balance. He too, fell over the edge, his cry abruptly ending when he hit the ice.

The second Klamath dropped on his hands and knees, keeping his torch low and active.

Pulamon raised his torch from the other end of the bridge. He gestured for remaining men to come back, as though they'd suffered enough loss and should give up the fight.

"I'm not leaving here until I kill that man," vowed Jones. "Here," he said, giving Pete his rifle. "I'm going to go get that torch. See those steps there."

He moved forward on his hands and knees carefully making his way around the Klamath warrior who stayed put. I could see Pete shaking, his eyes nervously looking around him.

Pulamon called again, and his warrior stood.

"Don't you try and leave Pulamon, or I'll give the order to have you all shot." Pete reluctantly turned the rifle on the warrior in front of him, completely ignorant of the fact that the native could disarm him in a milli-second.

Pulamon was trying to do the right thing, but I could see he needed guidance from me.

I gave a bird call and moved under a wide overhang. Shots were fired, the ricochets off the ceiling deafening. A buzzing began, the sensation increasing until the vibrations moved down the walls and underneath us.

"What is that?" asked Pete, glancing around.

"It's nothing!" yelled Jones. "Stay put."

Frightened bats had dropped from the roof above, flying down and into the company of the men, expressing their displeasure with wild screams. The men threw their hands up, trying to protect their faces, but the bats weren't attacking. They were causing panic.

It worked. Ignoring the warrior in front of him, the settler charged forward, off the bridge and down a corridor. The scream of repulsion was loud, the simultaneous crunching of feet upon millions of dung-eating cockroaches.

"Arrggg!!!" he yelled. I put the torch forward, watching his body overwhelmed with the cockroaches. If it had only been a few, he could have retreated. But his legs were knee high in the heavy bat guano, pinning him in place. The stings of a million cockroaches were paralyzing him. "I can't theee—" he screamed, flailing at his eyes, the word mutated as bugs went inside his mouth and ears. They might not eat him, but their poison in overwhelming numbers would prevent him from getting away.

His body crumpled, the slow death an awful one.

It should have been Jones.

From further up in the cave, I heard the sounds of fighting, yells of bloodshed, the screams of death and victory.

There had to be another way.

Jones was now on the lake of ice where he picked up the torch and reignited the flame.

I quietly slipped off my backpack, feeling for the spindle in the dark and the inscriptions for the pumice. If it could control water, I hoped that applied to the frozen version as well.

Noiselessly, I turned the top half of the orb to the left. I wanted punishment, not peace. A tremendous crack rocked the floor, a frozen earthquake splitting the lake of ice down the center in an uneven jag. Jones lost his balance and fell down on one knee, barking in pain. He got up, slipping and sliding away from the center as quickly as he could.

I turned the orb further, hoping to speed up the process. Up shot an ice shaft. It would have impaled Jones had he been closer. I kept turning it, and one after another, ice sprang up, then Jones fell down with a splash.

"What? Water?" he shrieked. "Pete, throw me the rope. Hurry!" Pete couldn't keep his rifle on the Klamath and help his friend, so he went around the Indian to the edge where the steps began.

Throwing the rope over the side he yelled, "It's not long enough!" The ice had started to drop into the melting water, the splashing and current increasing in velocity each time.

"Then come down further you idiot!" Jones cried. Pulamon and his warrior watched from the bridge, unmoved. I turned the top half once more, knowing what I wanted to see, but unsure how it was going to manifest itself.

A great rushing of water sounded like a jet engine being revved, the whir and ferocity of the noise including wind and force. It also included a scream which was distinctly female.

Pulamon looked upstream.

"Faster!" ordered Jones. The current was picking up, the sound of fury pushing the waterline higher. The water rose to Jones' waist, then mid-chest before he had the rope in his hands.

"Pull!" he screamed. The water rose higher as the tsunami-like water rushed around the man. Chunks of ice were in the current, cracking apart before they sank down into the black water.

"Hold on," encouraged Pete as he lost his footing. I couldn't have that man lose his life. I lunged forward, grabbing the Pete's ankle, holding him steady. It was barely enough. I flipped myself around, wedging my feet against boulders, adding my strength to the rope. Together, we pulled Jones closer to the edge.

At the same time, the female screams increased, sporadic shouts for help in the Modoc language, which were drowned out by the water. Still holding fast, I looked up to see that Pulamon had directed his warrior to the other side of the river. He was off the bridge now, carefully navigating his way along the edge, holding on to outcroppings and waiting. Pulamon untied a rope, dangling it down to the water.

"Pulamon!" I yelled, knowing that even as I spoke in English, he would be hearing it in his language. Such was the power of the ring I wore. "She won't be able to reach it!" I shouted. "The river is running too fast." I'd intended the water to take away Jones, not kill anyone else. And I knew who it was. It had to be Salia, the only female remaining in the cavern who would have been near the frozen waters.

Preoccupied, I hadn't seen Jones come closer.

I screamed, temporarily blinded by the excruciating agony that ripped through the outside of my left calf. Jones had rammed a long knife straight through my muscle, hitting bone. Pete was still holding to the rope, but without my help, he fell back, lost his balance and went head first into the water. His scream was lost in the frozen water, his head disappearing under the bridge.

He was a decent man, I thought in my rage of pain and fury.

No cougar was going to help me out of this mess, and if I left my body to jump into a bat, Jones would kill my physical self.

Jones twisted the knife and I screamed again, bright lights and darkness shooting through me with a pain I'd never endured.

I punched Jones with my right hand, trying to get the moment of peace I needed to throw myself into him. On the exhale, I pulled the knife out of my leg, gasping again as I felt faint.

It wasn't enough. I couldn't get out of my body and into his.

The female screams came closer, the acoustics of the rock acting like a bullhorn.

In my haze of pain, I saw a head appear from under the shadow of the rock overhang. It was Salia, arms motionless and frozen in the water. The Klamath warrior leaned over, slipping as he reached his arm out, barely catching himself from falling as she was swept by in the current.

Pulamon was ready. He had looped his rope around one foot and attached it to a large stalagmite that had risen from the floor. He was over the bridge, his waist serving as the balance.

"Reach!" he yelled. Salia looked up, her eyes glazed with pain and surrender. Reaching with all his might, he stretched the rope until the individual threads started to pop, waiting for her to pass underneath.

Jones punched my wound, holding the rope with his free hand, exposing his chest. My calf was ripped, but my right leg worked just fine. Jones experienced the full weight of my right foot in the center of his chest, the force crushing the chest bones. His mouth dropped open, the air shoved out with such force he couldn't get any back in. If he didn't die of his bones puncturing his major organs, he'd die of suffocation.

But just to be sure…with all my strength, I kicked him between his shoulders, grimacing as my left leg scraped along the rock floor. At least I had the satisfaction of feeling his collarbones collapse into his chest, separating from his shoulder sockets. He careened backwards, creating a surge in the water. It was just enough to lift up Salia as she reached Pulamon's outstretched hand. He gripped her, adding his other hand, holding tight. Jones floated by, his mouth already full of frozen water, his broken ribs, chest and shoulder blades paralyzing his ability to move. His head sunk below the darkness of the bridge as Pulamon's warrior came to his side. Together, they lifted Salia up to the bridge.

The woman shook uncontrollably, her wet mop of hair covering her face. Pulamon moved it off her skin, her lips wet and trembling.

"My savior," she said, her teeth chattering. She closed her eyes and leaned in to him, still shaking when he put his arms around her.

The moment was broken by the continued shouts of fighting from further up in the tunnel.

"Pulamon," I called. He and his warrior turned to me. "Let me heal Salia and me. Then I must go."

CHAPTER 26

By the time I'd replaced the orb, the sounds of fighting had diminished. My leg was as good as new and Salia's scrapes and cuts were gone.

Pulamon glanced up the passageway, his body posture reluctant.

"They will not harm you," I told Pulamon. "You have my word." A growl echoed the sentiment. Pulamon stared at me first, then looked over my shoulder. The female cougar trotted from the darkness. She must have come through an entrance deeper in the tunnel, perhaps where Mia and Kahinsula emerged.

You called.

"Stay your weapons," I said to the men, dropping to my knee. The cougar approached, nuzzling my face.

"My friends are in danger, and so was I. Soon I must leave for good."

She looked up and past me, her growl menacing. *He is here*, she thought. I knew exactly who she meant.

Salia reached for Pulamon's hand, taking it tightly as she looked in his eyes. "Come with me," she asked.

"No," he replied. "Come with me."

I felt Salia's heart. She knew of Pulamon and his loss and had been sympathetic. She had also never had a man of her own within the Modoc tribe, and of the remaining men who were going to battle, none had expressed interest in her.

"Cage?" she asked. "Was this what you saw in your dreams?"

"No, it was what I saw on the rock. Go," I said softly. "Live your life and have love. If you stay here, you will die. They will understand."

Pulamon heard my words in his own language and tried to comprehend the meaning. The cougar waited patiently by my side.

"Show him," Salia requested.

I pulled my shirt over my head and watched Pulamon step back. The outline of the scar was glowing, the colored tattoo moving within the outline, a living image.

The cougar was in me, and I in it, forever.

"Pulamon, the Klamath tribe will continue to exist for all time, but the Modoc tribe will be—" I couldn't bring myself to say the word but he understood. "Through your children, you will keep her heritage alive."

He put out his free hand and I shook it.

"Show him another way out," I suggested to Salia.

She nodded. "Thank you. Come back and see us, if you can."

The three moved through the tunnels and into the catacombs, where hundreds of paths stretched for miles. They would emerge into safety, Salia with a new man, and a new life, free of the devastation that was about to occur.

When I arrived at the mouth of the cave, nineteen settlers were on the ground, gagged, hands tied behind their backs, feet wrapped in chords. Two men were wounded, one seriously.

They cringed at the sight of me. It took me a moment to remember why. The female cougar was by my side, quiet as a whisper on the wind. I didn't ask if I could heal them, and they couldn't refuse or get away, so I just went ahead. One fainted, and I grinned. I'm sure they believed they'd experienced some sort of voo-doo magic.

"Cage?" asked my father, cautiously.

I looked up. "She won't attack as long as you don't want to hurt me." My father bore wounds consistent with a brawl, a cut lip and bruised face, but he'd escaped major injury. "You decided to stay."

"I wasn't going to run off with the women and children," he said, sounding slightly offended. "At least if I died here, it would be an honorable death. Can I touch her?"

She growled. "Not if you want to keep your hand," I answered. The cougar gave her version of a laugh, but my smile faded.

I stood, knowing we needed to leave.

"Dad, I'll be back."

Can you please stay with him? I thought to the cougar. *I don't want more men to see you than necessary.*

I found Lapuan and Boncho. Their mouths were downturned, shoulders hunched.

"I must go," I began.

"Cage," Lapuan said, his eyes dark. "Kintpuash…" he stopped, seeing the leader draw near. I knew instantly what he meant. Kintpuash was stiff as a board, proud and haughty, the victor of a battle. The Kintpuash I knew didn't take glory in spilling blood.

"Ubel survived me killing General Canby," I murmured. "If he throws himself inside you, think happy thoughts. He can't live with that. Tell the others." Lapuan blinked his eyes once and left.

"I want to go out and get air," I said, loud enough for those close to hear, including Kintpuash. "Join me?" I asked him.

"Yes," he said, waiting for me to take the lead.

"I'm going to get my father. I'll meet you up there."

He'd learned that jumping into me didn't work because I knew how to get him out, but anyone else was fair game. Hopefully, word would spread among the remaining Modoc men, and the settlers were bound, tied and gagged. They couldn't be possessed. The horses could wound people, that was true, but they could also be shot.

I found my father, wondering if it went down as he said. Perhaps Kintpuash had given him the option to stay or leave with us. If the opportunity came up to learn how the conversation went down, I would. For now, he was coming with us by default. *We have to work on our family relationship anyway.*

I told my father it was time to go. As we walked, the cougar padded beside me. I shared all that had occurred with her, and the evil spirit within Kintpuash's body.

"Do not be fooled," I cautioned her. "Right now, he is not the kind warrior of his natural state."

My ancestors know of this demon. He used his powers to kill many of your kind.

"Can you keep the spirit out of you?"

Kee hee, she laughed. *I would like to fight him, and I would win.*

Boncho brought two horses, one for me and my father. His eyes told me he and the others knew of the evil spirit. It occurred to me that if a person in modern times were told that an individual was possessed by an evil spirit, 911 would be called, the Internet would be broken and the paparazzi would be summoned to document the entire thing. Here, it was simply accepted. Spirits of good and bad existed; they were the balance of life.

"Thank you, Boncho," said my father politely. He took his time saying thank you and goodbye to the men in the tribe who he knew. Lapuan didn't shake his hand, but he nodded his head at my father. The emotion behind a loss might be gone, but the memory was still there, like a cut that closed leaving a scar behind.

We emerged out in the open, the night warmer due to cloud cover. It felt like a summer rain shower was going to drench the earth.

"Good luck to you," I said to Kintpuash, holding out my right hand. He took it, immediately rotating my wrist, breaking his grip. I hooked my left foot behind his right, shoving him back. He didn't release my hand, and we fell back, me on top of him. He opened his mouth and I knew he was going to bite my finger clean off, taking the ring with him.

I felt the growl inside me and to my left.

No. Wait, I thought. *I can do this on my own.*

I closed my fist and he bit and tore the skin clean off my middle finger, taking the muscle as I jammed it into his mouth. His pain matched mine as his teeth crunched inward. We rolled, the fight of a one thousand-year-old spirit against another, using the physical bodies of a lithe, young man and an older, well-built warrior.

He threw me off him before I had a chance to lock his neck. I raised the ring to use it, then changed my mind. For some reason, I wanted to prove I could beat him without any other powers aiding me.

He smiled when I dropped my hand. He crouched, Kintpuash's well-toned body moving cat like. He lunged and I spun, he thrust up his arm and I caught it, lifting it in a move that would have put anyone else on their back. He flipped over, landing on his feet, his smile wicked.

The men had formed a circle, their stance loose, cautious. My father had no idea what was going on and yelled at me to stop.

"No," said Kaga. "They must fight."

"But he's meant to save him not fight him!" my father said.

"This was foreordained. They must fight."

Back and forth we went, his moves as fluid as my own.

Kintpuash smiled. "You can't defeat me," he hissed.

"And if you could defeat me, you would have done it," I retorted. "And just like in times past you will fail, and I will send you back to where you came from. This time forever."

He roared in anger, then dropped to the ground, as though his energy had left him. I felt the negative energy move around the room, a spirit in search of a host.

"Think positive," I screamed, but it was too late. My father ripped free of Boncho and Lapuan, their hold no match for the spirit that now inhabited him. In my rush to protect the tribe, I'd neglected to tell my own father how to keep the spirit outside his body.

"You cannot kill me," my father challenge, "and I will escape alive."

"But your new body is no match for my skills," I retorted without fear. Despite the mental knowledge of hand-to-hand combat, it took physical technique and skill. My father had neither.

We circled each other like gladiators in a colosseum. On the perimeter, Kaga was at Kintpuash's side, helping him stand. When he gained his strength, he called for a spear, ready to end my father's life right there.

"Shall I let him do it?" I asked the spirit inside my father.

Kintpuash had his spear shoulder height, ready to throw.

"Stop!" yelled my sister. "Kintpuash, what are you doing? Cage! What's going on?"

"Ahhh," murmured my father, his voice carrying a glazed tone of seduction that my father had never possessed. "Ubel is my name, pretty thing. This will be interesting, won't it?"

I paced the circle, on guard. I'd told Mia how to prevent his ability to take over the body. I only hoped she remembered.

"It's Ubel now inside Dad, for the second time, isn't that right?" I said for all to hear. "And before that, you were in

Kintpuash, who is now ready to kill him, just as I had to do with General Canby."

"You killed the General? Not Kintpuash?" Mia yelled at me. "And now, he's...how could you?"

"Easy," I replied, never taking my eyes of my dad. "The General had a rifle pointed at my head. Ubel just happened to pull the trigger, not the General. If I hadn't shot, others would have died. It was self-defense."

"But you missed," said the voice inside my father, clear enough for all to hear.

Mia's complaints were cut short as she fully comprehended the gravity of the situation.

My father stopped walking, he bent over, head in his hands.

"Ubel's throwing himself!" I yelled the warning.

"Throw...the spear at me!" my father cried, his true voice coming through as a tortured sound. "Now Kintpuash!"

The warrior-chief hurled the spear, straight through my father's chest, the black and white eagle feather flapping. He staggered backwards, arms out horizontal to either side, resembling a walking cross, his face tortured agony.

Mia dropped to her knees, hands on her mouth, then she too, put her face in her hands. She had started crying, and it was enough. Her gulp stopped and she looked up at me, terrified.

"He was in me and I got it out," she cried.

I looked up and around. Ubel was here, *somewhere*.

She looked up and around, her panic moving from the darkness to Dad.

"Heal him," Mia gasped. "You have to!"

I stood straight. "I can't, Mia. I'm sorry. If I do, Ubel will take over his body again. He doesn't have the will or ability to keep him out."

"Cage, do it!" she screamed, jumping up, trying to tear the backpack off my shoulders. I jerked away, which made her fury uncontrollable. Boncho came up behind her, placing his arms around her chest and she bit down. As before, Boncho held his grip, unflinching.

The sound of flight was above us, and I knew He had found his chance to escape. The thousands of bats were leaving on their nightly excursions.

"Mia, we must get out of here before he returns. Do you understand?"

"Let me go!" she demanded. Boncho constricted her arms tighter, but it was Kintpuash who moved in front of her. Roughly, he put a rope in her mouth and tied it.

"You know our language, hear me," Kintpuash commanded. "That creature will kill everything in its way, including you. Your father asked to be killed, to save you, his child."

He pulled the ends tight, their gaze locked. Rebellion, love and fury built up in her eyes. A horse broke free of its stall and ran at full speed.

"He went from a bat to the horse," I announced. "Watch over my body," I commanded Kintpuash, "and don't let her leave."

"I need you," I thought to the cougar. In two paces, she was at my side. The next moment, I was in the cougar and we were chasing down a horse, one with four hooves that could break my cougar's jaw, stomp her head or crush her insides.

And all the while, my father was taking his last breath, surrounded by the tribe and my sister, who could do nothing for him.

Suddenly the horse in front of us reared, bucking its front legs at the hiss of a rattlesnake. When it stopped, my cougar body jumped to the left. The coiled reptile struck again, missing my front paw by a sliver. Up I jumped on the rock, my tail twitching, watching the animal. From above, I heard a stamping, and my shoulder was pushed, the bump painful throwing me off the rock. The victorious bleat of a ram confirmed what had hit me from behind.

It is all around us, said the cougar.

"Kill it in any form," I thought back.

I lithely jumped back up on the rock, my paws attaching to the slick rock surface as easily as the rock. Rams were dangerous, but no match for the claws and fangs of this deadly killing machine. Just as I pounced, the ram dropped its head, the spirit moving into a larger animal. It ran straight towards me, and I leapt high into the air, clearing the lethal horse, watching the ram below me.

I guessed this would be harder, the cougar thought with a bit of annoyance. I laughed. She was an incredible animal.

The clap of a thundercloud rolled across the open landscape, lightning strikes hitting the lake. I waited, tail twitching, wondering where the spirit was going to land next.

The horse took off again, and we had our answer. I ran after it, but knew it was going to be impossible to keep up with the horse for long. I either needed to take it down, risking injury, or let it go.

After a half a mile of running, I turned around, heading back to the Modoc tribe. Vultures flew overhead, diving down.

Look there, she thought to me. A body was face down in the water.

"Can we reach it?"

I waded into the stream easily swimming to the center. I nipping the body with her fangs, drawing it to the shore. I clawed the chest to turn it over.

Jones. He was finally dead.

"One less man to worry about," I thought.

She was purring with delight when her tail went straight. The next instant, my legs were running at full speed, up and up, climbing the side of the mountain, leaping straight over bus-sized boulders, the pace so intense I wasn't going to ask what she knew.

My cubs, she thought to me. Ubel had found them. He was going to use them to kill one another, and then kill her.

The horse outside the den was dead, its nose was bloody and scraped, as though it had run head first into the rock. Two of the cubs were already clawing at the carcass while the third was watching calmly.

I will kill them all if I must, thought the cougar fiercely, already stalking her young.

"No, you won't!"

A hawk flew by and I leapt out of the cougar, straight into the bird. I flew directly in between the cougar I loved and her male cub, getting swiped in the process.

The cougar growled in frustration and regret. Even in my spirit form, I felt the intentions of the evil one.

"Tell them to think of love, kindness and compassion!" I mentally yelled to the cougar, who immediately did as I said. The male cub growled and pawed the ground, and then dropped. The mother immediately gathered the three within her protective limbs, as Ubel searched for another target.

This time, it came in the form of a much larger bird of prey. The eagle screamed and I barely had time to dip as its talons ripped out a section of feathers on my left wing. I faltered, hitting the highest branch of a pine tree. The bird had two times my wing span, and the only thing that could save me was my agility and speed, but both were now gone. Before I could react, the claws of the eagle gripped both my wings, tearing my cartilage. Higher and higher it took me, constricting its claws as it flew, nearly severing my wings in half. My body wasn't dead, but it would be the moment the eagle reached its highest point and dropped me. Then I would land, my body crushed and my spirit dying with it.

With a cry of victory, he opened his talons. Down I spiraled, my wings broken and shredded, the earth coming closer and closer. I fell onto the soft branches of a cedar tree and heard its whisperings.

I have you, the great cedar said to me. His words called to the cougar. *She is coming.*

Here I was, in another form, and the tree still knew me, saving me once again.

Emotion welled within in, the energy of life keeping me sane and alive.

The eagle circled the tree, intent on finishing me. Squawks filled the air, overlapped with lower pitched twitters, the kind an irritated bird makes when a threat is approaching the nest. The branches were filled with black and multi-colored birds, the crows and sparrows flying around me and then out at the eagle, pecking its great wings and eyes.

The deliberate circle of confusion kept the eagle at bay as I fell. From branch to branch, I was gently dropped, down to the base, where the cougar waited.

Wearily, and with sadness, I apologized to the hawk and thanked it for the use of its body. It barely answered, dying as I left its body for the cougar.

Grief started to fill me, and I fought against it. *I can't let it in me.* The cougar's strength gave me renewed energy and determination.

Let me take you home, she thought to me.

The eagle was still above, screeching, waiting for the body of the hawk to fly. I threw my spirit into the cougar, and then we ran fast across the plains, back to the lava beds. I had the sentry in sight when I felt a ripping across my shoulders. The eagle had found us.

I rolled, the eagle releasing me as my shoulders hit the ground. Up went my claw, but the eagle was faster, slicing across one my eyelids. Blood filled my vision, but I was fast enough to tear through the underside of his left wing. I danced on my hind legs, rising full height as the eagle flapped backward. Dark dust clouded my vision, but I crouched and jumped, turning my head sideways to avoid the talons, my own claws extended.

The eagle's razor sharp nails covered my face completely, gripping my head as its beak went for my eyes. I furiously ripped my neck around, taking the claw and the bird with it, throwing it the side, directly into a rock. The eagle hit with such force that foot-long feathers came off, floating in the air.

I clawed the bird as it dropped, ripping into the belly of the bird. Coyotes howled in the moonlight as I sliced the bird again and again.

Finally, the rush of adrenaline faded, and I stepped back, licking my paw clean.

They are coming, she thought to me. From the howls, I knew it was dangerous for the cougar to stay any longer. A large pack could overtake a cougar, no matter how fast or strong. And she was tired.

"May I never see you again," I thought to the spirit inside the eagle. The eyes dimmed at my words, then went glassy. The bird was dead.

CHAPTER 27

Kintpuash and the others had taken my father's body and placed it aside a pile of sticks.

"They are going to honor him," Mia said, her voice hollow. "They've asked if they can put him in the sacred grove, with their people. You know," she said, looking up at me with vacant eyes. "The place where we were the first night."

I nodded. She looked back down at our father, moving the hair from his face. Someone had covered the hole in his chest with clothes, perhaps Mia. I didn't ask.

"I'll be back," I said. The cougar walked with me to a boulder away from the group.

"Let me heal you," I thought to her. The lacerations on the back were not deep, unlike the claw marks on her face. "You will have something to remind you of me," I said, hearing the sadness in my own voice as I removed the orb.

When she was whole, she licked my face and I put my arms around her. My mother first, and now my father was gone. I had to be strong for Mia, but who was strong for me?

Your animal spirit. I will always be within.

I nodded. It was only going to get worse, and I couldn't be a part of any more death. At least the evil had been killed within the eagle.

He can reside in any living thing, thought the cougar to me. *Beware.*

I touched her for what I knew would be the last time.

"Goodbye," I said quietly, the words floating on the air. She purred, went around a large lava boulder, and was gone.

We watched the fire grow, licking the bottom of the funeral pyre. I felt Mia's heart breaking as the flames consumed the bottom layer of sticks. The outline of my father's body blurred behind the smoke, then became one with the flames.

Mia gripped my hand, shivers of grief vibrating into her cold palm. I was glad she was here, as hard as it was to see Dad. This way she had closure of knowing what happened. Perhaps Kahinsula had been inspired by telling Mia to return to the lava beds. She knew the way, Kahinsula assured Mia, who reluctantly left.

The men were humming while Kaga said a traditional Modoc prayer. It was sacred, we were told, not to be repeated, but used only for those who had given their lives for others.

My father had been welcomed, reviled, redeemed, and finally forgiven. He was going where he belonged and deserved to go.

When the flames started to subside, Kintpuash stretched his palm out to Mia and she took it. They entered the cave together and I held back.

Boncho came beside me, asking if I was hungry.

"Starved."

The women had left two months of food supplies at Kintpuash's request. I forced the date from my mind; that's when the siege would end and Kintpuash would be taken. It was history, and I had failed to change it once. I wasn't going to try again. At least the Modocs were going to return the men to the settlement the following morning, an event in history neither Mia or I remembered.

During the meal, Lapuan sat beside me, eating silently. There was nothing else to say. We would separate as friends and eating together was enough.

When we finished, I walked with Kaga to the sleeping cavern. On the way, we passed the rock wall of the petroglyphs. I paused. The snakes had come and attacked, the cougar had fought the eagle, and the woman…Salia had been saved by Pulamon.

"Kaga, you were wrong. These happened, here," I pointed, "but this one did not." I told him about Pulamon saving Salia's life. "I'm not supposed to change the future, but I did."

"You are the Spirit Warrior."

"And yet I couldn't do more."

The petroglyphs remained static. There was nothing left for me to learn from this place.

We reached the sleeping cavern, where many of the men were already lying under blankets.

"Remember your dreams," Kaga quietly encouraged. *They will tell you all.*

I drew the wool covering up to my shoulders, the warmth of the underground heat comforting. I hadn't seen Mia since she entered the cave with Kintpuash, but I wasn't worried. She was smart and responsible; he was honorable.

Keeping my eyes open was no different than closing them; it was utterly black. An emotional detachment had begun as I watched my father's body burn. From our arrival, Dad had hinted he expected his life was going to end here, if not in penance for Nolina, but because of his neglect after my mother died.

Now Dad was free.

I hadn't cried during the burial ceremony, nor was the feeling of sorrow within me. This was only one more step in our journey, but I wouldn't say that to Mia, not yet. Her request for his healing and my rejection wasn't going to hit her for a while, and I feared when it did, her emotions were going to be extreme.

Exhaustion overtook emotional numbness, but I didn't know my eyes had closed until I started dreaming. My father's spirit was in the sacred burial area, his soul floating on the air, with the other spirits of the Modoc people. He was consigned here, within the protected glade. Perhaps one day, I'd have the skills or tools I needed to return and make him whole.

You can do it, his spirit whispered to me. *You can make our family whole.*

The spirits around him swirled, taking my father with them. The darkness of the clearing lit to a light blue with the sunrise. It seemed hours before the sun made its way up and over the mountains. When it did, I was awoken.

"It's time," said Kintpuash. He gave me two satchels of smoked meats and berries, a container for water and a new shirt. Mia was waiting at the entrance, her own water bag and food satchel strapped to her fanny pack. Her eyes were full of emotion, as was her heart. I purposefully chose not to explore her feelings, thinking it an invasion of her privacy.

At what point had we evolved from teenagers to adults? I wondered.

When we lost our innocence.

No other words were said as Boncho handed me a torch. We turned down to the catacombs, walking until I recognized the spaghetti-like strings handing from the sides of the rock walls.

"You're sure you don't want to stay?" I asked her quietly. "You can. I won't stop you."

"He's going to die, Cage. I'd get my heart broken twice and still be alone. No. Let's go."

Accepting her decision, I pulled out the orb. Mia touched my left arm, and we waited as the light started to glow in all directions. I put the torch on the ground, the flame quickly dying out. It had only been two weeks, but it felt like months had passed.

When the light hit full midday bright, the familiar sound of cracking began, and the wall started to open, bit by bit.

"Here we go again," I said, walking forward. We stepped over the threshold at the same time, into our future.

The end

AUTHORS NOTE

The idea of Chambers first came to me when I was traipsing up, down and through Captain Jack's stronghold as a kid, walking on the underground rivers of ice, literally getting lost in the catacombs and spending days underground in the miles of tunnels consumed much of my free time every year during summer break, all the way through college.

The notion of a spirit warrior evolved as I spent days with Native Americans Indians who believe that some have the gift of "throwing energy." In the western world, this is generally known as 'energy work,' but Native Americans view and use this gift quite differently. One person within a tribe, usually once a generation, has the gift of throwing energy, for positive or negative use. I was told, and shown evidence, where an individual used his gift for personal gain. He effectively manipulated gamblers to win money, affected the outcomes of business decisions and other very specific (and tragic) circumstances where people were hurt and he would financially benefit. This man was eventually brought to justice by his own tribe.

While this normally occurs in a man, females also receive the gift of throwing energy. I spent many hours with an Indian woman who discovered her gift when she was five years old. She could manipulate others do to her will, but fortunately it was identified early on, and the elders in her tribe showed her how to use her talent for positive purposes. Now in her mid-seventies, she has spent all her life using her gifts to help victims of physical or emotional abuse improve their lives.

I took this notion of energy and went further, to the concept of throwing spirit; moving in and out of others.

Regarding a spirit world, (a theme that starts in this book and continues throughout the series), a famous Native American, Crazy Horse, shared a vision he had with Black Elk (see Historical Notes):

> *"Crazy Horse dreamed and went into the world where there is nothing but the spirits of all things. That is the real world that is behind this one, and everything we see here is something like a shadow from that one."*

Crazy Horse also described his horse floating and moving differently above the field (thus, "Crazy Horse") in his powerful vision. It's been said that he was able to move in and out between the spirit realm and the physical world, able to see both, and so his courage and power was greater than most men. (Excerpted from the website Angels and Ghosts). I combined this notion with that of the ability to throw spirits.

The Native American people of this land hold a special place in my heart, and I tried to do the story justice although I've not delved into the vast historical issues between the Klamath and Modoc tribes.

As for my own connection with the land, my grandfather homesteaded Medicine Lake with a partner, building a summer cabin in the remote, 7,000-foot-high mountain location in 1913. He died at 100, leaving behind six children and over sixty grandchildren. My own mother was born in Tule Lake, California in 1939. We are now fourth generation full or part-time residents of that area, the love and value we have for the land and people mixed with guilt and regret for building the settlement to begin with. In the hundred-plus years, we have tried to honor the Native American people, and this book is my attempt to do that by sharing just a fraction of the history of the region and its people.

HISTORICAL NOTES

Kintpuash (Captain Jack). Best known as Captain Jack, Kintpuash led his warriors to reclaim a part of the Modoc homeland. On the advice of Muleo, the tribe's spiritual advisor and medicine man, Kintpuash attended the peace meeting where he shot General Edward Canby, mortally wounding him. He was led to believe that if he killed the "leader" of the Army, they would leave his people alone. Kintpuash and three other warriors were found guilty of murder and hanged. Today, he is most famous for holding off a force of 3,000 US soldiers with a group of only about 50 warriors. The Modoc National Forest protects that expansive area of the Modoc Indian tribe, and many monuments stand to honor their efforts to defend their lands.

(Old Chief) Sconchin. When thousands of emigrants began entering the Modoc territory, Sconchin ordered his tribe to resist, which they did for nearly for thirty years, beginning in 1846. On his command, the Modocs, led by Hooker Jim, attacked a train full of settlers, wherein 62 of the 65 persons were killed, including women and children. In a revenge attack, the settlers killed about 50 Modocs by a river, including women and children. Revenge attacks continued by both sides until the US Army was called upon to restore order. Historians calculate that at least 300 persons from both sides, men, women and children, died in the conflict. Note: the correct, historical spelling of the name is Schonchin, but for ease of pronunciation and readability, I chose to drop the first 'h.'

Muleo (referred to as Curly Joe or Curly Headed Doctor by the white settlers) was the chief spiritual advisor for the Modoc Indian Tribe. He attended the peace treaty meeting with the Army, and he later acknowledged he told Kintpuash that if the leader of the Army was killed, the remainder of the US Army would leave. Muleo was subsequently forced to leave the area with the rest of the Modoc Tribe but was not hanged for his role in the murder. He was Hooker Jim's father-in-law.

Hooker Jim was a Modoc warrior and son-in-law of Muleo, who ultimately betrayed Kintpuash (Captain Jack) to save his own life. After white settlers killed the Modoc women and children by the river, it was Hooker Jim who led the raids killing white settlers over a period of time. He also regularly led raids on the Klamath tribe and the U.S. Army. The Army requested that Kintpuash deliver Hooker Jim to them, but Kintpuash refused. When the siege of the Modocs in the lava beds ended, Hooker Jim turned on Kintpuash and testified against him in exchange for his life. He was exiled to Oklahoma with the remainder of the tribe and died in 1879.

Scarface Charlie (War chief). When Kintpuash was hanged, Scarface Charlie was made the Modoc chief and moved with the tribe to Oklahoma. He was known as a ferocious but fair warrior who was also a skilled craftsman. He designed a typeface to transcribe the Modoc language and built a line of furniture which supported him when he was replaced as the tribal leader after only a year. This was due to his refusal to acknowledge white men as 'true leaders' of the Modoc tribe. He died of natural causes.

Boncho, Kaga, Lapuan, Pulamon, Kahinsula and Salia are fabricated. Kaga does mean Chronicler in certain Native American dialects. The legacy story of love and strife between Pulamon, Lapuan and Nolina is fiction. However, the Klamath and Modoc tribes had a history of intermarriage, as well as fighting with one another.

Toby (Winema) Riddle was a Modoc native who married a white settler named Frank Riddle. Winema means "woman-chief" in Modoc, and she was given that name as a young teenager when she single-handedly rescued a group of children caught in a cascade, saving them from drowning. She was fluent in English and played a pivotal role during the settler's integration of the Modoc lands. During the peace treaty meeting, she saved the life of Alfred Meacham and was later awarded a military pension by the United States government for her role in the peace process. She and Frank had one son, who she named after the individual who took over after General Canby died. She was also invited to attend presentations and events with Alfred Meacham, who wrote several books about the Modocs and her role in the war. She died in 1920.

General Edward Canby was assigned the task of assisting the settlers in the Northern California area and negotiating treaties with the resident tribes. Historical accounts confirm he did not honor his initial agreements, creating additional conflict and hatred between the Klamath and Modoc Tribes, who were in a state of friction prior to the settlers and US Army arriving. He was killed by Kintpuash (Captain Jack).

Medicine Lake. This former volcanic crater sits on Modoc Lands, although non-native Americans have built private residences on the water's edge and in the surrounding hills. Lookout Point, the Burnt Lava Flow and Glass Mountain are within driving distance, and within forty minutes of the lake are all the caverns described in this book.

The catacombs exist under the miles of hardened lava flows. Like many of the famed ice caves, much of the catacombs are now closed to the public, but the hanging threads of lava and cylindrical tubes are still in place.

The Fleener Chimneys. Named for Sam Fleener, who homesteaded the area nearest the chimneys. These structures are the result of lava that shot out from underground flows, all approximately fifty feet deep. For the purposes of this book, I took creative license with the heat/material puffing out of the tubes. They are dormant. However, unnamed tubes exist within the Lava Bed National Monument that resemble termite hills, and stand five-six feet tall. They are not named after any one individual, and are the result of lava shooting upwards, but leaving hardened cones that resemble upside down tubas.

The Modoc National Forest is approximately forty minutes north of Mt. Shasta, or about five hours drive north from San Francisco. Klamath Falls and Tule Lake are just over the California-Oregon border.

Captain Jack's Stronghold. This entire region can be walked in about two hours' time, up and over, down and around, to and through the caves, caverns and blockades used by Captain Jack and his small band of warriors to hold off the U.S. Army.

During my research, I learned Native Americans view the "spirit world" is not a place to be feared, but celebrated, and that death is simply a door into the next world. I found two quotes that I chose to use. One is from Black Elk, a Lakota Sioux. The other is from Chief Seattle, for whom Seattle, Washington is named after.

In a famous address given in 1854, Chief Seattle spoke of being connected with the spirit world. He addressed the afterlife, ghosts and spirits and how each affect and interact with the living. "There is no death. Only a change of worlds."

Black Elk, a Lakota Sioux medicine man, had much to say about the Spirit co-existing with the physical world we know. I took inspiration from a direct quote from Black Elk, attributing it to Kaga. It is that: "...at the center of the universe dwells the Great Spirit, and that its center is really everywhere, it is within each of us. The Great Spirit is everywhere, he hears whatever is in our minds and our hearts, and it is not necessary to speak to him in a loud voice." Another quote from Black Elk is this: "Peace will come to the hearts of men when they realize their oneness with the universe. It is everywhere."

ABOUT THE AUTHOR

Before she began writing novels, Sarah was an internationally recognized management consulting expert. Her two dozen books have been translated into four languages and are sold in over 100 countries.

BOOKS IN PRINT

Contemporary Fiction
In a Moment
Danielle Grant Series
    Made for Me (book 1)
    Destined for You (book 2)
    Meant to Be (book 3)
A Convenient Date

Suspense/Thriller
Above Ground
Global Deadline
Incarnation Series
    Incarnation (book 1)
    Incarnation: The Cube Master (book 2)
Chambers Series
    Chambers (book 1)
    Chambers: The Spirit Warrior (book 2)

Non-Fiction and Business
Author Straight Talk: The possibilities, pit-falls, how-to's and tribal knowledge from someone who knows
The Overlooked Expert: 10th Anniversary Edition, Turning your skills into a profitable business
Sue Kim: The Authorized Biography: The greatest American story never told
Navigating the Partnership Maze: Creating Alliances that Work

REFERENCES & RESOURCES

Web site: www.sarahgerdes.com

Instagram: Sarahgerdes_author

Made in the USA
Monee, IL
25 July 2025